Ralph Compton:
The Hunted

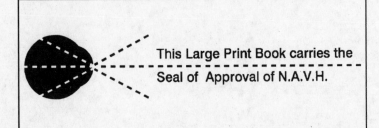

A RALPH COMPTON NOVEL

Ralph Compton: The Hunted

Matthew P. Mayo

THORNDIKE PRESS
A part of Gale, Cengage Learning

GALE
CENGAGE Learning®

Detroit • New York • San Francisco • New Haven, Conn • Waterville, Maine • London

GALE
CENGAGE Learning®

LIBRARY OF CONGRESS CATALOGING-IN-PUBLICATION DATA

Mayo, Matthew P.
    Ralph Compton : The Hunted : A Ralph Compton Novel / By Matthew P.
Mayo. — Large Print edition.
        pages cm. (Thorndike Press Large Print Western.)
    ISBN-13: 978-1-4104-6347-0 (hardcover)
    ISBN-10: 1-4104-6347-8 (hardcover)
    1. Large type books. I. Title.
PS3613.A963R35 2013
813'.6—dc23   2013037092

Published in 2013 by arrangement with NAL Signet, a member of
Penguin Group (USA) LLC, a Penguin Random House Company

Printed in the United States of America
1 2 3 4 5 6 7 17 16 15 14 13

THE IMMORTAL COWBOY

This is respectfully dedicated to the "American Cowboy." His was the saga sparked by the turmoil that followed the Civil War, and the passing of more than a century has by no means diminished the flame.

True, the old days and the old ways are but treasured memories, and the old trails have grown dim with the ravages of time, but the spirit of the cowboy lives on.

In my travels — to Texas, Oklahoma, Kansas, Nebraska, Colorado, Wyoming, New Mexico, and Arizona — I always find something that reminds me of the Old West. While I am walking these plains and mountains for the first time, there is this feeling that a part of me is eternal, that I have known these old trails before. I believe it is the undying spirit of the frontier calling me, through the mind's eye, to step back into time. What is the appeal of the Old West of the American frontier?

It has been epitomized by some as the dark and bloody period in American history. Its heroes — Crockett, Bowie, Hickok, Earp — have been reviled and criticized. Yet the Old West lives on, larger than life.

It has become a symbol of freedom, when there was always another mountain to climb and another river to cross; when a dispute between two men was settled not with expensive lawyers, but with fists, knives, or guns. Barbaric? Maybe. But some things never change. When the cowboy rode into the pages of American history, he left behind a legacy that lives within the hearts of us all.

— *Ralph Compton*

CHAPTER 1

"That's what you got for me? That?" The dealer nodded toward the cards laid before him. His words came out too loud, and as if he'd been waiting long minutes to say them. The thin man with oiled mustaches, black visor, and arm garters shook his head and winked at the gawkers gathered about his table.

Across from him, his customer sighed and closed his eyes for a moment. He was a mammoth man with a broad back turned to the rest of the room.

The dealer and the others clustered by the table flicked eyes at each other, then settled back on him. The player's rough-spun coat, the dark color of axle grease, strained across the shoulders as he brought a hand up to scratch the stubble on his face. "I'm out," he said quietly, nodding toward the table.

"You about were anyway." The dealer

shifted his cigarillo to the other side of his slit mouth and winked at the watchers. Their soft laughs chafed Charlie, but he'd earned them. Coming in here half lit and feeling as if he knew more about playing blackjack and bucking the tiger than any man alive. Heck, three hours and he'd spent more time running from it than wrangling the tiger, and what did he have to show for it? A whole lot of empty in his pockets.

He had his emergency five-dollar piece in his vest and that, plus his mule, Mabel-Mae, and his meager kit, was about all he had in the world now. Three hours earlier he'd been halfway to owning a sizable chunk of land in a pretty mountain valley. Now he'd set himself back by two years — that was how long it had taken him to earn that two thousand dollars. Those two years had all but killed him, he'd worked so hard. And now? Now he was two years older, and as his father used to say of his family's lot in life, he was poorer than an outhouse rat.

"Hey, how about letting someone else take up space in that chair?" The dealer squinted one eye against the slow curl of silver smoke rising up the side of his face from the cat-turd cigarillo. Charlie wanted to smear the smugness off his face, but he'd avoided jail for too long now to cozy up to the idea of

8

being near broke and tossed in the calaboose in Monkton, Idaho Territory.

He pushed away from the table, the chair squawking back on the boot-worn boards. He kept his eyes on the dealer's the entire time he stood, taking longer than he needed to. It wasn't much, but showing off his height was about all he had. It worked. The dealer's grin sagged at the corners and his cigarillo drooped as his eyes followed the big man's progress upward.

He'd not been there when Charlie sat down at the table, so he didn't know how big the fellow he'd been mocking was. And what he saw was a giant of a man, closer to seven feet than six. Charlie was wide enough at the shoulder that by now, at thirty-eight years of age, he naturally angled one shoulder first through doorways and ducked his head a mite. It didn't guarantee he'd not rap his bean on the doorframe — there weren't too many weeks of the year when he didn't have a goose egg of sorts throbbing under his tall-crowned hat.

Charlie's stubbled jaw — he'd not taken time to clean up before hitting the saloon for the first time in many months since he'd sold off his latest claim — was a wide affair beneath a broad head topped with brown curls, tending to silver, forever trapped beneath his big hat. It added nearly another foot to his height, but he didn't mind. It suited him somehow. His hands too were wide, callused mitts with thick tree-branch fingers more suited to dragging and pounding and stacking than tapping out cards. He should have known better than to think he could best the house.

The dealer eyed Charlie's hands covering the entire top of the now-wobbly wooden chair he'd been seated in. He swallowed once, began to speak, gulped again as the big man took his time straightening his coat, squaring that mammoth hat. The big man still didn't look away from the dealer's face.

The dealer finally managed to whisper, "Thank . . . thank you for your patronage, sir."

Charlie nodded once, turned, and heard the dealer let out a stuttering breath of relief. Despite his new financial situation, Charlie half smiled. At least he had his size. It wasn't worth much, but this big body could, by gum, still earn him a day's honest wage most anywhere labor was needed.

The big man strode the length of the narrow room, making the long walk toward the front of the saloon, the floor squeaking and popping under his weight. Everyone he passed gave him the hard stare. He felt

10

certain they all knew he'd lost all but his shirt.

Midway to the door he passed a cluster of men at the end of the bar. He felt relief that they were chattering among themselves and not concerned with him. Then he heard a voice that about stopped him in his tracks.

"Shotgun? Why, by God, it is! As I live and breathe, it's my old friend, Shotgun Charlie Chilton!"

Though it had been many long years since he'd been called that, Charlie's step hitched, as if out of dusty reflex. He paused right there in the middle of the room and closed his eyes. He knew a couple, three things: He should have kept on walking, he'd never had many friends and most of them had died away in the war, and the man who all but silenced the room with his drunken shouting was no friend. Anybody who called Charlie by that old name was no one he wanted to know anymore — and should by all rights be dead by now anyway.

Charlie knew he should have kept right on going out that door, headed to the livery where he'd intended to bed down for the night in the stall beside Mabel-Mae, his old mule. And then come tomorrow he'd lick his wounds out on the trail, put some distance between himself and the town of

11

Monkton. And once he did, he'd cipher out a way to earn money again, make up for the last couple of years' wages he'd blown at the faro table.

Though Charlie knew all these things and thought all these things, he still opened his eyes and slowly turned to face his past. And that's when what had begun as one of the best days of his life, which had gotten pretty bad, got a whole lot worse.

For who he saw annoyed him to no end. Jacob "Dutchy" Erskine. They had called him Dutchy because he looked as though he might be a Dutchman, though he wasn't any more Dutch than Charlie was the king of China. But the fool was grinning at Charlie, and judging from his rheumy eyes and leering mouth, his boilers looked to be half-stoked with liquor too.

Charlie turned back to the door. He hadn't gone another step before the voice stopped him again. All eyes were on them both now. Even the lousy banjo player in the corner had stopped.

"Shotgun Charlie, as I live and breathe!" Dutchy slid away from the elbow-smooth bar top and stumbled the few steps toward Charlie.

The drunk man was still a good couple of strides away when Charlie held up a hand.

"I . . . I don't know who you are, nor what you're after, but you've mistook me for someone else."

The man halted, weaving in place, his smile drooping. "What? Charlie . . . aw, you're funnin' me."

Charlie pinned a broad forced smile on his wide, windburned face. He looked left and right, nodding and smiling at the staring faces. Seemed as though there were a whole lot more people in here than when he'd come in. He felt his cheeks redden even more. Curse Dutchy for a fool.

"I'm telling you . . . fella," he said in a lowered voice. "I ain't never seen you before. Now do us both a favor and back off."

"No, no, I ain't neither. Come on over here, meet my new chums. You can buy us all a drink with your faro winnin's." Dutchy's smile turned pinched; his wet eyes narrowed. "Unless you'd rather reminisce all about the old days right here in the middle of the bar." He raised his arms wide to the room.

Charlie saw the two missing fingertips on Dutchy's left hand. They had healed poorly after they'd been shot off long before Charlie ever knew him. The hard pink scar nubs looked like pebbles or warts, and Charlie

13

had always wanted to pare them off with a knife. If they had been on his fingers, he'd not have been able to live with the look, nor, he suspected, the feel of them.

Dutchy giggled, looked around at the silent, expectant faces. "Maybe you'd like to tell 'em all about the last time we seen each other. Wichita, wasn't it? Something about a lousy Basque, wasn't it? All them sheep running all over the place, and Charlie here, he . . ." Dutchy stopped and leaned forward. "What's the matter, Charlie? You look like you seen a ghost. Maybe one of a little girl? One who's been all trampled by a . . . horse?"

It had been a long, long time since Charlie had dreamed of the little girl. But it hadn't been any longer than that afternoon that he'd thought of her. He'd been walking on into town leading Mabel-Mae when he'd seen the children playing before a white-painted schoolhouse a few streets away from Monkton's main street. He thought of her every day, in fact, and this man, this damnable Dutchy, was fixing to rip it all wide open again.

Big Charlie Chilton had tried hard since that accident to make sure he was slow to start a thing. But once he set to a task, he dedicated himself to it and rarely gave it

14

less than his all. But when his great ham-sized right fist drove like a rock hammer square at Dutchy's grinning face, Charlie hadn't known it would happen. Like the old days he'd worked so hard to put behind him. No warning, just action. He hated the fact that it felt good when his tight knuckles jammed hard against Dutchy's leering face.

The strike happened so fast that the entire room was still silent, listening with rapt attention to the drunk's account. The next thing they all heard was a muffled snap and Dutchy's head whipped to one side as if he were gawking at a passing bullet. His body followed suit and spun in a dervish dance before slamming into the bar leaners behind him. They parted fast and let Dutchy drop, his head clunking the mud-scraped brass rail.

The early gasps had given way to scraping chairs and now yammering as standing people leaned, trying to get a look at the collapsed victim.

"He dead?" someone asked.

As if in response, Dutchy groaned and rolled his head to and fro, the left side of his face already swelling and purpling.

An old man with a cob pipe leaned close over Dutchy. "Naw. It was his jaw that cracked." He plucked the pipe from its

15

customary spot in his mouth, the groove worn by it in his teeth. "He ain't dead, but he ain't gonna be right by a long shot for a long time to come, mark my words. . . ."

That was the last thing Charlie heard as he bulled his way through the double front doors, the glass panes rattling as he pawed them shut behind him. His big granger boots punched squelching holes in the slushed mud of the early October street as he stepped off the sidewalk. The livery. That's where he had to get to. Had to get on out of here before someone set the law on him.

Charlie didn't hear the doors open and close again behind him, fast footsteps hammering the boardwalk in the opposite direction, toward Marshal Watt's office.

CHAPTER 2

Mud muffled the blue roan mare's slow steps. Two women bobbed in time with the animal's measured pace, a pair of carpetbags jostling in counterpoint draped on the horse's rump behind the second rider. Mud caked the hems of their layers of limp skirts, of once-gay coloring that would have looked right on a warm, sunny spring day. But on this darkening autumn afternoon in the hill country of the western edge of the Rockies, their clothes, horse, bags, and skin took on the bleak, russet hues of spattered mud and the grime of long days spent traveling hard. The horse's gaunt frame worked to continue on, but she slowed, then stopped. A last step ended with a forehoof paused in the air, as if in middecision. Finally she set it back in the ice-rimed mud and stood still, head bowed against the coming dark and numbing cold.

"Delia?" the larger of the two whispered

to the woman in front of her in the saddle. "Are you awake?" With a shawl-wrapped hand she gently nudged the smaller woman.

The figure nodded, finally said, "Yes, yes, I'm here. So cold, Hester."

"I know, Delia. Me too, but we have to get to that town. I swear I saw lights a few minutes ago. That next rise ought to put us in view of it again."

Delia forced herself to sit upright. "Do you think that might be Gamble?"

Hester hesitated. "No way of knowing yet. I expect we have a distance to go first, dear."

"Will Vin be there?"

Again, Hester paused before replying, "I expect he will be in Gamble, yes. Waiting for you. But I don't think we're quite there yet, Delia."

The younger woman didn't respond.

"Delia? Is the pain . . . is it bad?"

Delia shook her head. "No, no. But I will be glad to rest for the night."

"Me too, sister," whispered Hester. "Me too." With that, Hester tapped her heels to the horse's barrel and the tired beast resumed her slow progress up the slope in the road before her.

CHAPTER 3

"If you all will recall, I said a whole lot of months ago that Jasper Rafferty was one man none of us should climb betwixt the covers with."

A collective groan rose throughout the low-ceilinged log saloon. An errant gust of icy wind chose that moment to whistle through a gap beside a poorly carpentered window opening. One of the men, a middle-height fellow with a thick, bristly black beard and big bony hands, the fingernails on which were mostly black from stray hammer strikes, leaned back in his spot on the split-log bench and poked the wadded flannel scrap back into the gap through which fine snow danced.

The gathered individuals included most of the living residents of Gamble: two dozen men, two women, and a patch-haired black dog that slept under the stove — an annoyance only when he got spooked and woke up too fast, stinking up the place as he singed the hair on his head on the stove bottom. Or when he waited until he came inside to shake off after a swim in the brook, splashing ineffectually for the darting mountain trout that lived under the cutbanks of the raw mountain stream that ran alongside the camp. But even the dog, whom they all called "Dang Dog," had largely given up on that frigid practice once the weather began hardening off the top of the water, a state the flow would soon remain in for many months of the foreseeable future.

The man who had spoken, a small bald man with enormous dragoon mustaches, one Clayton Eldridge, hooked his thumbs behind his leather braces. He fancied himself a mayor of sorts of Gamble.

He began to repeat his claim but was cut off by a fat black man wearing a brown bowler shiny from age and with a number of playing cards stuck at angles in the brim. "Now, I know you can't be talking of the same conversation I was present at, Clayton, for as I recall . . ." He looked around himself at the other residents of Gamble and smiled. "The only sounds you made were sort of grunting, suckling noises when mention of whiskey was made."

Eldridge's jaw dropped open and his eyes

widened. "How dare you, Luther!"

But the self-appointed mayor's cries of protestation were swamped by jeers and hoots from the rest of the group. The noise subsided as a burly, pock-faced woman, gray of tooth, and with once-red hair to match, rapped a wooden spoon on the bottom of a blue spatter-ware pot. "Simmer down, already. Simmer it!"

She held the pose, glaring at each man in turn until they all left off guffawing. Then she nodded. "The point of this gathering wasn't to yammer about who's right and who's wrong. Seems to me we all been wronged by Jasper Rafferty. We were saddled with him as our freighting outfit because him and that lawman bankrolled most of Gamble. But part of that deal is that we get the goods we wanted brought up here to this forsaken rocky knob surrounded by timber and peaks."

"What's your point, Sheila?" Eldridge worked his thumbs up and down his braces as though he were waxing them.

"Point is, *Clayton,* that we should get what we're paying for. We been sending our gold down there and in return, we been getting a whole lot less than we was promised."

"What's this 'we' business anyway?" The black man smiled and sat back against the

21

log wall, his callused hands resting on his paunch. "You got a mouse hidden in your dress, Miss Trudeaux?"

The place erupted in laughter once again. Sheila stifled a smile and nodded, waited for it to die down. "Only thing no bigger'n a mouse in my dress lately's been you, Luther."

"Now, look," said Clayton Eldridge, shushing the laughing crowd with his hands. "We all know what we're getting at here. And if we're going to keep in any sort of manner at all until spring, we'd do well to send someone to track down our supplies. I know those Shoshoni got us pinned down here. No one knows that more than I do. I lost my only boy. . . ."

His voice cracked, and the gathered folks all looked at their hands, their feet, anything but at Clayton's quivering lip and wet eyes. His son's death had been a hard blow on them all. The boy had been well liked. More so than ever after he was found, flailing and gagging on the talus slope below the diggings that day in June, pinned by an Indian's arrow. It had laid the boy low but had taken a long time to kill him. He had mostly bled out there, so it hadn't taken him long to die by the time they got him back to what they jokingly called their "town."

22

Gamble consisted of a cluster of log structures, a few with plank additions tacked on with the coming of the gold, some sporting store-bought roofing tin, and felt paper. The saloon they sat in on this very night, though a log affair, had two fancy hand-turned posts someone had brought up on the back of a mule. They'd replaced two cobby-cut pine poles in the center of the porch with the fancy turned ones flanking the steps. From then on — mostly with the help of the gold strike shortly thereafter — they had begun to feel that Gamble might not be one of those two-bit, two-month towns no one could recall five minutes after the gold dried up.

The boy, Selby, had died and they'd buried him on a pretty knoll not far from the buildings. Clayton, much to their surprise, dug harder than ever. When asked why he stuck, Eldridge said it was because he would never leave his boy. He'd had to leave his wife's grave back where he and the boy had come from, in a town somewhere on the ocean in Maine, and he'd never forgiven himself for abandoning her. He said when he struck it big he was going to have her dug up, carted all the way to Idaho Territory, and reburied beside their boy.

"Who in their right mind would go to

Monkton?" said Luther. "I, for one, would bet a whole lot of ore that Rafferty did send up the supplies. I bet Marshal Watt made him do it. You know why the freight wagon never made it through. That foul Shoshoni laid 'em low and scattered our goods. Took what they wanted, then scattered the rest. And as far as Rafferty and the marshal are concerned, they did their part."

"At this point, it doesn't matter much who did what," said Clayton Eldridge. "Just that we can't afford to sit still here all winter and we can't afford to go. But we can afford, maybe, to send a rider out, get help. Who's up for it?"

"The Italian, where's he at?"

"Sleepin' off a hard one from last night, I expect."

"How does he do it? I didn't think there was much booze of consequence left in Gamble."

"He gets himself in Fancy's drawers, that's how." The man's voice, silent until then, drew attention from all.

The second woman in attendance paused in lighting a half-smoked cigarillo she'd pulled out of her brassiere. "Screw you, Proudhorn."

"Not likely," said Proudhorn, stroking his big black beard. "But I'll go."

24

"Go where, exactly?" said Sheila Trudeaux, folding her arms.

Samuel Proudhorn stood, stepping back away from the bench he'd been sharing with three other men. "To find out if it was the Shoshoni who got to our goods before the goods got to us."

There wasn't much sound in the room at his comments, though all eyes were on the broad-chested man with the big beard and big hands. He was not a particularly tall man, but Samuel Proudhorn, with his deep voice and its strange Cornish accent and his oversized facial features, boots, and hands, struck them all as a big man even in stature, nonetheless.

"Well, now, don't let's all break into a chorus beseeching me to reconsider." His eyes seemed to narrow in that way that told them he was probably making a joke, though with that beard they could never see for certain if he was smiling.

"That's mighty kind of you, Samuel, and I think I speak for all of us here" — Eldridge spread his arms in a gesture he hoped showed he was including the entire room — "when I tell you that we appreciate it mighty. But on second thought, I wonder if we shouldn't wait another few days."

"No, no." Proudhorn circled around the

table. "We've seen more sign than ever of Indians nearby. We're all looking over our shoulders at the slightest noises when we should be concentrating on turning out the richest ore strike of our lives. All the signs of sizable riches are here. And yet we aren't even hunting as much as we should for fear of Indian attack. And let's not forget that winter comes early in the Bitterroot Mountains. No." He waved a hand and pulled a big-bowled briar pipe from his vest pocket, rooting with a forefinger in the bowl. "We have taken far too much for granted. Assumed safety just because the Shoshoni to the east of us have been somewhat placated. All the gold in the world won't mean much if we're dead, either from starvation or scalping or both."

Again, the room filled with the stone-faced silence that usually greeted Proudhorn's blunt observations. Blue-black smoke clouded upward from his pipe, and his eyelids fluttered beneath it. He blew a plume of it outward. "Don't look so horrified. I merely said what we've all been thinking for weeks now. And don't tell me you don't trust me."

The rush of voices made him smile again, and this time he laughed too, so his fellow Gamblers knew he was kidding. "I tell you

26

what, you can all split my share of the diggings in the event that I do not return. That should convince you I intend to see this thing through. Because I'll be cursed for eternity if I am going to give up my precious gold to you all!"

"A drink to Samuel Proudhorn!" shouted Sheila, and the men offered up halfhearted cheers, hating that the Cornishman seemed to outman them once again, but as a feeling of relief worked its way into their thoughts, they cheered a little louder.

The next morning, the bushy-bearded man had saddled his buckskin mare, strapped on his big skinning knife and Enfield percussion pistol, and mounted up. Sheila Trudeaux slipped a precious nearly full bottle of whiskey into his saddlebag and rebuckled it. He watched her but only smiled with his eyes. She winked at him and said low enough that the others couldn't hear the words, "Good luck, Samuel. Come back to me."

He nodded once to her, then looked at the rest. "I'll be back as soon as I'm able. With answers at the least, and preferably leading a train of supply wagons. Maybe, if we're lucky, soldiers will already be out and about, taking care of the blasted heathens."

"No, no, do not bring too many of the damn strangers up here to Gamble, Meester Proudhorn!"

They all turned to see Vincenzo Tantillo standing behind them, his arm draped over Fancy's shoulder. "Because eef you do, I will, uh, how you say, fight you for the gold, no?" His handsome smile spread wide across his darkly stubbled face. The smile did not reach his eyes.

"Ignore him, Samuel," said Sheila, smiling up at the man on the horse. "Go with God."

"I thank you. I hope I won't need his assistance, but if it is required, far be it from me to turn him away." He raised one of those big bony hands to the fawn brim of his slouch hat, nodded once, and headed south out of Gamble proper, leaving behind the tiny settlement, the buildings arrayed as if scattered by a drunken dice roller.

Samuel Proudhorn knew he would have to follow the ragged cut of the wheel-rutted trail down out of the mountains, alongside the icy flow of the feeder streams that in spring became pummeling freshets, to the lower valley, where the freshets would feed the Salmon River that would eventually lead him to the town of Monkton. He also knew that between Gamble and Monkton, there were a host of deadly elements, not the least of which were the rogue Shoshoni and the fickle caprices of Mother Nature.

By his careful count, he was beginning his fourth day out from the settlement he had called home, for better or worse, for much of the last year. Gamble had few redeeming qualities, in his estimation. Most of the baser points could be found in her inhabitants, but he had made the best of it. For all their coarseness, Samuel had found most of them to be of a giving, caring nature, and so he had tried in kind to reciprocate.

In truth he would have departed long before, having a hankering to try his hand farther west at panning on the wide, promising streams of the lower Oregon and northern California region. But then in midsummer they had struck pay dirt, many of them, all at once, and they had all agreed in the saloon one night that they would do their best to keep the strike a secret, though for how long they could do so remained a mystery.

Since nearly all of Gamble's occupants had been staked by the wily merchant, Jasper Rafferty, and, consequently, Monkton's Marshal Watt, who was part owner of Rafferty's Mercantile, they naturally had to be told of the promising diggings at Gamble. But they all had agreed that few others should be told.

All had gone along well then, as each of them worked like dogs to get as much easy ore out as possible. It was feared by them all that one or more of them might soon tire of the labor, cash in their personal claims, and skedaddle, leaving the rest of them open to well-known savage practices of large mining outfits, the very folks Rafferty and Watt wanted to bring in to Gamble, come spring.

That one or more of the big mining corporations would come in was inevitable, blasting roadways and bringing with them thousands of men, all with families. Stores, gambling houses, saloons, laundries, eateries, liveries — such grand-scale mining would be the ruination of small personal fortunes. It would also be the gateway to large personal fortunes, but for far fewer of them than any supposed.

Samuel Proudhorn knew this only too well. For he had been one of the early discoverers of color at Pikes Peak. And he had been a younger, more foolish man then, and had sold his early efforts, diggings that had seemed to him little more than promising short-term holes. He had doubted very much they would yield more than what he was able to pry from them in the short months he had been there. So when a large firm had come in and offered him four thousand dollars, he leaped at the offer, signing away all rights to his claims.

And two months later, in between bouts of drunkenness in Breckenridge, he heard that the Eastern Amalgamated Corporation had struck a fortune in gold on his old claim — it tested three thousand dollars to the ton — and in the years since, had proven up as one of the best claims ever, worth more than one million so far.

So to have the opportunity at another fortune at his fingertips, Samuel Proudhorn found it was worth the effort of putting up with Gamble's other denizens. He could also endure the hard, long, labor-filled days, the ragged hands and aching back, leg, and arm muscles. He also welcomed the tender, if misguided, ministrations of Sheila Trudeaux, proprietor of the town's saloon and sporting house, such as it was. He even justified the necessity of making this trip that none of them would have dared make. Yes, it was all vital to preserving his take. And this time he would not waste the effort.

As if waking from a dream that never changes, Samuel Proudhorn was dragged from his musings by the grunt of his horse,

Sassy, whom he'd had charge of for five years. Never had she let him down, rarely faltered in her footing, and never nipped an arm or threw him, nor made overtures to pluck from him a pound of flesh. But the grunt was a sound he'd not heard from her in a long time, long enough for him to have forgotten momentarily that it meant she'd become nervous and wary.

And in the finger snap of time following it, he saw her left ear twitch, and when her head turned to the side he saw a nerve pulse in the soft hollow above her eye. Then he felt a punch to his left thigh, and a pucker of black-red blossomed unbelievably on his trouser leg. The realization he'd been shot hit him with a searing pain that in an instant coursed through his body, flaming outward from the raw new wound. He kicked with his right leg at the horse and hunched low.

I should pull my rifle, he thought. *I should try to find out where they are.* One hundred things he knew he should do before another instant passed him by flooded his mind. They left as quickly when he heard a howl to his right, then another to his left. They were the shouts of at least two men, excited, crazed men filled with a killing frenzy of bloodlust. Samuel had heard it before, had witnessed it in the eyes of poker players sure of themselves, drunk on nothing more than the power of their conviction as they bet it all.

He had now begun to catch glimpses of them, Indians by the look, perhaps the Shoshoni, as he broke Sassy from the trail and veered to softer earth that she might gain better purchase on. But it wouldn't matter, because another punch, harder this time and in his shoulder, shoved him from the saddle, pitching him hard to the rising blurry ground.

Samuel Proudhorn's head bounced on a gray boulder; mint green flecks of moss flew up when he hit. His hearing pulsed as if he were underwater, and his eyesight dimmed.

The last thing he heard was loud yipping noises, not unlike coyotes taking turns sinking fangs into a lamed fawn. The last thing he saw were the faces, not of men, but of demons, leering demons from beyond the grave. And he knew he would never get to enjoy all the finery that his precious gold would one day offer him.

CHAPTER 4

Samuel Proudhorn had never awakened so fully and so quickly in his life, and to such sharp hot stabs of pain. It felt as if his entire body were being roasted on a spit. There, before him, over him, one of the leering demon faces. It leaned closer, and then it smiled a wide, toothy grin and its hand delivered a stout smack, backhanding him in the face, snapping his head to the side. Pain flowered up his left side, laced him like lightning. What was happening?

"Wake, white man! Wake!"

The leering demon howled at him — was it speaking to him? It was all Samuel could do to keep his eyes from closing, from trying to force away the pain, the hot tears such pain pushed up and out of him.

Crack! His head whipped to the left. *Smack!* To the right.

"What . . ." He tried to speak, but his tongue felt as though it were thicker than his wool blanket rolled so tight tied behind his saddle. Yes! That brought to mind Sassy, galloping . . . he'd been shot. *Oh no, no, Samuel,* he told himself. *This cannot be. You have too much to do yet. And the people of Gamble, your friends, those people you kept at arm's length for so long, the only real friends you've had in a lifetime of roving. You have let them down. You have doomed them, the weak souls of Gamble.*

Seconds later, a great gush of water poured over his face and Samuel sputtered and coughed, jerking himself side to side, but he was held down by something. The spastic thrashing hurt, yet the water had helped clear his mind. And what he saw made him wish he'd stayed incoherent.

Two Indians stared down at him, their decorated buckskin clothing and faces offering a confusing sight of color. The stink of them as they moved closer was the smell of animals, of raw musky rage, sweat, and anger and wood smoke and blood. How many were there? Just the two? Samuel looked about as best he could, and saw he was tied down, staked out with leather wrappings. His eyesight began to cloud, limiting what he could see. Soon he tasted a warm wetness on his lips, knew it was blood, perhaps from a wound to his head.

The demonic Indians murmured among themselves. Samuel could see two now, both men, and their prodding, kicking, and laughing had begun to enrage him. He gathered a shout and tried, tried again, and got it half out before one of them drove a hard, tight fist into his mouth, snapping his head to the side again.

Behind him, a cry arose and Samuel, weak as he was, tried to look in that direction. He saw one of the men standing beside a horse, his horse, Sassy. She still looked to be upright, unharmed. What would become of her? *Stop thinking like that,* he told himself. *Figure a way out of this.*

The Indian held aloft his bottle of whiskey, still mostly full. Samuel had not allowed himself to indulge in its splendors these past nights on the trail. Now he wished he had. Or else had dumped it out.

But the Indian hooted and gasped with the fiery rush of the rough whiskey.

"White man, what do you want here?"

Samuel turned his head back to face the man looking down at him. This one didn't seem interested in the least in the whiskey shenanigans of his friend.

"This is not your land, not your people, and yet you whites come here, take everything that we have and leave nothing for us

36

but death and sickness. No more, white man. We will go into tomorrow without you."

"I . . . don't want anything," said Samuel, trying to shake his head. It seemed important to convince this man that he wanted nothing but to live. For that he would leave here forever, never come back, would gladly forsake the gold, all of it. He would leave here forever.

But the man was having none of it. Even laughed at Samuel's tearful efforts at convincing him of this.

Soon the effects of the whiskey drove the other man to shout and snarl, to dance and sing in his native tongue. Where did this one learn his English? A missionary? For all Samuel knew, the Indian could have traveled back East for his education. Did any of it matter? Soon, as if in answer to that last question, the miner's thoughts clouded over with pain.

The first arrow jerked his eyes wide. Any previous pain he'd felt had been galloped over by this fresh, hot flame — a pain that ripped a scream from his throat as though a hand had reached in and dragged it up from his guts. Samuel screamed until there was no breath left in his body, and this seemed to be what the Indians wanted, for they let him fill and empty, fill and empty his lungs over and over.

And with each cry, he jerked, pinned to the ground as before, by the staked leather thongs he had seen earlier, and now by the long shaft of the feather-topped arrow jutting from his left shoulder. He could not move that part of his body, could feel nothing of it but pain. The hot, raw stink of sweat and dirt and of his own blood filled his nostrils.

More smacks to the face, more kicks to the chest, none of it mattered anymore. Not until the second arrow, driven deep into his right shoulder, pulled more screams from him. Then more water to revive him. He saw the same man standing over him with a long shaft — a spear, this time. He bucked as it drove into his guts, and he felt every slice and sting as the other of them, howling and mad with drink, set to work on him with a knife.

Water and hard slapping awakened Samuel Proudhorn once again. Large, rough fingers pulled his eyes wide, forced them open.

"What do you want here on Shoshoni land?"

Samuel tried to think — what did he want? Nothing, he wanted nothing from him, from the land. He wanted to pass through, to be gone from here. That was all.

Another slap and the fingers forcing his eyes wide, forcing him to watch as a knife, Samuel's own knife, always kept keen-edged, wagged into view before the leering face.

"Wha . . . ? What are you going to do?"

Samuel had wondered fancifully in the past that if he were ever caught by a scalping Indian, what could they possibly do with his hair, seeing as he was nearly bald? But now he knew, for the Indian let go of Samuel's eyes and snatched the mass of Samuel's blood-and-spittle-soaked beard in a begrimed, bloody hand and lifted Samuel's head off the ground.

"No!" shouted Samuel, but his cries only seemed to goad the man on. Other shouts drowned out Samuel's sobs. Sobs that became screams once the man began slicing at the skin beneath Samuel's great bushy beard. The screams died in a guttural gagging sound, but not before the Indian had peeled half of Samuel's face free.

CHAPTER 5

"Folks just call me Charlie. Big Charlie."
He tried to hide the trembling of his fingers
by rebuckling the straps holding Mabel-
Mae's load in place. The animal's girthy
body swayed slightly from his efforts.

"I wonder why that is."

Charlie glanced at the marshal but saw no
humor in his dark, staring eyes. The man
had all but sneaked up on him not but two
minutes before when Charlie had been busy
gathering his gear. Too busy, he guessed, to
hear. That and the wind had picked up
outside, rattling a loose plank and raising
dust along the floor.

"The man I hit, did he say anything?" Big
Charlie looked over the mule's back at the
marshal. Even in the lamp's dim light, he
could tell the lawman's eyes were studying
him, wondering why he'd ask that.

"Nope. I personally saw that he can't do
much more than whimper and bleed and

snot himself. You broke his jaw in a hundred pieces, Big Charlie."

Charlie wanted to sigh and whoop, all at once. As far as he could recall, Dutchy also couldn't write, so chances of him blathering to anyone about Charlie's past were slim. Despite his slight renewal of hope, Charlie still wanted to drag Mabel-Mae on out of there and get gone. Instead he nodded and retied a rope he'd already dealt with twice, hoping the marshal wouldn't stand there much longer. But in that, the lawman continued to disappoint him.

"I reckon I'll be on my way, then."

The marshal rested a hand on Mabel-Mae's rump, patted her. "Now, see, that's where you're mistaken, Big Charlie."

"How's that?" Charlie felt the small fist in his gorge tighten. Any warmth from the rum toddies of earlier, and the fevered flush he felt in dropping Dutchy to the floor, had left him, cold and still inside, long minutes before.

"I got a number of folks in the Royale Gaming Hall told me they swore they heard that the man you accosted had accused you of being someone whose name might ring a bell with me. Might go so far as to say that should I care to dig through the pile on my desk, I would likely find a dodger on a man

41

fitting such a description as you sport." The marshal nodded slowly up and down, taking in Charlie's full height.

Charlie shook his head. "No."

For the first time since he came into the stable, surprise raised the marshal's eyes. "No? Uh, which part, exactly?"

"There ain't no dodger on me." He tugged a rope, let his big hands drop atop the load on Mabel-Mae's back. "Not anymore."

"Served your time, did you?"

"Something like that."

"Then you won't mind walking on up to my office for a spell."

Charlie sighed. "I told you, Marshal, I ain't riding the owl-hoot trail."

The marshal shucked his sidearm as fast as Charlie had seen any man ever do the deed, and peeled back the hammer at the same time. "Oh, but I insist, Big Charlie. You see, a man can't pop another man with a bone-breaking love tap like you did to that drunk fool back there and then ride off without so much as a by-your-leave."

Charlie guessed that small speech would have drained the talk out of pretty near any other man. But the marshal here was apparently made of sterner stuff, for he kept on prattling, even as he wagged his pistol at Charlie.

"In my town, you see, we have a little something called law and order. And I like to keep them one after the other, like that. Law first, then order. I'm the law, and I do a decent job of keeping the order. Hired to, in fact." He followed Charlie out the front door of the barn.

"But you, Big Charlie, you took the order part to task and apparently, finding the law wanting, why, you up and popped that man."

"He was asking for it."

"Mm-hmm. And I could ask why. But I won't. Because I like my guesses just fine. I'm afraid the truth might peel them all apart till you get to the softness in the center and find the onion's gone bad."

Charlie didn't really know what this man was going on about, but he hoped it would stop soon. Was he going to be arrested? Tried for a crime? Kept until the marshal proved to himself that Charlie was no longer a wanted man? He reckoned he'd ask a few of these questions once they got to the law dog's office, but right now he was doing all he could to walk without knowing where he was going, somewhere on up the street. They headed toward the busy part of the main street, right up there where all the nosy folks were out on porches, watching the marshal parade him back on up there. He felt as he had when he'd walked through the bar.

"A man's past hangs on him like a coat he can't shuck, Big Charlie." The marshal's voice was closer than he expected, and lowered. "No matter if he's atoned or not, the public is a fickle thing. I know this for a fact, having served it in various capacities for a long damn time, Charlie Chilton. Keep going. It's the single lit window up there on the right."

Men, women, even a few youngsters stared in near silence at him. The night was turning cool, crisp. It felt good on Charlie's face, his cheeks already heating up again under the scrutiny of the townsfolk.

"Now, then," said the marshal once they were inside the office. But he didn't finish his thought. He nodded to a straight-back chair before his desk. "Have a seat. I'll fetch us some coffee."

Somewhere along the walk, the lawman had holstered his Colt. Charlie looked around the small front office, taking in the usual features, the open-face gun cabinet, the desk with an identical chair behind, the desktop a layout of neat stacks of paper and orderly items looking as though they belonged where they'd been placed. Also sitting atop the desk were a tin cup with a number of writing implements poking from it, an unlit lamp on the corner, and a ring with three skeleton keys. And under it all, the dark wooden surface had been scuffed and scarred and gouged and carved and stained by who knows how many lawmen before this one.

Behind him the marshal slid a coffeepot back onto the low sheet-steel stove's top. "I noticed you don't wear a gun, Charlie."

It wasn't a question, but it was, just the same. He waited a moment. The marshal set a cup of steaming hot coffee on the edge of the desk before him. "No, sir. Been a long time since I . . . needed to."

The marshal dropped into his own chair and nodded, blew across the top of his coffee. "I looked like you, I guess I wouldn't need anything other than those." He jerked his chin at Charlie, indicating his big hands.

Charlie looked at them, kept his forearms on the chair's armrests. He flexed his big, callused paws, let them hang over his lap. "I reckon." A moment of silence passed; then Charlie said, "Say, Marshal . . ."

But the man held up his hand. "I am Marshal Watt, by the way. And I know what you're about to ask me, Charlie. But I will hasten to that point before you, if I may." He didn't wait for permission but barreled right on ahead. "I believe we may be able to help each other."

Charlie's eyebrows pulled together like two great rodents greeting each other. "I don't see how. . . ."

"It's like this, Charlie Chilton." He leaned forward, elbows on his desk, and stared right at Charlie.

Given that the man had used his full name again, a name folks from his past would know him by, Charlie guessed it was some sort of offer he wouldn't be able to refuse too easily. If at all.

"I am a married man, Charlie." He paused.

Charlie guessed that meant he should say something. "Well, that's nice for you, Marshal Watt, I'm sure."

"No, no, it isn't, Charlie. Not in the least. It's a venomous relationship that because of who I am and what I am, I am locked into this marriage until death do us part." His eyebrows rose for a split second, as if he were mentally exploring the possibilities of death parting one of them from the other earlier than nature might intend. Charlie guessed it wouldn't be the marshal from his wife, but the other way around.

46

"You see, Charlie, that man you hit earlier, he was part of an outfit hired to work for Jasper Rafferty, a man who had contracted to run a freight trip soon."

"Who on earth would hire . . . him?" Charlie realized too late that he'd all but admitted he had known the man.

The marshal smiled. "I like you, Charlie. You are a good judge of men. And the idiot who hired the man you punched, and a handful of others besides, is my brother-in-law, Jasper Rafferty. In fact, when Jasper showed me the crew, I asked him why he'd hired such barrel scrapes. 'Because they came cheap,' he told me. Can you believe the man?"

The marshal smacked his hands on the desktop and stood, obviously disgusted by the talk of his brother-in-law. "Would that his sister, my wife, had the same cheap streak. But no, sir, not a chance."

"I still don't see what this has to do with me."

"Charlie, I am in a position to offer you one of two things. One, you can sit in my jail for a long time waiting for a court date."

Charlie almost stood, but the marshal's hand dropped with the instinct of a striking viper to his holster. "Or you can sit back down and listen to the more interesting half

47

of my offer."

Charlie eased back into the chair and nodded, knowing for sure he wasn't going to like much of anything he was about to hear.

"The trip that is to be made on behalf of my brother-in-law and me — much to my chagrin, I am also in business with the man — has been postponed several times for want of a crew. Now that Jasper finally has arranged a crew, said crew has lost one member, a member who, if what I am told is to be believed, was a knowledgeable teamster. And if that trip does not run, Charlie, do you know what my life will be like? It will be unpleasant, to say the least. I suspect that foolish Jasper and his morbid little wife and fat children will all have to move into our very home, a small affair at the best of times that offers little respite from my wife's constant pestering."

"So . . . you want me to go in . . . his place? On that trip?"

"That is what I am on the cusp of saying, yes."

"Oh. Well, I'm not so sure. . . ."

"You don't seem to understand, Charlie Chilton. And as much as I hate to be indelicate about it, you don't have much of a choice, now, do you?"

"It's like that? Jail or some crazy freighting trip?"

"It's about like that, yes."

"But I'm a free man. I haven't done anything wrong."

"Except for disturbing the peace in my town, laying out someone in the Royale Gaming Hall with a singularly impressive blow to the head. Stoving him in so hard that he is unable to perform the task he's been hired for."

Charlie sighed. "And that puts you in a tight spot. So you put me in one, huh?" He stood, sudden decision hastening his movements, the chair stuttering on the floor. "No, sir, no, you can't do this to me. I don't reckon you have enough of anything to keep me here."

The marshal sat back and stared up at Charlie. Charlie stared down at him. In the center of the other half of the small room, a knot in a hunk of firewood popped, and the stove ticked with the heat.

"Fine. I expect," said Marshal Watt, "that Judge McElroy will be through sometime . . . oh . . ." He consulted the wall calendar. "Along about December."

"December? But that's nearly two months away!"

The marshal smiled. "Or January. He likes to spend Christmas in Salt Lake with his brother's family. Oh, but don't you worry, Charlie. The cell back there is usually empty, so you won't have to share too often. And the wind often blows from the north, and since the cell's barred window is on the south side, you won't feel much of the breeze. The food? Oh, it's downright edible. Nearly so anyway. How that woman ever convinced the town she could cook for the prisoners is beyond me." He smiled again. "My wife. That's why I take at least one meal a day at Hazel's Hash House, on Sixth Street. A man has to eat. But why am I telling you that? You obviously know what I mean." He nodded at Charlie's robust girth.

The big man poked the air in front of Marshal Watt with a finger like a stick of dynamite. He spoke through gritted teeth: "Dagnabbit, Marshal. I don't like being railroaded, not one bit."

The marshal nodded knowingly. "I'll bet you don't. No man worth his salt does. But you're not married to Ethel. I almost forgot to mention that the job does come with recompense."

Charlie's eyebrows met in a questioning look.

"The position pays."

Charlie almost smiled. "How much?"

"Knowing my foolish brother-in-law, a

man whose very existence is a testament to frugality, I doubt it is very much at all." He leaned forward and in a lowered voice said, "But it will be more than the distinct lack of coins in your pocket at present."

"How did you . . . ?"

"It is my town, Charlie. I am paid to know everything that goes on here. And I found out in fairly rapid fashion that you lost your shirt at Wilkie's faro table this afternoon. I'm guessing you could ill afford the loss."

"You guessed right."

"So does that mean . . . ?"

Charlie sighed. He settled back into the wooden chair and reached for the cooling cup of coffee. "Tell me about this trip."

The marshal nodded and leaned back in his chair. "It's a freighting run up into the Bitterroots of our very own Idaho Territory, to a mine camp up there, place by the name of Gamble."

"That far, this late in the season? You ever been up that high in the fall, Marshal?"

"As it happens, I have not. I am a Southern man by birth and inclination, relocated here to this outpost as far from magnolia blossoms and beautiful belles as a man can be. Curse me for being a man of my word. Curse me for a fool." He looked back at Charlie. "Pardon me for being wistful. I gather from your reaction that such a trek at this late date is ill-advised."

"You got that right, and then some."

"Then it's a good thing it begins tomorrow morning."

"What?"

"Bright and early, yes, sir. Now, you may spend the night here and in the morning you can collect your things and I'll show you to the freighters' camp. And before you protest, I'll tell you that I've seen the best of men, when faced with tantalizing temptation, make mistakes they regret for a long, long time. You are looking at one of them, in fact. With that in mind, you will indeed spend the night in the back cell. But I will make sure you get extra blankets — and a tray of food from Hazel's Hash House and not from my own harpy's kitchen. Deal?"

"Do I have a choice?"

"No, sir, as a matter of fact, you do not." The marshal smiled and extended his hand. Charlie noticed the other hand still hovered by his holster, thumb lightly hooked in the belt. They shook.

"And Mabel-Mae?"

The marshal looked surprised for the second time that night. "That your wife?"

Charlie smiled, shook his head. "No, not me. Never had one of those, never will.

Mabel-Mae's my mule, back yonder at the stable. You already met her."

"Oh, sure. I'll see that she's taken care of for the evening. You have my word. But I will stable her with Skunk."

"Skunk?"

"Yeah, best liveryman in town, but the creature will not bathe to save his life. Can't understand it. Stock don't seem to mind, but his customers come and go quick. Now that I think on it, maybe that's why he chooses to remain so smelly. One way to get out of dealing with the public."

Charlie nodded. "And my . . . name?"

"As far as I'm concerned, there's no paper on you . . . Big Charlie."

True to his word, the marshal made sure Charlie had a stack of blankets, moth-eaten, but all to himself. And Watt returned with a tray heaped with food. It went a long way toward satisfying Charlie's impressive appetite.

That night, as he stretched out on the hard plank bunk, Charlie thought back on the long day and decided that it could have ended a whole lot better, to be sure. But on the other hand, it nearly ended a whole lot worse. Sure, he'd lost his life's savings, but he still had Mabel-Mae, his health, his reputation, such as it was, and his freedom, of sorts.

He also had a job, something he sorely needed, especially heading into winter. But north into the Bitterroot Range, in late October? That was a fool's mission, make no mistake.

Nearly asleep, he chuckled, because he was the fool on the mission.

CHAPTER 6

Jasper Rafferty hadn't been down to the freighters' camp since they'd arrived two days before. Now it was dark and he'd wished he'd gone an hour earlier, while there was still daylight. He hated leaving town for much of anything unless he was riding high in his barouche, and he never liked to touch the bare ground out here along the river if he could help it.

He'd seen his share of snakes, but always from as far away as possible. But who knew what the foul creatures did at night? Didn't they come out of their holes in the dark to hunt and find warmth? What if they sought him out — wrapped themselves right around his ankles and . . . ? Just then he stepped on a brittle length of old branch. It snapped and he pinched out a high, girlish cry.

A few moments later, he saw a low bloom of lantern light, and footsteps approached.

"That you, Rafferty?"

Rafferty recognized the voice as that of the coarse little freighting boss, Everett Meecher.

"Well, I swear, it is you. I admit to being a bit disappointed. By the sound of it, thought maybe it was a little girl from town, come to show us her attentions." Meecher doubled over in a squeezebox wheeze that tailed off in a coughing fit. The lantern swung up and down with him, the wire bail squeaking.

Meecher spat what sounded to Rafferty like a hand-sized gob of phlegm, then said, "Come on to camp, then. I reckon you got some mother-henning to do, so we might as well get that out of the way. And grab that stick while you're at it. Take all we can get for the fire. It's fixing to be a cold one tonight."

Rafferty froze, wondering if he should go back for the stick. Then thoughts of bending down and wrapping his fingers around something cold and slithery turned his innards to stone and he ran straight for Meecher's lantern light.

Once they reached the freighters' camp, Meecher handed him a tin cup of hot coffee, set the pot back on the flat rock beside the fire.

"Thank you, Meecher." Rafferty sipped, looked around the camp.

Meecher caught his eye. "Don't worry your head, Rafferty. The men are in town, getting potted up one last time before we load up and hit the trail tomorrow."

"That's what I'm here about, actually."

"Oh?"

"Yes, you see, one of them, the man named Dutch?"

"Dutchy, yeah, what of him?"

"It seems he's gotten himself in a bit of a pickle. Been punched pretty hard by someone. Got himself laid out good and proper for running his mouth. He was hit by a man some of the folks in town seem to feel is an outlaw."

"Hell, how bad is Dutchy hurt?"

"He is alive, but his jaw's broken and he can't stand on his own. I think he'll be laid up for quite a while, by the looks of it."

Meecher stared into the dark toward the lights of the end of town, as if waiting for his men to emerge from the dark at any second. Finally he sighed and said, "I can't leave the teams. I'll wait till they get back, then see to Dutchy."

"I think, Mr. Meecher, that this would be an ideal time to, well, to . . ."

"Out with it, Rafferty."

"I feel we should call off the trip." Rafferty liked how that came out, much easier than he had expected. He was already picturing where the stock for the wagons would go in his store and warehouse. The town of Gamble would have to wait out the winter by tightening their belts.

His know-it-all brother-in-law, Marshal Watt, wouldn't like the idea, but really, where were the people of Gamble going to go? And who would visit them? Snow would soon seal them in, giving him and Watt time to get their investors lined up.

"Call it off?" Meecher gritted his teeth, the makings of a smile barely tugging his mouth corners. He looked behind him, as if at other men, then back to the thin, nervous man standing before him. "You'd like that, wouldn't you?"

Meecher kept the raw smile stretched wide and nudged his hat back on his head. "Seems to me you made a deal with them folks up in Gamble to get this freight on through. They'll be socked in tighter'n a bull's backside before too long and they won't have a lick of flour, nor coffee, nor dried fruit, nor nothing. Not to mention me and my men and the pains we took in getting here at your request. You'd go back on that? On your word, Rafferty?"

"I never said that. I never said anything of the sort. It's just that with the Dutch fellow laid out, well, it doesn't make any sense to push on, you one man short and all."

Meecher stared at him hard. Even though he was not a large man, Everett Meecher had a habit of demanding attention wherever he went, simply by being himself. That much Rafferty had noticed from the first day the little scowling man and his crew had arrived in town, the only ones to have responded to Rafferty's too-late feelers for a freighting outfit.

"What of it? We got five wagons, five men. Simple."

"But," said Rafferty, "you need a backup man, someone to take up the slack should one of your men come down with something." Rafferty half turned away, swallowed hard. Not looking at the older man, he said, "No, I'm afraid my mind's made up. I can't risk it —"

"Since when did you know anything about freighting, Rafferty? You did, you'd know them people up in Gamble should have had their supplies long before now." Meecher squinted. "I don't know what you're playing at, but if you think you can weasel out on me, you best think again."

Meecher came at Rafferty again with that

stiff little finger, prodding into his chest with each phrase uttered. "I got all the men I need!" Prod. "And I got all the wagons I need!" Prod. "So you just be ready with the goods first thing in the morning at your storeroom, you hear me? We'll be there and so will you!" Prod.

Rafferty stared wide-eyed down at the vicious little man, saying nothing.

"You got me, Rafferty?"

"Yes, yes, sir, Mr. Meecher. I . . . I'll be there."

"Then git gone!" Meecher turned back to the fire, his arms wrapped around himself, brooding into the flames.

It was a long walk back to town, made worse by the fact that Rafferty's lantern went out with more than half of the twenty-minute walk still ahead of him. It seemed to him that he might well freeze to death or be bitten to death and partially consumed by snakes before he could reach the town.

It would only be much later, in bed next to his angry stick of a wife, that he would recall someone telling him that snakes denned up in cold weather, all winter long.

But for the remainder of his walk, the one thing that kept him heading toward the town's lights was his increasing anger, not with Meecher, though he would dearly love to see the last of that rank man, but with himself for not standing up to the little tyrant. He should have known dealing with Meecher was like dealing with his wife — you never can win an argument with such belligerence. But now he was stuck and had to honor the contract — unless he could make his brother-in-law, the marshal, order Meecher to go away and find some other town to bother.

For the first time in long minutes, Jasper Rafferty thought that maybe he'd come out of this deal okay after all. Yes, sir, he'd pay a visit to the marshal, try to convince him of the wisdom of canceling the trip altogether. Then see if he might not be interested in running that freighting outfit right out of town.

CHAPTER 7

Rafferty decided to postpone his visit to the marshal until he double-checked the store for the night. He hadn't been there for five minutes before he heard a rapping on the back door. His first thought was of his wife, Edna. Maybe she'd left something behind after they had closed up for the day. The children were forever in need of a sweet or requiring liniment, or making some other demand for goods from the store shelves he could ill afford to give them, not when creditors were a constant threat in this business.

His wife had once been a woman who could make a penny scream she pinched it so hard. But once the children came, she indulged them in ways he never would have suspected of her in the days when it had been the two of them, a young couple seeking to establish themselves in Monkton and make a mark there. She was still frugal in most matters, to be sure, but not where the children were concerned. It was irksome.

But as Rafferty moved to the back door, hastened by the repeated knocking, he knew it could not have been her. She would have her own key and would have used the store's front door. Who could it be, then? Perhaps one of the freighters — maybe they had found out somehow about his attempt to cancel the trip. He stopped in the dark of the storeroom. They might be angry . . . and drunk.

The knocking resumed, but it didn't sound like the rapping of a drunken or angry man's knuckles. He hesitated before the door, swallowed once, and in a voice he hoped sounded deep and menacing, he said, "Who is it? What do you want?"

Scuffing sounded, as if someone in boots had stepped backward on the wood of the loading platform. "Hello, sir. Pardon me. . . ."

A woman's voice. Jasper sucked cold air in through his tight-set teeth. And not his wife. That's what he needed, some woman trying to rob him. Or worse! "What? What do you want? I am a busy man." He paused, then said, "And I have a gun."

The woman's voice came to him closer now, close by the other side of the plank door. "No, sir. We don't want trouble, only to find out if you are Mr. Rafferty — we were told that your supply train hasn't gone on to Gamble yet."

What could this all mean? Why would a woman want to know about the freight trip? It was no voice he recognized, and he fancied he knew everyone's voice in Monkton.

"I am Jasper Rafferty. What do you want with my supply train?"

He heard a weary sigh, and lifted free the two timbers barring the door. As he swung the door inward, he held aloft his lantern and saw a woman in dark dress standing back from the door. He nodded out of politeness, but was ready to slam the door in her face should she do the slightest thing he didn't like.

"I am Hester O'Fallon. My sister, Delia, is back there." She indicated over her shoulder at the dark. "Sitting on our horse. We are on our way to Gamble and had thought we would have to travel there alone. But a woman at the eatery, the Hash House, told me that your supply train to Gamble hasn't left yet."

"That would have been Hazel. Yep, she would tell strangers my business."

"We aren't asking for anything from you,

Mr. Rafferty. Merely to be allowed to follow along. We'd appreciate the company. And we don't really know how to get there on our own."

"My freighters are on a business trip to Gamble. This is no silly mercy mission. They are a rough outfit looking to make good time, and I won't tolerate anything that might slow them down."

"I can assure you we won't slow anyone down, sir."

Rafferty sighed, then canted his head and looked her up and down again. "This is the sort of thing that folks usually have to pay for. No different than buying a ticket on a steam train, you know."

"I understand that, Mr. Rafferty. And we can pay our way."

Now, that was more like what he had in mind. A business transaction. "I tell you, Miss . . . uh . . ."

"O'Fallon. Hester O'Fallon."

"Right, Miss O'Fallon, you see, this trip's more complicated than that. I am willing to charge you, say, ten dollars each."

The woman's shoulders sagged as if under a great weight. "I need to buy supplies and that would leave us nearly destitute. I am sorry, Mr. Rafferty, but we'll have to go it alone. I thank you for your time, sir. But I would like to purchase a few items from you tonight."

"Where will you go?" Rafferty didn't really care, but he'd become a bit curious about them and their need to get to Gamble. He wasn't keen on anything fouling the trip, and Watt would certainly not like new faces headed to Gamble. It flew in the face of the air of quiet they were trying to lend the town until spring.

"Tonight I will try to find accommodation at the town marshal's office."

"Why? Why would you go to the law?"

"To see if we might stay there the night. We have stayed in empty jail cells before."

Rafferty shook his head. "No, no. That won't do. Marshal Watt won't like that at all."

"Why not?"

"Well . . . you're indigent, right? That means you're lawbreakers."

"Mr. Rafferty, just because we are not wealthy does not mean we are indigent. We are travelers, nothing more, nothing less. Despite what you say, I will risk a visit to the town marshal. He may be able to offer us some sort of help. We will see you in the morning, sir."

"Oh, very well, then. You may as well stay in my stable out yonder. We don't have a horse at present, our last delivery animal having come down with colic some months ago. There you'll find hay, and I daresay there are oats, what the mice haven't carried off anyway. It even has a door."

"Thank you. Now, seeing as how the store is still open — the back door, at least — I would like to buy some items from you."

Rafferty didn't move, so she continued. "Two wool blankets, bread, cheese . . . and laudanum."

"Aah, so that's it, is it?"

"No, sir, Mr. Rafferty. Do not mistake what you hear. My sister is ill and that is the only thing that eases her increasing pain. I would like two bottles of the stuff, for I fear it will be an unpleasant journey."

Rafferty stared at the woman for a moment longer, not sure if her story was true. She didn't look like one of those laudanum fiends, but who could tell? Finally he nodded and opened the door wider.

"Come inside," he said. "I'll get the things you need. Stove's nearly out, but I'd wager what's left of the coffee's still warm. You can take the pot out with you, and two of those cups there by the stove. Just see that you return them in the morning. Speaking of morning," he added as he picked items from the shelves, "see to it that you're up

67

early. Those freighters will be loading up and heading out, and not waiting for a soul, I reckon."

She nodded.

"But let me be the one to make your presence known, when the time is right. Elsewise, they will leave you here. And I for one wouldn't blame them." He stuffed a loaf of bread in an empty coffee bean sack. "You're going to need enough food for the trip, you know. Those freighters won't likely be pleased to share with you."

She paused, and it seemed to him he had brought up something she hadn't mentioned. "You could buy supplies from me, enough to maybe get you by. Especially if the freighters share their meat with you — I daresay they expect to shoot game on the trail."

"That would leave us with nothing once we get to Gamble."

"Not much of anything to spend your money on there anyway, Miss O'Fallon. There are things a woman can do in a mine camp, I've heard tell, to make a dollar. I expect you'd make out all right."

She straightened, looked him in the eye, at his half smile, then at the items he had lined up on the shelf, among them two bottles of laudanum. She seemed to come to some inner decision, nodded, and reached in the folds of her clothes for her coin purse.

CHAPTER 8

Charlie woke to the smell of coffee. Still dark, but he reckoned dawn wasn't far off. He yawned and stretched his full length on the bunk, much of his lower legs dangling off the end, and his shoulders hanging off the side, despite the fact that he'd tried in the night to sleep on his side. The outer door squawked open and in walked the marshal, a cup of steaming coffee hooked in one hand, the key ring jangling in the other.

"Good morning, to you, Big Charlie."

"Morning, Marshal Watt. I sure hope you intend to let me out about now, because as much as I hope that coffee's for me, I can't put a thing into this body until I . . . well, you know."

Marshal Watt smiled and cranked the keys in the lock. The cell's iron-strap door swung wide. "Just back there to the right, you'll find a single-holer. Can't miss it. In fact, you'd better not miss it."

Soon the two men had made their way down to the freighters' camp. Mist hung low along the river bottom, curling like smoke from a slow fire through the willows and gnarled stubble of bankside scrub brush. The trail, a two-rut wagon path, wound along the Salmon River.

"What sort of man would take on such a dangerous late-season job, Marshal?"

Charlie's question made Marshal Watt stop. Without looking at Charlie, he said, "You take a guess and you'll be half right. Let's say they wouldn't have been my first pick. Come on, you'll see soon enough."

Charlie smelled the tang of an early-morning campfire before he saw the glow of the fires, two or three of them that he could make out through the ground-hugging fog. Presently the dark, bulky shapes of oxen, then a telltale bray of mules. A mixed outfit? Hardly seemed professional.

"That you, Marshal Watt?" A small man ambled toward them, the mist parting around his bowed legs. Charlie took measure of him as he approached, chest height to Charlie, but lean. He looked to be solid, maybe old enough to be Charlie's father, with a bristly beard more gray than black, and with quick eyes that seemed to take in everything all at once. He strode right up to

Charlie, not something the big man was at all used to, given his impressive size, and especially not from so small a fellow.

"I'm Everett Meecher, and I'm told you're a handy man with a fist."

Charlie drew in a big breath, dropped the paw he was about to offer up for a handshake. "I —"

"Normally wouldn't make no never mind to me, but Dutchy was a decent hand. And now he's so stoved up he can't hardly go. Can't talk, can't ride, can't do nothing. I got to leave him here. So I figure you owe me."

"Well, now, I reckon I don't owe you a thing. He's the one who started it."

"Not the way I heard it. Yeah, that's right, a couple of my boys was there. You'll meet 'em presently."

Charlie rasped a big hand across his beard stubble. He'd about had enough of this situation, marshal or no. "Like I said, I don't owe you or any man a thing in this life."

The marshal coughed, looked at his boots.

Charlie folded his arms across his chest. "But as it happens, I do need a job. I'm running a little short on seed money just now." No one said anything. Finally Charlie said, "If you ain't interested, then I'll leave you to it." He turned to go.

Meecher trod a circle around the campfire, kicking at whatever lay in his path — an empty milk tin, a small frying pan with bacon fat thickening, a last handful of finger-sized twigs. "Hang fire, I need a driver."

He beelined for Charlie again and though he only came up to the big man's chest, and weighed barely what one of Charlie's legs might, Everett Meecher thrust a callused finger up at Charlie's face. "I ain't convinced you're worth it, but you're a big enough boy. You'll do, I reckon." He turned away, then said over his shoulder, "I don't suppose you're handy with a gun."

"Don't carry one."

"That ain't what I asked, is it?" Meecher turned, hustled up to the lawman. "Marshal, this is the best you can do? I got a run to make and you bring me a man who weighs half as much as a wagon and don't carry a side-arm?"

"I carry a Green River knife, good enough so far."

"Oh, that's useful. I'll be sure to look for you when I need a beaver skunned out." Meecher shook his head and walked away, mumbling to himself.

Marshal Watt and Charlie watched the little man walk beyond the campfire to the

73

empty wagons.

"Nice fella," said Charlie.

"Meecher grows on you — not unlike a fungus, come to think on it. I had occasion to stand him a drink in town the night they arrived, and believe it or not, I think he's a straight arrow. Or was at one time. You wouldn't know it to look at him, but Meecher used to have quite a freighting firm, made regular runs from Salt Lake on up to Montana Territory, hauling flour, hardware, ore crushers, all manner of mining equipment, as a matter of fact, you name it."

"It's his outfit that worries me." Charlie eyed the crew, which looked to be made up of four men, in addition to Meecher, roughnecks all, by the looks of them. None of them looked particularly clean, as if scrubbing off in the river would never occur to them.

Their clothes, from rough-spun cloth shirts and fur vests to buckskins, were slick with grease and sweat stains. They were a hairy, patch-bearded bunch — not things Charlie could hold against them. Life on the trail was always a hard thing. But there was something else there, maybe the looks they shot his way. He seemed to recall a couple of them; might be they were in the bar. He'd been so busy trying to shut up Dutchy that he'd not paid much attention to the other faces around him.

"Marshal, I count four of them, one of the old man, and me. That's six, and by my tally, they have five wagons. That leaves but one man for each wagon with one to spare. Now, that's a tight-to-the-bone outfit."

Marshal Watt nodded. "That it is. I'll be headed back now. See you in town in a while, Charlie. I'll have your mule ready at the store — unless you'd rather leave her here in Monkton. I'd make sure Skunk took good care of her while you were away."

"Thanks just the same, but I reckon I'll take her along. After this trip I doubt I'll want to wander on back this way. Might be I'll hole up in Gamble for the winter, see if I can't make a fortune rooting for gold."

"Hmm," said the marshal, walking away, his voice fading as he headed back to town. "You're welcome to, of course, though I've heard there's not much promise of gold. . . ."

Charlie waited a few moments before striding over to meet the others. The first was an average-height thin man with looks under his beard stubble that Charlie knew the ladies would find handsome, something he'd never been, and a trait he'd long ago gotten over envying in others. The man was solid, broad shouldered beneath a once-red long-handle shirt. His hard face and set jaw had the look of a confident man. His quick, flinty blue eyes, ringed with red veins, reminded Charlie of old man Meecher's.

"You'll be Big Charlie, huh? Any truth to the rumor that you're also Shotgun Charlie?"

The question pried up a bitter taste in Charlie's gorge and set his teeth to grind. The man who spoke must have seen evidence of it on his face, for his eyes widened for a moment. "Aw, never mind. Only . . ." He stepped closer and lowered his voice. "You might have my uncle Everett convinced you're up to the job of driving for us, but I'm the real boss here and you ain't nothing but a hired man who ain't wanted nor needed. You keep that in mind."

Charlie felt his face redden and as he opened his mouth to bellow back something that would set the man in his place, Everett Meecher shouted, "Enough of that pissing contest. Rollie, introduce him to the boys and then get to work. We got to finish rigging. We still got to get to town and load up, got a long day ahead."

Rollie, who Charlie now knew as Meecher's nephew, nodded to the three staring dubs behind him. "The one in the buckskins there is Norbert, the fool in the middle with the pretty teeth is Beauregard." The man smiled wide, revealing pitted black stubs and a mouth black with chaw juice.

"His friends call him Bo, but you can call him Beauregard." Rollie smiled as if he'd said something truly clever. "And that bald piece of work over yonder is Shiner."

Charlie figured he'd at least try to be civil. He gave them a quick nod. "How do, gents? Good to meet ya."

The four of them laughed and headed to the wagons, shaking their heads. Charlie sighed, not for the last time that day, more convinced with each passing minute that he should have made a run for it with Mabel-Mae the night before.

"In for a penny, in for a pound, Charlie, old boy," he said as he readjusted his hat and headed for the wagons and the little man shouting orders.

It took them another twenty minutes to clear the camp and finish harnessing the beasts. Despite the ragtag appearance of the outfit, Charlie was pleased to note that the horses, mules, and oxen all appeared well cared for. One wagon was packed with feed for them. The rest were empty, canvas and ropes piled in the back, ready to cover and tie down the loads from the store in town.

"Would have left sooner," said the old man, coming up beside Charlie. He flinched, not having heard Meecher's approach. This seemed to please the old dog. "But the smithy was busy and some of 'em needed new shoes. I won't take to the trail without starting my beasts off right on foot. I can do what needs doing on the trail, but I start 'em right."

Charlie didn't know what to say, so he nodded. "Yes, sir. Fine bunch of beasts they are too."

That seemed to please the old dog even more. Meecher smiled, rocked back on his heels. "I take it you're a man who knows his way around a critter?"

"I reckon so, yeah. Grew up on a farm Nebraska way. Not long ago I drove ore wagons in Colorado."

"Good to hear. You'll be driving the oxen. Seem to suit you." Meecher laughed so hard he bent double and wheezed. He straightened up, dragged a shirtsleeve across his tearing eyes, and rolled a quirly. "Couple things you got to know about me. I don't abide drinking on the job, only at night. And don't let me catch you eating more than your fair share of the vittles. But most of all, I see you abusing my stock in any way, I will personally kill you with these bare hands."

He said this last through gritted teeth. And as he said it he shook with a bubbling rage that seemed to come out of nowhere. His face turned a bright red. If Charlie didn't know better, he would have sworn the man was joking with him — especially since he couldn't picture Meecher doing much more to him than bruising him. But no, Meecher was obviously serious about his animals.

"Yes, sir. Sounds fair to me."

CHAPTER 9

An hour later found them nearly loaded. That part went quickly, with all men pitching in, and Rafferty's hired help making the job even quicker. Meecher hopped in and out of the wagons, double-checking the positioning of each crate and barrel and sack. His attention to everything going on in his wagons impressed Charlie, and he decided that if there was one person on the crew who might turn out to be decent after all, it was old Everett Meecher.

It sure wasn't his nephew, Rollie, nor any of the other three — rough cobs all. Charlie knew he'd better keep his wits about him. They looked to be the sort to gut a man because they felt they might get away with it. And being in the wilderness and all would surely offer them such temptation.

Soon enough, all loads were tarpaulined and lashed down six ways from Sunday. And about then, Marshal Watt came walking up the street leading Mabel-Mae, Charlie's kit lashed atop. "Here you go, Charlie. You sure you won't change your mind? Skunk would take good care of her for you."

"Naw, thanks, Marshal Watt. But like I said, I don't see myself heading back this way for any reason once the job's through. Might as well take along Mabel-Mae and my gear."

"What in tarnation is this, now?"

Charlie, the mule, and the marshal all flinched as Meecher appeared beside them, his already ratty felt topper scrunched in his fist as if he were trying to squeeze water from it.

"This here's Mabel-Mae. She's my mule," said Charlie.

"I can see she's a mule, but what I can't see is her on the trail with us!"

"Then you can call us quits right here and now, Mr. Meecher. 'Cause Mabel-Mae goes where I go, and that's that. She'll trail along. You won't even know she's here."

Meecher circled the animal, running a hand along her side, up her neck, patting her lovingly. "Well, see to it, then. I reckon one more beast won't harm nothing." He turned on Charlie, that finger poking in his face again. "But you feed her out of your own stores, you hear?" He stalked off, muttering.

"I hadn't counted on that," said Charlie, looking at Mabel-Mae.

The marshal cleared his throat. "How much do you reckon she'll need for a few weeks on the trail, Charlie?"

"Huh? Oh, a couple sacks of feed corn, some oats would do the trick, but, Marshal Watt" — Charlie's voice grew quiet — "I only have a few dollars. I don't have the money to . . ."

"I know, Charlie. But I do." He crooked a finger at one of Rafferty's assistants and told him what to bring. "And make it snappy, boy."

"Yes, sir," said the lad, and scurried off toward the storeroom.

Watt turned back to Charlie. "As it happens, the shopkeep's my brother-in-law, as I believe I mentioned last night. So we'll let him worry about the expense, okay?"

"I can repay you, or him, just not right now."

"No need to, Charlie. You're doing me a big favor as it is. Consider it a thank-you."

Charlie grinned, stuck out his hand, and the two men shook on it.

"One last thing, though, Charlie." The marshal stepped back and raised his voice so that all the men heard him. "The trail you're headed for? I don't have to tell you how bad it can be at the best of times — she's carved out pretty well by regular wagon traffic, but it's still rugged and rocky. And this time of year you have snows to deal with. And an old trapper, fella by the name of Pawnee Joe, came down to town from up that way last week. He said the Shoshoni are active this fall. Something's got them stirred up — I expect it's the army, or more likely someone found gold on their land again and they took offense. Can't say as I blame them."

"You an Injun lover, law dog?"

Everyone turned to see who had said it. The only one of them smiling and not looking around was Rollie Meecher.

"Hush your mouth, boy," said his uncle. "You'd do well to cut a wide swath around any Injun you find. I'd just as soon take a different trail altogether, but we ain't got no choice."

If the marshal had been offended by what Rollie had said, he didn't let on. He spoke to the boss of the outfit. "My advice, for what it's worth, Meecher, is to make it a fast run. As fast as the terrain allows anyway."

"I aim to . . . if everyone in this town can

quit palaverin' and telling me how to run my affairs!" The old man crab-walked past the wagons toward the front of the line. "Now climb aboard! We got trail to cut!"

Charlie looked once more at the marshal, who was smiling and shaking his head. The lawman caught his eye and gave him a quick salute. Charlie nodded, double-checked Mabel-Mae's lead rope, then climbed aboard the seat on the last wagon, behind the four oxen he guessed he would grow tired of seeing all too soon.

"Hooooo!" Everett Meecher's voice rang out loud and clear. As the sun continued to rise, the wagons rolled, hubs freshly greased, loads lashed down tight, and animals fed and rested.

As Charlie's wagon, the last in the train, passed by, Jasper Rafferty led a thin roan out from behind the last building at the end of the street. But it was the horse's load that Charlie had to look at twice.

Rafferty stared straight at Charlie, his jaw thrust out and eyes flinting sparks, as if daring Charlie to say something. Rafferty shook his head in warning, and then cut his eyes toward the front of the train. "Ho there, Meecher. Hold up!"

Within seconds, Jasper Rafferty had explained the situation to Meecher, right there in front of Charlie, the other freighters, and what townsfolk had turned out to see the supply train leave. Even Rafferty's somewhat business partner, the departing Marshal Watt, paused and warily eyed the proceedings.

Everett Meecher squawked and sputtered like a hen on a nest of snake eggs. He circled the halted wagons twice on foot, waving his arms and kicking at the frozen ruts of mud, at the dirty runnels of brown water beginning to form in the morning sun's heat. He seemed oblivious of the chuckles of the slowly gathering townsfolk at his antics.

When Meecher finally came to a stop beside Charlie's wagon, he stood staring at the two women, his arms folded. "No, no, and again, I say no. Ain't no way any women, least of all two of 'em, and on a half-dead horse, to boot, are coming on my freighting trip into Injun country. Rafferty, you are a jackal and a rascal and you ought to be hung high for this."

Jasper Rafferty responded by turning his red face away, letting go his hold on the horse's bridle, and walking back toward his store.

"I ain't finished with you, Rafferty!" Meecher's voice cut through the air like a sore-throated rooster's too-early crow. It had no effect on the storekeep. But the marshal strode on up.

"What on earth is the matter here, Meecher?" He looked from the women to Charlie to the scarlet-faced man.

It took another minute for Meecher to come out with his version of the story, which involved being saddled with passengers and not being paid for such, and on and on. All the while, Charlie watched the two women and saw the larger of them, the one riding second, grow angrier. Finally she slipped to the ground, and he caught a glimpse of her bloomers as she slid off the horse. He closed his eyes and chewed the inside of his cheek, felt his face redden.

When he opened his eyes, her gaze raked his as she strode up to the two men and folded her arms. She waited until they both stopped arguing and looked at her.

"Fine. Now, my sister and I are bound for Gamble. I foolishly paid Mr. Rafferty good money for passage to be included as part of this freighting outfit. If there's something about this you don't like, I suggest, Mr. Meecher, that you take it up with him. As for my sister and me, we have our own supplies, our own horse, and will be no bother."

There was stillness for a moment. No one spoke; then all at once half the freighters began shouting. Meecher howled like a scalded cat, and Marshal Watt was forced to drown them all out.

Charlie watched as the marshal led the woman and Meecher off a few yards and spoke low to them. Meecher's outbursts became less frequent, until he merely stood there shaking his head, not looking at the woman. He threw up his hands, as if admitting defeat, and stalked past Charlie to the gaggle of freighters, and they all clucked loudly at each other about the situation.

The marshal continued to speak with the woman, walked with her to the horse, where the other woman, a smaller thing and more frail looking — certainly paler about the face, it seemed to Charlie — sat as if it took effort.

He could tell the thin lawman was using his sizable talking skills to convince the women that they would be in grave danger on the trip, that they'd not be welcome, that they might not be looked on well, nor for that matter treated too kindly by the freighters. That it was a long journey with angry Shoshoni running wild all throughout the hills.

And from what Charlie could tell by the marshal's movements, headshakes, and waving arms, none of it made any difference to the woman. He appealed to the younger woman on the horse, but she turned away, that tired, glassy look in her eyes staying with her, almost as if she hadn't heard him.

Marshal Watt, sagged and defeated, walked up to Meecher and the others and spent another few minutes convincing them of something that Charlie couldn't quite hear but could guess at.

Finally Meecher came back to Charlie. "Me and the boys have decided that since we ain't got no choice, and since you're a big fella to be on thin ice anyway, and since you're riding drag here, you'll be responsible for seeing that them two womenfolk don't fall too far behind."

"Me?" Charlie stood in the wagon, fixing to climb down. "Now, see here —"

"No, sir. You owe me, boy." Meecher moved close to the wagon wheel, halting Charlie as he tried to step down. Meecher spoke in a lowered voice. "They got to go with us. That's all there is to it. And you got to watch 'em, boy. Anything happens to them, I'll never forgive myself, nor you neither."

Charlie held there, half down out of the wagon, traded another spitfire glance with the woman on the ground. She stood, defiant, arms folded, by their horse. She was a good-sized girl, he noted for the first time. She had long, reddish brown hair, sort of tied up in back, but much of it had come loose. It didn't seem to bother her. Her eyes were big, green, if he had to guess at that distance, and her cheeks were red and bright with the morning air's nip, her complexion not at all like that of the other one.

The marshal appeared beside Charlie, laid a gloved hand on his forearm.

"Hey!" Charlie jumped back. "Marshal Watt . . . I wish everyone would quit doing that. Scare a man half to death."

"What? Listen, Charlie, you have to promise me you'll look after them. The two women."

"Not you too? Aww —"

"Charlie, believe me, I've tried. But I can't arrest them for something they haven't done. If I went around telling law-abiding people what they could or couldn't do, I wouldn't be a marshal, I'd be a dictator."

"Well, go ahead and be one of them, then, whatever it is," said Charlie, disgusted and not at all convinced he needed the responsibility. "So long as I don't have to take charge of them two women. I have enough troubles, dang it."

"Look, Charlie. I've given Meecher money

to help justify the extra food those two women are bound to need on the trip, but that alone won't keep them safe. Make sure the other men treat them square, okay?"

Charlie gave up, sighed, and nodded. "What's their story, then, anyway?"

The marshal looked back at the women, the one standing, still staring at them, her mouth set in that same hard line. "They're sisters. The one on the horse is ill and they need to get to Gamble. Why, they wouldn't say, but —"

"I know, I know, you ain't one of them dictators, so you can't do a thing about it."

Marshal Watt smiled. "That's about it, yep. You feel you can do your best?"

"That's all any man can do, I expect, Marshal Watt." Charlie climbed aboard and nodded once to the lawman. Within a minute, Meecher's reedy voice cut through the morning air once again. And this time, they headed out of town without looking back. All of them but Charlie. He looked back once to check on Mabel-Mae, and saw the two women on that tired horse, doing their best to keep up.

CHAPTER 10

Blue Dog Moon tossed the picked-clean deer rib into the flames of the small cook fire. He watched it heat, the marrow bubbling and spilling out the end of the white bone.

"That is the best part of the bone," said his older brother, Son of Cloud.

Blue Dog sighed, but did not look up. He sat on his side of the fire, lazily sucking his teeth and playing at the whites' game of cards. It was something so many whites and his people found of interest, but he could never understand it.

Blue Dog looked at his older brother sitting beside him. "Even as I desire to kill every white I see, I spend time pursuing the ways of the whites. I do not understand that."

Son of Cloud smiled. "Do not forget that our mother was a white. But she is long dead. You never knew her and I barely remember her. And now that Father is dead too, we are no longer welcome among the people we thought were our own."

They sat quietly for a long moment, and then Son of Cloud continued. "And that is why we are here alone. We no longer have any of our own people. We" — he waved a finger back and forth between them — "are the only blooded people either of us will have. Perhaps that explains your fascination with such things as whiskey and cards."

The younger man said, "Bah," but did not look up.

"I only sat down here to talk with you because you look like an old woman, alone and brooding with your thoughts."

Blue Dog spun, his eyes wide. How dare Son of Cloud speak to him in such a manner! But then he relaxed — his brother was laughing silently. He should know better by now. "They should have named you the 'Trickster,' " said Blue Dog. "It is all day with you, isn't it?" But Blue Dog too had to smile.

Soon they fell silent, listened to the flames crackle the wood, the faint slap of the cards.

"I have heard that the Crow accept money and trade goods with the whites at the place they call 'Gamble.' " Son of Cloud now stared at the fire.

"That is because the Crow are weak and will soon be fat and hairy and stink like the whites."

Son of Cloud nodded, then looked at his younger brother and smiled. "Again I say, do not forget that we are half white. Blood cannot be changed, even though we were raised by our father's people. Maybe you are jealous of the Crow, eh?" He nudged the sullen young man in the arm.

"Bah!"

"Oh," said Son of Cloud, his voice louder, as if addressing unseen guests across the fire. "Blue Dog, I have seen you drink the whites' whiskey. And I think you liked it!" He nudged his younger brother again, both of them nodding at the memory of the stuff they had encountered so recently.

It left enough of an impression on Blue Dog that he wanted more, and licked his lips at the thought of it. Son of Cloud was far less impressed with the fiery liquid.

"Soon enough, then," said Son of Cloud. "For that white man we stopped on his way down out of the mountains from Gamble, the one who owned those cards? He said that they expected wagons filled with food and other things the people at Gamble would need for the long winter to come."

Blue Dog looked at his brother, eyes wide.

"They will be things, then, that the Crow might need also?"

Son of Cloud nodded. "I think so, yes."

They were silent again; then Blue Dog said, "He was no man."

"No. He cried like a child and then died much too quickly." Son of Cloud shook his head at the grim task they undertook. "I would prefer to fight them than to kill them outright, with so little resistance." He looked at Blue Dog. "I am beginning to doubt that the whites have a warrior of worth among them."

The brothers pulled their blankets tighter over their shoulders and stared once more into the hungry flames.

CHAPTER 11

They had traveled, slow but steady, for hours. The trail had been in much better shape than Charlie guessed it would be. It was nearly a regular road with a great many trees having been chopped and sawed with a crosscut, then dragged out of the way. The recent rain and snow had softened the wheel-rutted trail in a number of low spots, and the beasts took extra urging to roll steadily onward. Charlie didn't like to lay the lines too heavily on the backs of the oxen, but there were times when he had no choice. And the brutes took it, straining against their yokes but never breaking stride.

A number of times, Charlie glanced back over his shoulder at Mabel-Mae, who walked on, uncomplaining as he knew she would. Not much perturbed that mule. She could carry a full load or Charlie or nothing at all and she always wore the same quiet look on her face, as if she were always thinking of something more pleasant somewhere far off. Charlie found himself envying that, particularly since he had mired himself in this latest kettle of muck and saw no way out of it but to bull on through, much as he'd always done in life.

Always after looking at Mabel-Mae, he'd risk a peek at the women on their old horse. They were still there, closer than he expected they'd be, and it seemed that the one who'd argued and won with Meecher and the marshal was always looking right back at him, catching his eye with a gaze that bothered him something fierce. Seemed as if she wanted to stab him for checking on them. A hundred times that morning, he cursed the marshal and Meecher for saddling him with them.

Hours into the day, they came to a low spot, wide and open alongside the Salmon River, the same flow they'd been more or less bumping up against for the past hour. The road led to the thick waterway, then out of it again on the other side. And boy, did that water look cold to Charlie! Ice had formed across much of it, the early-season scrim that thinned the farther from the banks it crept. But it grew thicker with each passing hour that the temperature stayed stubbornly low.

Charlie guessed that in another month, that ice would have formed a solid surface clear across, each side meeting in the middle and strengthening with every freezing slap of water underneath.

For now, it was still mostly open in the middle, but it looked colder than a grave digger's backside. He didn't relish the thought of having to lever a boulder-stuck wheel in the middle of it. The sooner they crossed and put the river behind them, the sooner Charlie would begin to enjoy the fine fall day again.

Meecher halted the train with a hearty "Hoooo-yah!" and the five wagons ground to a halt. The men set the brakes, coiled the lines, and hopped down from their hard bench seats, stretching and rubbing their backsides and moaning as if they had climbed up out of the gutter after a three-day drunk. It felt good to Charlie to step down, for certain, but he wasn't all that sore.

He expected none of the others, save maybe for the wiry little Everett Meecher, had done much in the way of hard labor in recent days. They looked to him like soft, drinking men who worked when they had to and loafed away the rest of their time. Men like that never sat well with Charlie.

He aimed to work hard, as much and as

long as it took, to buy that quiet place in the mountains, all to himself, the little valley with plenty of game, a river for fishing, and timber enough to build a fine home. A place he could go and be alone forever and a day, and not have to work at freighting or much of anything else that didn't suit him. He might even take up whittling. He had the urge to carve little animals now and again, a dog maybe, or a bear.

Charlie sighed. That would have to wait now, maybe for another couple of years. He cursed himself at the thought of losing all that money at the faro table. What had he been thinking? He shook his head again, as if to shoo away a fly. In his experience, thinking never did help solve many problems. And he'd spent much of the morning wasting time thinking about his long-gone money and the faro table and Dutchy and Meecher and the rest of them. And the women too.

He looked up to see Norbert wading out into the frigid water of the river, a long pole, riddled with spiky branches, thrust out before him, testing the depth. He had reached far into the middle of the river and nodded back to Meecher, who stood on the bank shouting orders to him, indecipherable over the rush of the river.

"I'll wager it's deeper than it looks," said Charlie to the women, who now stood beside their horse. He hadn't necessarily been looking for conversation, and in that he wasn't disappointed. The sickly looking one kept her sullen face pulled, while her protector, the larger girl, cut her eyes once to Charlie, then back to the river.

He was about to tell them they ought to move around, stretch their legs, maybe visit the side of the trail while they had the chance. If he read Meecher right, that squawking old man would get across the river as fast as his beasts' legs and the wide wheels of the wagons would carry them.

For that matter, Charlie was mighty surprised that the old man had allowed sense to prevail and had taken the time to sound the river bottom. In Charlie's not-insubstantial experience, these mountain rivers could be deceiving. Each spring the hard-charging freshets ran bold and cold, feeding into these flowages and carving all manner of new eddies, gullies, washes, and hidden rips. They could suck a man and horse under and hold them there, thrashing like twigs in the current long enough to break every bone and suck the air from their lungs for good.

And that's when they saw the tall, thin,

buckskin-clad Norbert lose his footing. One second he was there, nodding and shouting something unheard to Meecher, and the next . . . gone. Everyone onshore, even the two women, gasped as if they'd watched their favorite horse break a leg on a race course.

They saw nothing for a long moment. Then farther toward the opposite bank than they thought possible, Norbert's head popped up, flopping on his shoulders. Then he was gone again, back under the roiling surface.

Charlie sliced free a spare roll of hemp rope from the side of his wagon and uncoiling it as he ran, he jammed one end into Everett Meecher's old horned hands. "Tie this off to something stout!" he shouted as he scrabbled for the other end. He looped it about himself and snugged it around his chest, securing it with a double bowline. As he did so, he heard Meecher yell to the other men.

"You useless bastards get over here! Rollie, back that second wagon around, get her ready to yank these boys out of there!"

Charlie didn't wait to see if they did as Meecher bade; he trusted that they had. And he plowed into that half-frozen river, angling downstream to where he saw Norbert's skinny leather-clad body, hung up on a bobbing, bony deadfall tree, one arm weakly slapping at the ragged edge of ice forming from the far side. The man's head barely bobbed above the surface of the gray-green water.

"You hang on, Norbert! I'm comin'!" To himself he said, "Charlie's coming, all right. Only he's getting mighty cold and he don't know if he can make his legs work much past the middle of this river. . . ."

As soon as the water topped his boots, they filled, and the numbing cold sucked the breath from Charlie's lungs. He kept slow-stepping forward, though his chest convulsed with shallow breaths. He moved as fast as he could, jamming his boots down hard with each step, bracing his legs against the current.

He also took care to keep his legs far enough apart that he kept what balance he could muster — too close and he could be knocked clean down by a rogue thrust of water. With each step Charlie felt sure he was about to topple downstream. He knew that if that happened, he had to aim his feet downstream, keep his arms above the water, and the back of his head upstream so that he might have a chance at breathing through the ordeal. He'd have to keep angling toward a bank, either side, and hope he didn't take on too much water before he made it.

Charlie glanced back once when he heard a raspy shout — his quick glance showed him that Everett, Rollie, Bo, and Shiner had arranged the wagon and lashed the rope to the tailgate, and each stood one behind the other, hands on the rope, ready to pull him back as soon as he muckled on to Norbert — if he could get to him in time.

Charlie glanced back once more over his right shoulder and saw the two women, also at the shore but downstream. Both looked worried. The bigger girl held a hand to her face as if stopping herself from saying something. He thought maybe he caught a look in her eye that was softer than the ones she'd been sending his way all day. *My word, but she's not half bad,* thought Charlie as his boot inched forward into a big hole in the river.

The instant numbing pain stung him all over, like millions of tiny needles jabbing into him without letup, over and over. He wanted to scream, but his nose and mouth filled with river water, colder than ice. It froze his eyes into throbbing knots of gravel.

Something tugged at him from behind and in a fraction of a second he felt convinced it was some great underwater creature snapping and tearing at him, unwilling to let him go. Was that what death felt like? Coming up hard on you like a fish on a worm?

Charlie, you're a fool, he told himself. So intense was the burning pain of the freezing water, he'd forgotten that a rope was tied around him and was probably being yanked by the men back on the shore.

He thrashed and flailed and managed to drift downstream enough that he once again felt bottom beneath his boots. His arms swung up and broke the surface first, as if clearing a path for the near-solid water. Before his eyes, the flesh of his hands turned purple, the very color of a favor girl's fancy dress.

Where it had been a shallow, labored thing before, his breath now stuttered in and out with a freight-train speed that scared him. He was sure it would never again settle down. Having seen he had gained his feet, the men ashore stopped yanking the rope. For that he was grateful.

Then, above the gush and roar of the water, so much louder in the river than from the bank, he heard a moaning that tapered off to a long, drawn-out whimper. To his left, not more than ten feet from him, he saw Norbert, as the man let go his feeble hold on the branch and slid into the icy, greenish flow.

As Charlie dived forward, his teeth clacking together like seeds rattling in a gourd, he hoped the men onshore would give him slack enough to get to the man. It might already be too late. Norbert hadn't drifted far, as the current here had slowed. It took Charlie two lunging dive moves forward to reach the man.

Norbert floated facedown, as if he were trying to see something on the bottom through the murk. His long gray-black hair fanned around him, and a beaver-skinned stick had eddied and caught in his armpit. Charlie took one more hard step, felt sure he was not even moving since he couldn't feel his limbs, and tried to grab Norbert's waterlogged buckskin shirt. But his arm wouldn't do what he asked of it.

Charlie tried again, stumping his way forward, his mouth chattering beyond all control, and managed to swing a meaty arm onto the man's back. Had to get him turned over or he'd be a goner for sure. Charlie put all he had into making his frozen arms work for him — they felt like two ice-covered lengths of stove wood — and it was enough to get them both on top of the man. He worked them forward up to Norbert's neck, as if he were snagging something in a pond to drag it to shore, and in this manner managed to drag the man's limp shape to him.

"Get your head up, get your head up!" was what Charlie tried to say. But all he heard from himself were low moans. It worked and Norbert began to spin over onto his back.

The men onshore must have thought he had good hold of Norbert, for they began pulling on the rope and pulled Charlie away from the drowning man. He fought against them and pitching forward, with his chattering teeth he grabbed a puckered ridge of buckskin shirt across the broadest part of the man's back. It was enough to drag Norbert back to him.

He worked his hands around the man's shoulders and wedged them as best he could up under Norbert's chin. The folks onshore pulled harder than ever.

Charlie had no idea how long it took to get to shore. It could have been the time it takes to swallow a mouthful of hot coffee; it could have been a year. The next thing he recalled he was on his back on the bank, coughing and retching. He felt hands trying to push him onto his side. He tried to help.

As his senses came back to him, he

shouted, "Norbert? He make it?"

No one answered for a few moments, and Charlie worked to lift his head. He saw the men hoisting Norbert upward by the middle, facedown, working his belly with a fist as if kneading dough. It looked as though it was working, for with each thrust, water gushed and then drizzled out of the skinny teamster's blue mouth.

Then someone shouted, "Yeah, he'll live, I reckon."

Then he heard Everett Meecher shouting about getting a fire built. Charlie grabbed the spokes on a wheel beside him and worked to pull himself upright. Whoever had been pushing on him had left. He saw, as he was halfway to standing, the two women dragging deadfall wood, flood branches, anything that might burn, building a fire. Everett scurried to them, shouting something, and they parted away from him while he kneeled and put match to tinder.

Charlie felt sure it would be too late. He'd never been so cold in all his days. So cold he was hot, in an odd way. Even when he'd been caught in that squall in Colorado, crossing that frozen lake while he had the ague a few years back, he thought he'd been ready to die then. The cold had racked his body for what seemed like days. Wouldn't leave him be. Lucky for him he'd been traveling with an old sourdough who'd built a fire and helped drive the fever from him.

But this time it was far worse than that. He tried to look around to find Norbert, but he couldn't see him. Then he did, stretched out on a wool blanket that the men gripped in their white-knuckled hands as they hustled him to the new fire. Charlie felt as though he was about to lose his balance, but it was the women pushing him.

"Can you walk?" the larger of the two said. He looked in her eyes and didn't see the flash of anger he'd seen earlier, just concern. He nodded, unable to form any words, barely any thoughts.

He managed lurching stumbling steps, a woman on each side of him, but though he couldn't feel much, he could tell the one on his right side, the frailer of the two, wasn't doing much more than being in the way. Should he fall he'd probably crush her.

Everett Meecher must have seen the same, for he edged in between her and Charlie and draped Charlie's big arms over his shoulders, never once letting up with shouting orders. "Get Norbert's clothes off'n him, and someone help me with this big blasted bear of a man. I can't hardly hold his froze limbs up myself, and the only other help we got is a couple of women."

His sputtering drew Shiner to Charlie's side. The bald man tried to edge the big girl away, but she jerked her head to the side and said, "Help the old man over there. He's weaker than he looks."

Meecher howled and shook his fists all the way to the supply wagon for blankets. By the time Meecher made it to the fire, Charlie had dropped to his backside beside the flames. All he wanted to do was stick his head right in the fire. He leaned around it and looked at Norbert.

The man, he could see, was breathing. As they slid the buckskins from his legs, Norbert's skin was a deep blue. Charlie looked down at his own hands and saw they were now more red than purple. He took that as a good sign.

His own legs felt funny, as though they were being moved. He worked to shift his gaze and saw the bold woman had straddled his leg and was tugging on his boot, yanking it off for him. He smiled — or thought he did. Mighty nice of her. And he got to watch her backside too. Then she stopped and saw him. He hoped he wasn't still smiling.

She started in on the other boot. His socks

came off with the boots and he hoped his feet were presentable. They weren't — they looked blue and purple and all splotchy. *Not good, Charlie, old boy.*

"I'm going to have to help you with that shirt and those pants, mister. You can't stay in these clothes — they're keeping the heat out and the cold in."

"She's right, dagnabbit. Now do as I say and get them duds off, Big Boy."

Charlie spun his head around — it was Meecher. He had no idea what they were both yammering about; he felt fine. Better every second, in fact. He reckoned that fire was doing the trick.

They yammered some more, but he didn't care a whit what they were saying. Now that he was warm, he thought he might as well take a bit of a nap. He closed his eyes and felt something touch his face. Maybe it was rain or snow. There it was again. He opened his eyes, not really wanting to, and it was that woman, pestering him again.

"You can't go to sleep, you have to stay awake. Do you understand me?"

"Keep slapping on his face like that. I'll get these duds off'n him," Meecher shouted as if the entire camp needed to hear everything he said. Charlie found it annoying, especially for someone trying to get some

109

shut-eye.

"No, no, no, lady. We'll attend to his long-handles. You keep on whomping his face, keep him from dozing off. That's it. I don't know what you ladies are used to, but this here is a workingman, and this ain't no pleasure palace. Now avert your eye!"

Meecher was in high dudgeon and Charlie almost had the strength to chuckle or beg him to stop tossing his wordy abuse at the ladies. But he gave up on either and worked to will strength back into his hands. All of a sudden they hurt like the dickens.

Seemed as if a lifetime had passed, and then Charlie was coming around again and his body was starting to throb like a hammer-struck thumb. He'd rather sleep, but darn if they weren't letting him. Felt like someone slapping him. Who on earth would dare to do that to him?

He forced his eyes open again and saw that it was near dark. The fire was snapping and blazing to beat the band right beside him. And right in front of him, he saw a woman's face, that woman, the bold one, who had kept chucking hard looks at him all morning. There she went again, with a hard look — and she followed it up with a slap! Then another!

"Wake up and stay awake, mister. I have

plenty to do without you dozing off all the time."

She certainly didn't sound friendly. But just the same, Charlie figured he'd better heed her dire warning and work to keep his eyes open, for what reason he wasn't sure. But she seemed serious.

Soon enough, he found it all too easy to stay awake, for his body pained him something fierce. It must have been worse for Norbert, because Charlie heard him howl like a kicked dog every time anybody tried to drape the blankets back on him.

CHAPTER 12

Son of Cloud closed his eyes and tilted his head back, sniffing the air. It smelled to him like snow. Not tonight, but maybe late tomorrow. He pulled in a bracing draught of crisp air. Yes, tomorrow night would be a stormy one. He missed the long season of cold. It had been far too long since he'd felt the promise of heavy snow. Others of their tribe had complained and constantly sung the songs that would hasten spring's arrival. Not Son of Cloud.

Soon the snow would slow down the travelers. And if they received enough of it, the wagons will be useless. Yes, thought Son of Cloud as he watched his brooding brother, for the hundredth time, paw through the white man's bags. What did he find so fascinating about the white? The only thing of value he had to offer was the fine adornment his face hair had made to his lance.

He looked up at the dangling beard, the puckered knot of skin to which it was attached mostly covered by the long, thick hair the color of sooty snow.

Since the rest of the tribe did not want them and would no longer work to rid the whites from the mountains, then Son of Cloud and his brother, Blue Dog Moon, had decided that they would be the ones to do so. They might never see eye-to-eye with the rest of their people, but they would die one day knowing they had done all they could to keep their home free of the whites.

As if reading Son of Cloud's thoughts, Blue Dog said, "The whites made much of the river today. Those two fools acted as if they were thirsty enough to drink the whole thing."

Son of Cloud smiled, nodded drowsily, his eyes still closed. "They are the whites — of course they want it all."

"I want only to kill them and be done with it."

"Have patience, brother. We will wait until they are deeper into the mountains, where it will be harder for them to run." He opened his eyes and looked at the young man whom he had raised without much help by the tribe. He smiled. "And then we will have fun, eh?"

The younger man returned a grin.

"Don't forget that no matter how many whites you kill, you cannot kill the part of you that is white."

Blue Dog threw the bags to the ground. "You say this over and over — reminding me that I am tainted, that part of me is white!" He spat the word from his mouth as if it were poison.

Son of Cloud barely moved, and still smiled. "Yes, and part of me is too. We must grow to accept it and live our lives, or fight against it and die with them."

"Bah. You talk too much and say too little." Blue Dog Moon stalked off toward the horses.

Son of Cloud sighed. For once, he wished they had more whiskey.

CHAPTER 13

By the time the bold woman brought him a tin plate of hot food, stewed meat hunks swimming in beans, Charlie could feel his legs again and had been working on willing his toes to move. It had taken some doing, but the little nubs had roused to life after a while.

"Thank you, ma'am."

She nodded but said nothing. Charlie held the plate by one edge, and with the other hand he pinched the wool blanket closed. Still she stared at him. Finally he realized that she was offering a tin cup of coffee too. He set the plate in his lap. All this awkward maneuvering seemed to amuse her. Charlie couldn't be sure, but in the dancing orange glow of the fire, he swore he'd seen her smiling.

"Lucky it's only October, I reckon."

"Yes, you are. Any later and . . ." She

spoke in a low, quiet voice, and shook her head.

"Something wrong, ma'am?"

"You . . . risking your hide for him?" She nodded across the fire.

Charlie's spoon paused halfway to his mouth. "I reckon he'd have done the same for me."

She snorted a laugh. "You really think that?"

"Well, yeah. Yeah, I do, as it happens."

"Did you see any of his so-called friends diving in to save him?"

Charlie kept his mouth closed, knowing what she was driving at, then shook his head.

"And do you think he's any different?"

Charlie swallowed a mouthful of coffee. "That ain't the point."

"Then what is, might I ask?" She stood then, and folded her arms across her chest.

"I reckon it ain't something I can explain. Thanks for the food."

She walked away, still shaking her head.

That is one perplexing woman, thought Charlie, shifting his attention back to the plate of hot food. He could eat ten of them.

Everett Meecher toed Charlie in the leg with his boot. "You going to make it, Big Charlie?"

Charlie smiled and nodded. "I reckon so, Mr. Meecher. Question is . . ." Charlie's face darkened and his brow furrowed. "How's ol' Norbert doing?"

"Don't you worry 'bout him. Norb'll be fine come tomorrow," Rollie Meecher piped in, gesturing with his chin toward his sleeping friend. "Wasn't any big deal. Man fell in the river, is all." He upended a bottle and swallowed long on it.

That got his uncle spinning again. "Not a big deal? I swear you fell out of too many trees as a youth. Must have landed on your head."

"You had any sense you would have rolled the wagons right across. Any man could see you don't need to go telling one of us to wade out there. That was foolish, Uncle Everett. Plain and simple foolish. You're the one was dropped on his head. And you're the one to blame for Norbert nearly dying out there!" He thrust an arm toward the river, a source of constant rushing sound not far away in the dark.

"I don't recall seeing you or any of them other useless fools over there trying to save Norbert's hide. 'Bout time you tighten up."

"You ain't my father, old man. I don't need you telling me what to do." Rollie dragged his shirt cuff across his mouth.

"No, but you need my money, don't you? And my booze, I see. Yes, sir, always take, take, take, but what do you give? Nothing. And why? Because worthless trash don't give, it takes. Bah, you wouldn't make a patch on your father's trousers."

"You're right, I ain't like my father. He was just another stupid old man, like you." Rollie must have known what his words would do, because he handed the bottle off to a grinning Bo and squared off, away from the fire.

For a moment Charlie thought maybe the men were playing games with them all, putting on some sort of show. He had thought they were fond of each other, being uncle and nephew and all. But then Everett ducked his head low and, growling, drove himself like a charging woods pig at Rollie's legs.

Rollie must have experienced this display of ferocity in the past, because he sidestepped at the right moment, grinning as he did so, and immediately squared off again. His growling uncle spun, undeterred, and as if spurred on by Shiner's and Bo's hoots, he lunged at Rollie once more. This time the younger man muckled on to Everett, driving blows tight in. Charlie heard the thumps of bony fist on solid flesh.

The two sparring men flurried on at each other, their hard-earned breaths pluming into the chill night air. Rollie feinted toward the flames, then away. Everett countered and stepped backward, driving one of Norbert's legs hard against the other. The prone man groaned loud and low.

"I tell you what, boy —" Everett didn't finish his thought, because Rollie landed a hard right fist on the old man's knobby, stubbled jaw. Everett backed up a step, shook his head as a wet cur shakes off water, and like the surly little dog he was, he resumed his growling, lunging attack.

His uppercut to Rollie's jaw fell short of the mark, grazing the younger man's cheek and ear. It must have stung, because Rollie clutched at his face, seething. He bent low, cradling his head, and Everett drove in close again.

Charlie could take no more of the foolishness and struggled to his feet. He still felt chilled and unsteady — he couldn't feel his feet yet — but something had to be done.

He stepped between the two of them and clapped his big paws on each of their shoulders, forcing them to stay apart. "Enough!" he bellowed, his head dizzy with the effort. "One thing for you all to take out your worries on each other, but I got a problem with both of you when you start stepping on helpless folks."

Charlie nodded toward Norbert, who had drawn his legs up and lay on his side, red-faced and moaning.

The sight of him made Charlie even angrier, and he pitched the two struggling men away from each other. They both stumbled to a stop and the entire camp, even the groaning man, fell silent. They all stared at Charlie. Then Bo started giggling, followed by Shiner and Rollie, all three pointing at Charlie. He looked down and saw he was naked as a newborn baby. He'd dropped his blankets when he stood.

Even in the fire's weak light, Charlie felt sure his face had reddened more than it ever had in his life. He glanced sideways toward where the two women sat, huddled together, wrapped in a blanket against a log on the far end of the fire. And of course, they were both watching him, smiles on their faces. If it had been any other sort of situation, it might be nice to see them really smile for the first time all day, but by gum, not at his expense.

He made sure to keep his back to them as he eased himself as fast as he could back down on his blankets. He tugged the woolens over himself as best he could and

120

wished he could pull them up over his face. He rarely ever went without clothes any time of year, save for the odd strip-down-and-scrub-up in a mountain stream in his beloved high country. Always in summer and always with a handful of river sand for soap. It about tore the skin off him, but he liked how it made him feel — tingly and alive all over. But this was not one of those times.

Everett sat down stiffly near Charlie, put one hand out toward the fire. He sipped from his own cup and Charlie thought he detected the faint sweet tinge of whiskey on the air. Soon enough the old man reached in his coat and slipped out a small bottle. "Thank the Maker that fool nephew didn't smash my bottle."

Charlie heard a tiny *punk* sound as the cork popped free. "You should take another nip, Big Charlie. Keep you from shivering."

"*Another* nip?"

"Yeah, you had a few swallows earlier. Thought it might help with your shakes. That woman over there didn't seem to think so, but hell, what does she know about men's ailments?"

Charlie shrugged and accepted the small bottle. He gurgled back a snort and choked on the fiery trail the whiskey had burned down his gullet. His eyes watered as he handed it back. "Thanks, Mr. Meecher."

"Yeah, call me Everett."

"Okay, then." Charlie nodded.

"Boy ain't had no right to talk against my brother that way. Ellroy was a good man and a good brother to me. We started the freighting business way back before that viperous pup was whelped." Everett swigged the bottle and cut his eyes toward the far cluster of men, talking among themselves and passing their bottle back and forth.

"I thank you too for pulling me off him," said Meecher. "I'd like to have killed him. We was that close to mixing it up in a big way and I ain't never lost a scrap in my life yet."

"You know, Everett, I believe that. Somehow I believe that." Charlie smiled at the fire, wondering what else this day might have to offer.

"This is to be my last freighting trip, Charlie, boy. I been having a rum run of it these past few years, figure it's time to call it a day. Taking on Rollie was a mistake. I had no choice, of course. I made his father a deathbed promise, but he's been a trial, has that boy. Too much of his hussy mother in him."

He swigged again, licked his lips. "The

whoring creature up and ran off when the kid was still wet, left Ellroy and me to care for him. But the boy's an expensive keeper, he is. I ain't been able to bring myself to turn my one and only family member loose. But I'm getting close. He's blown through all our money, ruined my reputation as a freighter. I lost it all but this."

Meecher waved the bottle at the dark surrounding them. "I'm down to it, Charlie. The raw bone. But this time, he swore to me he'd keep it all tight and right. Ha. We get through this trip, I'll have enough to last me, give him some so he can do whatever it is he plans on doing — it sure as hell ain't freighting. He's too lazy for that. I don't know why I'm telling you all this anyway."

After a few minutes of silence between them, Charlie cleared his throat and said, "Mr. Meecher, I mean Everett, you mind if I ask you a question?"

The old man looked at Charlie, one eye squinted. "Depends on what sort of answer you're expecting."

Charlie didn't quite know what that meant, so he did what he always did in life when something didn't make sense, he plowed on ahead. "There's heavy snow all but on top of us, and from what Marshal Watt told me, there's also a rogue band of

Shoshoni been spotted out here by some trapper friend of his."

"There a question in there somewhere, Charlie?"

"Yes, sir, I mean, well . . . don't you think Marshal Watt should have worked a little harder to keep us from taking this trip? I expect you know more than me how dangerous a run like this is, and at this time of year, and in this sort of country, to boot."

The old man closed his eyes and grinned. *The whiskey must be taking hold,* thought Charlie. *He's up and fallen asleep on me.*

Then Meecher spoke. "Ain't no wonder in it at all, Charlie, boy. That Jasper Rafferty ain't the only one who bankrolled this trip, nor, I would guess, the very mining town of Gamble."

Charlie's eyebrows nearly met in the middle. What was Meecher getting at? And then it occurred to him. "The marshal? He's —"

Meecher leaned close. "Yeah, yeah," he said, in a husky whisper. "Don't go flapping your mouth about it. "Why else do you think he'd let us up and go on a fool's errand like this? He wanted to see his share of the profits. You were nibbling close to it before, Charlie. So keep chewing and ask yourself this: If the marshal wasn't invested himself in this venture, do you think a law-man worth his salt would have let us go on the trip, let alone send two women along?"

"Profits from what? The supplies for the town?"

"Good gravy, boy. Just how long did you spend living under that rock of your'n?" Meecher leaned even closer, almost resting his chin on Charlie's blanketed arm. "Gold, fool," he said in a whisper, cutting his eyes quickly to his nephew. "Gold up in Gamble. Rumor has it it's a mighty big strike and Rafferty and the marshal are doing their best to keep a lid on it, least until spring. Promised me a decent spot at the diggin's if I could get these supplies up yonder before the snows plugged this passage. It's the only way in or out till spring."

Charlie rubbed his numb fingertips along his jaw. "Big strike, huh?"

"That's what I said." Meecher nodded and sipped. "One of the biggest this or that side of the Rockies. Even them two women coming along wouldn't have slowed down the trip. You got any interest in it yourself?"

Big Charlie nodded. "I reckon I do at that." He looked at Meecher, concern lighting his eyes. "If there's room, that is."

"Yeah, Charlie. I reckon."

They both sat musing in silence a moment, and then Charlie whispered, "Why do you think they're trying to keep it hushed all winter?"

Meecher shrugged. "Didn't tell me that. But my guess is they're looking to bust it wide open in a big way. And the only way small-money men can do that is to hire one of them big mining outfits back East. You know, the ones with more money than sense."

"How big are you talking?"

"Put it this way, this here rutted trail would be a proper road and there'd be a half dozen mine camps between Monkton and Gamble. And Gamble'd be one of the biggest towns in the whole of Idaho Territory. Within months, mark my words. They'll have smelters and more men and machinery than you can imagine."

"What about the mountains? This place?" Charlie nodded at the dark.

"Mmm, I expect they'd hollow out the mountain till she collapsed in on herself. At least them warpath Shoshoni won't be a bother. All these whites probably scare 'em up into Canada." He giggled.

"Did the marshal tell you any more about the Indians than what he told me?"

"Naw," said Meecher. "But I can tell you it's a near-certain thing we'll end up scalped, but then again, maybe not." He wobbled his hand before him like a flopping fish. "We were desperate enough to need the work. . . ." He let the thought taper off.

"Bad as all that?"

"Well, Big Charlie. Other supply trains traveled this road a whole lot of times this summer, and only a couple of times did they see sign of Injun. Once or twice they was fired on, but for the most part, naw. I reckon if we keep our wits about us, keep our heads down and our hats covering our hair" — he winked — "we might make it through."

"Then what?"

"Then what . . . what?"

"Once we get to Gamble?"

"Why, I don't know about you, but I aim to take my earnings and set to digging. If the diggin's are that rich up there, we'd be fools not to."

"How we getting paid anyway, if you don't mind me asking?"

"Course not. I'm carrying some — since I demanded some money up front, and there's a man in Gamble going to pay us the rest, in dust, I expect, once we arrive. Rumor has it they're sitting on bags and bags full of rich ore and dust. I'll take dust as sure as currency. You?" Meecher cackled.

Charlie only nodded, his mind already on

the gold he could dig, the money he could make. Enough to buy his hidden mountain valley, someplace to hole up. Just him and Mabel-Mae, far away from crazy freighters and women who looked angry and stared back every time you looked at them.

CHAPTER 14

The next morning, Charlie felt surprisingly good, considering his dunking of the day before. He also recalled all that had happened afterward and wondered how much longer any of them could take being together, especially the Meechers. Uncle and nephew were so much alike and yet so different.

He helped Everett load Norbert into Bo's wagon. The rangy man in buckskins who almost drowned barely looked at Charlie — not that Charlie wanted thanks. He would have blushed had Norbert offered such, he felt sure. But at least, Charlie thought, Norbert was coherent and able to move his feet and hands. The woman was right: Any later in the season and they likely both would have died.

The oxen and mules and horses all acted fidgety, a good sign that animals wanted to move, to stretch their muscles and put some miles beneath their hooves. A sentiment that was shared wholeheartedly by Everett Meecher. Having lost half a day's travel yesterday, he was ready to make up as much lost time as he was able today.

He hopped down from getting Norbert settled and said, "You ride until you get your pins back under you, Norbert. And don't try to hobble down if you have to make water — lean over the side of the wagon, let her go."

"Since when did you become a nursemaid, old man?" Rollie shook his head, bloodshot eyes swimming wet and flinty in his stubbled, puffy face. Charlie had seen mean and hungover a few times in his day, but rarely did they show up so stark on one person as they did on Rollie's angry face.

"Shut your mouth, boy." Everett climbed up onto his seat and tickled the lines over his team's back. "And if you lay the lash on them mules today like you did yesterday, so help me I'll take another round out of you, boy!"

Rollie responded by shaking his head again and leaning back with a thin whip, he let loose. The long rawhide serpent unfurled fast and stung the air with a *crack*! just above the hip pins of those beasts. They jerked forward in anticipation of more of what they had received from the man the day before.

Charlie closed his eyes and waited for Everett's screeches to pass. He looked back to see Mabel-Mae traipsing along, followed by the two women, the older of them walking and the other aboard their horse. Charlie gave them a nod and touched his hat brim. He received a weak smile from the girl on the horse, and a nod with no hint of a smile from the older sister. *She is a tough nut to crack,* thought Charlie.

Everett Meecher took the lead and they rolled on out, cutting upstream of where the waterlogging episode took place. If the day before hadn't been so nearly tragic, the fact that Meecher chose a route that barely brought water up to the animals' knees would have been laughable.

Charlie was especially worried about the women, and wished he had made them ride across, but the bossy one was insistent and in the end he had begrudgingly given in to her stubbornness. She had mounted up behind her sister on that old roan and they crossed fine, trailing right behind Mabel-Mae. In truth, he had been more worried about their feeble-seeming horse. But the old mare stepped solidly, if slowly, picking her way across with the grace and delicacy that only long years on the trail can bring.

As soon as Charlie's team dug on up the opposite bank of the Salmon, Meecher continued on, not waiting a second longer than he had to. Charlie paused his team and waited for the women. Their horse looked tuckered, but he didn't want to leave them there — thoughts of Indians, mountain lions, snakes, wolves, and grizzlies filled his head until he shouted, "Come on, now, this is no place to dawdle."

They drew abreast of him and the bigger woman said, "And that side of the river was?"

Charlie set his mouth and shook his head. Would he never learn? As he got his team walking again, the younger, frail young woman said, "Thank you, Charlie."

Her voice surprised him. It was clear, but thin and delicate somehow, just like her.

"For what?"

"For waiting. It was kind of you. And my name is Delia." The girl indicated behind her with a slight move of her head. "She is my sister, Hester."

He smiled and touched his hat brim. "You're most welcome . . . Delia, ma'am." He cut his eyes to the other sister and his smile slumped. He nudged the team forward and spent the next ten minutes feeling bad about being so petty to Hester. He hardly knew a thing about her anyway.

He purposefully hadn't let himself speculate on why they were headed to Gamble, though the obvious reason that he didn't want to entertain was that they were sporting girls. And if what old man Meecher had said about Gamble's prospects was half true, they'd be setting themselves up for a whole lot of business.

The day stretched on, with the morning's promise of sunlight pulled away like a wink from a pretty woman who disappears in a crowd. The stark hide of aspen and the green masses of pine muted to dark shafts of shadow. The air took on a bracing tang that hurt Charlie to take in through his nose. Storm, sure enough. He looked up for further confirmation. What had been blue sky stuck with far-off white streaks a few hours earlier now bore the purple-black of a spreading bruise. The coming night would be cold, coldest yet, and he knew snow wouldn't be far behind.

Long past midday, Meecher's reedy yelp called for a halt. The front of the wagon train had reached a stream, and the animals of each team would stop, in due course, for a drink. While he waited his team's turn, Charlie stretched in his seat and worked his hands and feet again, flexing fingers and toes. He was sure grateful that had happened yesterday and not today, and it would have been a darn sight better if it had happened in July instead. Though these mountain waterways were cold any time of year.

The old roan horse was laboring long and hard, step by step toward Mabel-Mae, who still didn't seem perturbed by much of anything. Hester was walking again, leading the aged horse, had done so for most of the day, in fact.

Charlie sighed. "You going to take me up on my offer yet?"

They walked on up another ten feet, then halted and Hester said, "She's fine. Thank you."

"Yeah, well, she don't look fine to me." Just then the team ahead of him, Shiner's, rolled forward. Charlie clucked, danced the lines on the backs of the oxen, and they begrudgingly stepped into their load, the steel-rimmed wheels cutting grooves despite the stiffening mud. "Was my sister," he said as they rolled forward, "I'd put her on something stronger than that old girl."

"Well, she's my sister, not yours, so don't you worry about it none."

Hester's words were sharp-edged, and he heard Shiner cackle up ahead. Charlie reddened again, and he ground his molars, biting back a hard remark before it flew out of his mouth. It had been a long day so far, and the way Meecher was driving them, it was far from over. The last thing he needed was more of her guff.

His jaw muscles bunched and relaxed, bunched and relaxed, and he worked hard to not look at the women. Soon enough his team had slurped their fill and Mabel-Mae too. He didn't even look back when they crossed the stream and ground their way uphill. Within minutes of leaving the chill burble of the stream behind, the roadway narrowed at a hard spot and each wagon had to pause again while the one before it laid on the lash, snapping the air, each driver urging the team on with blue oaths.

Charlie's team crested the wide-topped rise, and the wagons ahead were easing down a slight hill before leveling off, when he heard a scream from behind. He turned in the seat, but given the twist in the trail and the rise, he couldn't see beyond Mabel-Mae. Even as he set the brake and clumsily began climbing down from the wagon, his thoughts were of hordes of savage Indians setting upon the women.

He hustled past his mule, his legs stiff and numb more from sitting all day than from his icy dunking, and bellowed to the women. "Hester! Delia! Hey!"

Within seconds he caught sight of them, still down close to the stream. They'd made it across, but that was about it. The horse had collapsed on top of Delia, looked to have pinned one of her legs. Hester was cradling her sister's head and kicking at the horse, but the animal's legs trembled, one hoof clacked feebly on a flat stone. The one horse's eye that Charlie could see was wide and bugged, and her lid quivered twice as fast as her wheezing breath.

"Oh, Charlie, help!" Raw fear had stretched Hester's features.

Charlie hustled down to them, assessed the situation quickly, and dropping to his knees, he jammed his hands far under the horse's side, behind the old saddle's cantle, and lifted hard with his wide upper body. Despite the fact that the horse was a shadow of its old weight, the effort was a hard one. But he managed to raise the bony beast up enough. "Drag her out!" he wheezed as Hester slid her sister to safety. Charlie lowered the horse and stood up.

Hester had already raised her sister's skirts and was feeling the girl's left leg. Charlie couldn't help noticing the girl wore long-handle drawers on her legs. He also couldn't help noticing that the girl wasn't much put out by the ordeal. She had a worried look, but not nearly as much as her sister.

"Is she okay?" Charlie kneeled and looked at the sickly young woman. "Delia? Can you hear me?"

"Nothing feels broken." Hester pulled down the girl's skirts.

"Maybe she's in some numb state. I seen it before. This drover tumbled off his mount . . ."

Hester shook her head. "No, it's the laudanum. She's numb from that."

"Don't talk about me like I'm not here," said Delia, a smile threatening her face.

Charlie and Hester traded looks.

"How's Angel?" said Delia.

"Who?" said Charlie.

"She's our horse." Hester nodded toward the trembling creature. "Can you help us get her up? I think she'll be okay if we get her on her feet again, let her calm down."

"Ma'am . . ." Charlie lowered his voice and said close to Hester, "That horse is played out."

"Yes," said the woman. "She needs her rest —"

"No, Hester. She's done. I should have made you listen yesterday." He kneeled and ran a hand along Angel's quivering neck.

"No, no, Charlie. You can't be right." She dropped down beside him and put her face to the horse's.

"If he told you that horse has reached the end of her road, missy, then he's right as rain." Everett walked down the slope to them. "Heard the ruckus. I am sorry to say this, but Charlie's right, girly. Trust me when I say it. I been around beasts all my life, and that horse is done."

Hester stood, pulled her ragged shawl tight around her shoulders. "How long do you figure she has, then?"

" 'Bout as long as it takes for me to pop her one." Rollie walked down to them, already pulling his Colt revolver.

"Ain't nobody going to fire off no guns in Injun country, you hear me?" Everett's voice barked at his nephew.

"We can't let her suffer, Everett," said Charlie, not pleased that he was sort of agreeing with Rollie.

"For once, I agree with Big Boy." Rollie offered a toothy grin to Charlie.

"No, no, and no, I tell you. Ain't going to happen."

"Oh yeah?" Rollie thumbed back the hammer and fired off a round, straight up into the darkening sky. He did so twice more, all the while keeping his eyes squarely on his

138

uncle's trembling face.

The wheezing horse spasmed with the sound of each shot.

The old man had clapped a gnarled hand on the scarred grip of his Colt Navy.

"You want I should keep on firing, Uncle Everett?" Rollie dragged the name, made the name sound like a taunt.

"Go ahead!" Everett dragged on his gun, but Charlie stayed his hand.

"No, Mr. Meecher. That won't solve a thing. One more shot won't make a whit of difference. Give me the gun and I'll do for the old girl."

The three men stood facing each other for a long moment. Then Meecher lifted his hand free and Charlie took the pistol. The old man was so angry he shook uncontrollably. Rollie's nervy eyes twitched, but he holstered his gun.

"Get gone back up there. I'll tend to things here," said Charlie to the pair of them, his big voice startling even himself.

He watched the men climb back up the hill, Rollie first, his uncle a few paces behind. Everett's hands clenched and unclenched as if grasping for something that wasn't there. Once they passed out of sight, Charlie stuck the pistol in his trousers top.

"Hester, not much time now. We have to

get going. Say your good-byes to Angel. I'll take Delia up to the wagon." He bent and lifted the girl before her older sister could protest. Delia, still in the grip of her pain medicine, seemed far enough gone that she still wore her almost-smile.

Hester regarded Charlie, who nodded at the horse.

"Go on, then," he said. "We'll wait for you."

He couldn't watch. This was a black afternoon, to be sure. Hester kneeled, smoothing the trembling horse's cheek and whispering. Charlie hoped she was saying enough for both women. She kissed the horse, then stood, her eyes wet but not tearing, and nodded to him.

They trudged up the hill and Charlie laid Delia on the ground beside the wagon. "I'll be right back." Charlie headed back down the hill.

"Charlie," said Hester. "I . . . need to get our things."

He nodded, smiled. "I'll bring them back up with me, don't you worry."

He strode back down the slope, kneeled by the confused, played-out horse, and gently slipped off the hackamore. As he ran the back of his hand along her face and offered her what he hoped were soothing sounds, Charlie vowed he'd somehow make sure this sort of foolishness never happened again. "Won't happen in my valley, Angel. I'd not have let this happen there. I wish I could have brought you there, old girl." He pulled in a deep breath and sighed it out. The horse groaned, her breath rasping harder now.

Charlie stood and cocked the revolver all the way back, bent to the horse, and said, "Your suffering's all gone, girl." Quickly he placed the barrel on her temple, closed his eyes, and pulled the trigger. As he opened his eyes, she sighed out her last, her trembling limbs relaxing.

Her eye filmed even as he reached to close it. He lifted her head, did the same with the other; then before he set to work stripping off the rest of the women's meager gear, he used the saddle to drag the horse as far to the side of the trail as he could. The saddle wasn't much to speak of, the blanket beneath a threadbare thing, and the two carpetbags tied behind were not in particularly good repair.

In death, stripped of her burdens, the old horse looked mighty frail. And Charlie again felt the pangs of guilt sicken him. He should have made them do as he had bade the day before. Thankfully they'd have to now. He trudged up the hill without looking back.

"We'll need to fix Delia a place in my wagon," said Charlie as he strode up to Mabel-Mae and plunked their gear on the ground, trying to ignore Rollie and Everett at the front of the wagon, still fuming at each other, arguing about something Charlie didn't care to hear.

"I don't think so, Big Boy." Rollie pushed by his uncle and stood facing Charlie, the women between them. "No way a woman is riding in this here wagon. No passengers but us freighters. Besides, they're bad luck — look what they done to that horse. No, sir, ain't no way those two are going to tire out my team."

"Your team?" Everett shoved his nephew hard, pushing Rollie into the wagon. "Who died and made you king of my mountain?"

"You old goat! Bad enough we got them womenfolk along this trip, we didn't never cipher 'em into our plans — you said so yourself!"

"Yeah, but that was before all this. Besides, they ain't hard to keep." He thrust a finger at Delia sitting on the ground. "That girl's sickly, you fool."

"You can say what you want to, Rollie, but that girl" — Charlie pointed a big finger at Delia — "is riding in that wagon." He pointed at his wagon. "And that woman there" — he pointed at Hester — "is riding on that mule there." He pointed at Mabel-Mae, who flicked an ear at all the commotion. "And that is that. Now shut up, the both of you."

Once more, the two chastened men did as Big Charlie bade. He turned his attention to arranging a spot for Delia in the bed of the wagon, taking care to ensure that nothing might jostle on the trail and fall on her. Once he had blankets and an extra canvas tarpaulin laid out over his own gear, he lifted the sick girl in and nodded to Hester to take care of her.

While she attended to Delia, Charlie rigged up their saddle on Mabel-Mae, who didn't seem to care one way or the other what was happening.

"Charlie, I appreciate what you've done," said Hester. "But I'll walk alongside just fine."

He sighed and turned to face her. "Ma'am, I ain't offering. I'm telling. This here's the way it's going to be."

Her face hardened and she thrust out her lower jaw.

"Now, you can shoot daggers at me all you like with them pretty green eyes of yours, but I'll heft you up onto Mabel-Mae if I have to. You understand me?" It was some moments before he realized his face was inches from hers, and it was but a few moments more when he realized what he'd said about her eyes.

"Fine, then." She strode to Mabel-Mae, a beast a bit taller than Angel had been.

"You want a hand?"

"No."

"Fine." Charlie climbed up into the wagon's seat. Behind him he thought he heard Delia giggling. He didn't look back but was relieved to hear the telltale saddle squeak of a seated rider.

CHAPTER 15

Not long after the sisters' horse expired, the sky darkened — a full hour before it should have — and snow began to fall. Not pleasant, easy flakes, but stinging granules, hard like sand. Another hour later, they made it to a sloping meadow butted to a decent pine stand. Just into the trees, they picketed the animals and made camp.

By the time they had a fire crackling and tarps arranged off the wagons, the snow still hadn't amounted to much, but the wind had increased, playing hell with the fire. They managed to keep it lit, and had stockpiled a decent stack of wood, enough for the night.

Charlie noticed that Everett kept to himself. Every time he tried to speak with the man, Meecher all but growled at him, and Charlie saw that he hadn't simmered down at all from the hubbub earlier on the trail. It was as if he couldn't stand being told off by his nephew, nor told what to do by Charlie.

The old grump finally sat off by himself, barely close enough to the fire to benefit from any warmth, and the entire time he held his hands stiff by his sides, clenching and unclenching his fists. Charlie wished he hadn't given him back his gun.

Norbert had sufficiently recovered throughout the day, enough that Rollie decided they should all celebrate. He cracked a fresh bottle of no-label snake juice, and he and his chums all hit it hard. Soon they were singing and hooting into the stiffening wind. The snow had begun to accumulate in the curl of leaves and against rocks, in the folds of the canvas.

"Here," said Rollie, thrusting the half-filled bottle at his uncle. "Take yourself a swig and calm your old-man nerves. You're making all of us nervous."

This struck Rollie and the others as humorous and their sudden laughter made Charlie groan. About the only good thing happening this night was that Hester and Delia had decided Charlie wasn't such a horrible person and sat with him on the other side of the guttering fire.

In the midst of this latest burst of laughter, Everett lashed out and knocked the bottle of whiskey from Rollie's outstretched hand.

He followed it by springing to his feet.

"Oh no," said Hester and Charlie at the same time.

It was as if the fight of the evening before was unrolling once again at their feet. But this time, Everett Meecher was stone sober and angrier than Charlie had seen any man. In the firelight, he saw a blue vein thick like a finger, pulsing down the middle of the old man's forehead. Spittle flecked from his mouth, his hands formed stiff claws, and he held his entire body tense like a lion ready to pounce.

Rollie matched him in stance, but he was taller, younger, and looser from drink. He still regarded it all as a joke. "Look at you! All crazy and wasting my good whiskey." His right hand lashed out and slapped his uncle's left cheek. The entire camp held its breath. Rollie laughed and followed with a hard smack to the other cheek. His uncle, eyes impossibly wide, screamed through clenched teeth and made to lunge at Rollie. But his hands grabbed at his own chest instead. His face sagged and he dropped to his knees as if poleaxed from behind.

Charlie jumped to his feet, and made it to Everett's side as the man flopped over onto his shoulder, half facing up, his purpled face already gone gray.

"Everett?" He lightly tapped the old man's cheek. "Everett? It's me, Charlie. You're gonna be okay, now, you hear?"

Hester bent close, stroked the man's forehead, but Meecher's eyes fluttered and his breath threaded to a trickle.

Charlie looked at Hester. "What do we do?"

She shook her head knowingly, aware of something he did not want to hear, not again this day, not again so soon. As if to confirm the awful truth, Meecher's head sagged to the side, and spittle trickled from his mouth. His body finally went limp in what Charlie guessed was the first time in years.

Charlie looked up at Rollie, who stood swaying, staring down at the scene, wide-eyed and puzzled. "You did this! You did this, you damn whelp!" He jumped over Meecher's body and drove a hard backhand at Rollie's face. "How do you like it?" He gave him another. "Huh? Feel good to you?"

He kept on for a minute or more until he felt arms tugging at him. He reached with his other hand, ready to deliver a fist to whoever was trying to stop him, but saw it was Hester. A haze of red, as if a wash of blood, dropped away before his eyes and he recognized the determination and fear warring on her face.

"Stop now, Charlie. He's beaten. You beat him."

Charlie lowered his throbbing hands and looked down at the whimpering, bloody Rollie, collapsed in a crying pile behind the log. Norbert, Bo, and Shiner had melted back against the log on which they sat, their own hands raised before their faces, in defense of the beating they were sure they were about to get from the enraged mammoth man.

Charlie smoothed his sleeves, said, "I'm all right now," to Hester, and regarded Everett Meecher's body at his feet. The dropped form reminded Charlie a lot of that old horse of earlier in the day. Once unsaddled of the burdens of life, both spirited creatures were nothing but frail old things good for little else but the boneyard. He bent to the old man and scooped him up. He almost gasped at how little Everett Meecher actually weighed.

He's half clothes and half nerve, thought Charlie. *And one-half of that mix is gone.*

He pulled down one of the tarps and with Hester's help, rolled the old man in it, then placed him carefully under one of the wagons.

They returned to their side of the fire,

keeping an eye on the four somewhat so-bered men on the other side of the waver-ing blaze. Much to Charlie's surprise, Rollie didn't have much to say. The men cracked open a fresh bottle of booze and hit it pretty hard. As the evening wore on, Rollie's face puffed up something fierce.

But they didn't make any moves toward Charlie's side of the fire. They did talk in low whispers, and that convinced the big man that he had better not let his eyes shut that night. Hester tended to her sister, dos-ing her with some of the laudanum. There didn't seem to be much to say or do. Everett Meecher, cantankerous, but oddly likable old man, was dead.

The more Charlie thought on it, the more convinced he was of his equal responsibility in the death, along with Rollie. If he hadn't shouted the old man down earlier, made him give up his gun and all but ordered him to shut up, hadn't shamed the man as he did, might be Meecher would still be alive.

Deep inside, he knew that Rollie was as much to blame, maybe more, and the old man hadn't helped matters either, being as tight-strung as he was. The thoughts yarn-balled in Charlie's mind and left him even more tired and more confused than ever.

Despite his best efforts, Charlie's weary

eyelids lost the battle with vigilance and he nodded off, his back against a pile of gear. The breeze had died down a bit during the night, and between the wool blanket and the waning warmth of the fire at his feet, he was downright comfortable.

Charlie woke as stark early light cracked through the cold-stiffened pines. The snow hadn't amounted to much after all. A warning shot, he reckoned. Low sounds like voices whispered, grunted, shushed each other, and he heard a dragging sound. Charlie ground his stiff hands into his eyes, shook his head to dispel clinging sleepiness. No sign of life anywhere else in the camp. The fire was blackened, dead, and cold. Dead. . . . And then he remembered the scene of last night. Everett Meecher, dead.

There was that sound again. He looked around, spied movement off near one of the wagons. The old man! Maybe something, a critter, was at him. Charlie rolled to his knees, stood up stiffly, and did his best not to make a sound as he crept low toward the wagons.

He rounded the corner of the last wagon and saw the four freighters kneeling, crouched around the body of who had been the boss of their outfit, Everett Meecher.

"What in tarnation are you boys doing?" In the mornings, Charlie's voice sounded even deeper, gruffer than normal, and this morning, after a night in the cold mountain air, it was a low, booming thing.

They all looked up at him, and Rollie, whose back was to Charlie, spun and stared at him. Charlie hardly recognized him. For the flicker of an instant he felt sorry for the man. Charlie had really laid into him, buttoning up the young man's eyes until they were nearly shut, puffed tight, yellowed, and purpled. And his bottom lip had swelled until it resembled a bright red chili pepper.

Charlie couldn't tell if Rollie was sneering or surprised, or if he could even see Charlie at all, so puffed were his eyes.

"You're the man I was looking for," said Rollie. The words came out pinched and forced, no doubt because of his misshapen mouth, which stretched wide in what Charlie assumed was a grin.

"What are you doing to Everett's body?" Charlie stepped closer.

"Why, Big Boy, I am taking what's mine. The old bastard's money, for one thing, and his Colt Navy revolver, for all the good the old thing is. He can keep his crusty old pipe and tobacco pouch. I expect he'll have no shortage of flame to set it alight where he's headed."

He wheezed a laugh and the other three followed suit, though their unease with the dead man was plain, given their downturned mouths, and the glances they cast at the corpse when Rollie turned back to Charlie.

"That's desecration. Leave Mr. Meecher be so's we can give him a proper burial."

"Oh." Rollie struggled to his feet, his Colt already in his hand. "I see how it is. You and that hussy yonder wrapped him up tighter'n a tick so you could get at all his money and the gun too. Huh? Don't tell me you didn't know the old fool kept all his cash in a special pocket sewed inside his trousers. Yessir. But I know. And you know how I know that, Big Boy?" He waved the pistol and stared at Charlie.

"Nope," said Charlie, thinking maybe he'd reached the end of his rope. He sure wanted to put less space between him and the talking end of that gun. Might be he could still best the fool out of it.

"I'll tell you, then, since you so kindly asked. You see . . . Big Boy, I am Everett Meecher's nephew. At least I was until he died. So that makes me owner of the freightin' business. And the wagons. And what's in them."

"No, it don't," said Charlie, afraid of

153

where this crazy talk was headed.

"Oh." Rollie cranked the hammer back. "But I do think so, Charlie. I damn sure do. I was his nephew, after all. His closest kin. You, on the other hand, ain't nothing but a thief and a . . . well, we'll save that for later, why don't we?" He stepped backward. "Right now you got work to do."

"What's that you're saying?" said Charlie, taking a step toward Rollie.

"Uh-uh-uh, not toward me. Toward him." He waved the gun barrel at the dead man. "Bury his bony old ass. Now."

Charlie's eyes widened.

"Yeah, you heard me, thief. Anywhere. I expect it'll be hard going for a bit, but the ground ain't froze clear through to China yet." This prompted a new round of forced laughs from his chums.

Under persuasion of the business end of that six-gun, Charlie retrieved a steel bar and shovel from a tool locker under the supply wagon. The bar was carried for use in repairing axles and levering the wagons out of rough spots. He traded a glance with Hester and offered her what he hoped was a reassuring smile.

Hester gave him a nod in return. "I'll help," she said, tucking a blanket around her sister.

"Nope," said Rollie. "Him only." He waved the pistol at Charlie and tried to smile.

Once Charlie located a decent spot that he felt would be a suitable final resting place for the old curmudgeon, he found that Rollie was right, curse his hide. The ground was hard as iron. But he kept at it, pounding and scratching away, and eventually, after a couple of feet down, he was rewarded with softer earth where the frost hadn't sunk down yet. He levered up clods of frozen earth, then scooped out the loose dirt.

It hadn't taken long before he was soaked through with sweat, despite the chill air. He rewrapped the old man in the tarpaulin, then carried him over and gently set him in the hole.

"Get on with it! We have miles to make up because of your foolishness." Rollie wagged the pistol and knocked back another slug of whiskey. Behind him, his hungover cronies slowly got the animals harnessed and rigged.

"Don't you want to say anything over him? He was your kin and all." Charlie leaned on the shovel, red-faced and sweating.

"Him?" Rollie laughed again, then grimaced and gripped his face. He'd split his lip, and blood welled out between his begrimed fingers.

Hester and Delia walked over to the grave by Charlie, and the three of them bowed heads. The two women looked at Charlie. He shrugged and Hester nodded at the body.

Charlie sighed and cleared his throat. "Lord, I . . . uh, this here old man, Everett Meecher, he was . . . well, sir, he was something else."

"I'll say," said Rollie, snickering and taking a pull on the bottle.

Charlie shook his head and continued. "The thing is, Lord, well, we'd appreciate it if you took care of him. And if you could, see to it that we make it to Gamble without too much fuss." He glanced at Hester and Delia. "I think Everett would want that." He gave Hester another quick look.

She nodded back.

"Amen," said Charlie.

The women echoed the word, and Hester bent for a handful of dirt to toss in the grave.

Rollie strolled over and said, "So long, you foul old bird." His finger squeezed the trigger and the wrapped corpse flinched as the bullet sliced into its middle, leaving a smoking hole in its stead.

Charlie lunged at Rollie. "What's the matter with you, you fool!"

The younger man backed up, stumbling a bit, but still managing to crank back on the hammer. "Nothing a dead Big Boy wouldn't fix. Now cover him up. We got miles to go yet."

It didn't take long for Charlie, with Hester's help, to fill in the grave and mound it over. They worked to secure rocks over the hump of frozen clods, and then Charlie drove in an old silvered branch at the head of the grave, and on a flat rock beneath it, Hester scratched in the old man's name and the current year. That was all they figured they could do, with Rollie pacing and fondling the six-gun behind them.

By the time Charlie hustled the two women over to Mabel-Mae, the sun had almost come out, but decided against the effort and ducked back behind the mass of low gray clouds. The mule stood, picketed and looking bored, and Charlie told the sisters to wait there for him. He retrieved their carpetbags from the wagon and carried them over to the mule. As he slapped a blanket on her back, he heard Rollie behind him.

"What are you up to, Big Boy?"

Charlie said, "I'm fixing to leave. I'm taking these women and my gear and my mule and we're walking out of here. And that is that. I have had enough." He turned to the wagon, reaching for his own gear. From behind, he heard a Colt crank back into the deadliest position of all.

"I don't think so, Big Boy. Oh no, no. You signed on for this trip, you see. And a deal's a deal."

Charlie turned to see Rollie a dozen feet from him, a wide smile on his face, the revolver's hard black snout once more aimed right at his own big chest.

Charlie let out a long, disgusted sigh. "I didn't sign on to wet-nurse a passel of crazies, no, sir. And that's all I'm seeing here. Leave us be and we'll leave you be."

"Not a prayer, Big Boy. Besides, where you gonna go?" Rollie smiled that split-lip grin, his swollen eyes creased into yellow-black slits. "We got us Injun killers behind, in front, to the left and right. You'd be dooming the poor, pitiful town of Gamble, with all that gold hid away and ready for the plucking."

Charlie's eyes narrowed.

"Oh yeah, you don't think ol' Uncle Everett was the only one who knew all about the wonders of Gamble, how it's fit to burst, how the town's filled with gold ore and dust and whatnot."

"I don't know what you're talking about." Charlie didn't think he sounded all that convincing.

"Oh, come on, Big Boy. I heard the old man telling you all about it the other night. So you know the big news. Makes it nigh on impossible for you to leave now, don't it? Besides, strength in numbers." Rollie leaned forward, as if he were sharing a secret, though he was still a good ten feet from the big man. Everyone in the camp had hushed and seemed to lean in too. "You need us more than we need you, *Big Charlie.* If that's what you're calling yourself now."

With the suddenness of a gunshot, Charlie realized that Rollie knew something about him, something he'd worked long and hard to keep quiet, keep hidden. He thought back to that bar in Monkton. Had to be he heard it there, maybe from that bigmouth Dutchy. Charlie sighed again. It was becoming a habit he didn't much like. And not being able to do anything about it was an even worse feeling.

"I can see from that look on your face that you have decided to throw in with us. Smart move for a dumb workhorse. Now get that junk loaded back on the wagon, get them hussies settled, and let's go. I'm the boss of this here outfit and you are sorely trying my patience."

Charlie ground his teeth together so tight he thought for sure they might powder, but he didn't care. All he wanted to do was snap that whelp's head off. "I should have finished you last night when I had the chance."

"But you didn't, did you? Let that be a lesson to you, Big Charlie." Rollie half turned, then looked back and said, "Or should I say . . . Shotgun Charlie? Now get a move on before I shoot that damned mule of yours. Right between its big, dumb eyes."

Charlie took a step forward but felt a firm hand on his forearm. He looked down to see Hester there, restraining him once again. They stared at each other for a long moment, the fog of blood rage fading from his vision. He backed down, and the air in his lungs seemed to leave him. But the feeling of wanting to cripple Rollie Meecher didn't.

CHAPTER 16

Charlie guessed that the day ahead was going to be a bad one, mostly because of Rollie Meecher. It seemed every chance he got, Meecher wagged that pistol in his direction and shook his head, as if to say, "Oh, you wait to see what I have planned for you later."

They'd stopped to let the animals blow and give them a feed from the nose bags. For themselves, they made do with a cold lunch. Charlie slowly chewed a second strip of jerked venison and sank his head down as low as he could into his sheepskin-lined coat collar. He'd offered the coat and other clothes to the ladies as the temperature dropped, but they'd declined, hauled out more of their own garments, and wrapped up in more wool blankets.

This was shaping up to be the worst day of the trip, and though he had doubted on previous days it could get much worse, it had managed to be so with each hour that passed. He tried to enjoy the view — though low dark clouds had scudded along above them most of the day, now and again a teasing shaft of sunlight lancing through and lighting the narrow cleft of a valley below the winding trail.

With the aspens skinned of leaves and the pines doing their best to reach the sky, Charlie saw all around them the rocky outcrops and far below, raw tumbledowns of shale slopes lining the river. As pretty as it was, Charlie knew it would be even prettier after a heavy snowfall. *Pretty if you're a bird, Charlie,* he told himself. *That way you could fly right on over it to someplace warm.*

That line of thinking dismayed him because he normally loved winter, looked forward to snow in the mountains. But this trip seemed to have pulled any hope and good humor he might have had right out of him.

"Charlie, can I ask you something?"

He turned to see Hester, her wool blanket wrapped tight around her shoulders and head, trailing off her like a serape. Her arms were crossed and he thought maybe her usual hard look had softened, at least for the moment.

"Ask away, ma'am."

"First off, you can stop calling me 'ma'am.' I'm Hester. Hester O'Fallon."

"Well, that wasn't really a question." Charlie smiled and nodded, touched the worn brim of his tall-crown hat. "But I'm pleased to meet you, after a fashion, Miss O'Fallon. I am Charlie. Uh, most folks call me Big Charlie. I reckon you see why."

"Yep. I've seen you naked."

Charlie's face heated up and he scuffed his boot in the dead grass by the trailside.

"Aren't you the bashful one?"

"Yes'm. You had a question for me?"

She regarded him a moment, then said, "A gun. I wonder why you don't wear one, is all."

"Oh, I got a Green River knife. Does me fine."

"That's not really an answer." Then she smiled and shook her head.

"No, ma'am, I reckon not, but it's as close as we're liable to get just now. Here comes Rollie Meecher."

And up strode the freighting outfit's new boss. Even from ten feet away, Charlie smelled the musky wood smoke, sweat, and boozy reek of the man.

"Ain't nothing I'd like to do more today than to let you two lovebirds chatter on and on, but we got time to make up. Now get mounted or be left behind." He turned to go, then said, "Oh, and I didn't really mean that. We ain't leaving you all behind. 'Specially not such pretties as them two women."

"You keep away from me and my sister, Meecher." Hester stood defiant, her jaw thrust out.

"Oh, is that so?" Meecher stepped closer, but still out of easy reach. "Well, we'll see about that. I may have taken a shine to that sickly one, I tell you. So you best tell your sister that she ought to shape up so ol' Rollie Meecher, the head of this here outfit, can have himself a look-see, maybe a little fun tonight. You understand me?"

"There won't be any tampering with the women, Rollie. You leave off of them." Charlie had angled in front of Hester, who looked none too pleased about it.

"Oh, I see how it is. You two got something going on. Then you shouldn't mind a professional man such as me taking up with your sickly sister."

"You touch my sister, jackass, and I will gut you where you stand."

"Ohhh." Rollie's puffy eyes widened and one corner of his mouth rose. "Bold talk for a dollar-a-thrill girl. Besides, she ain't likely to find herself a man who owns his own business, now, is she? Consider me an educator of sorts, what they call a professor. After all, you and her are headed up to Gamble to make some sporting money, am I right? Old Rollie could teach you all a thing or three about what your customers will be needing most from you."

Charlie balled his fists and stepped forward. Rollie winked and backed away from them, then shouted, "Get mounted. If I have to say it again, that mule gets one in the eye." His laughter echoed across the narrow valley.

"We play along, Miss Hester, and it'll all come out right, you mark my words." He offered her a smile, but all he got was her stern look.

"Charlie, I swear. Hoping that the best will come out of every situation won't make it so."

He couldn't think of a thing to say to that, so he nodded and climbed up into the wagon. She might well be right, but he was having a hard enough time fighting his own case of the sours that he didn't want to add hers to it too.

The next few hours passed in near silence, save for the increasing sound of laughter from Rollie, Bo, and Shiner. Norbert was still lamed from his dunking in the river, but looking as though he'd make most if not all of a recovery before long. Charlie guessed they were drinking again — still — and wondered if they'd miss Charlie and the women.

Might not even give chase, considering the fact that their animals were all pulling beasts, hooked up and slow to move anyway, and it felt as if more rough weather was on its way. The air felt thicker, tighter somehow, as if everything had a big pillow wrapped around it beyond where they could see, up in the heavens.

As much as Charlie hated to admit it, Rollie wasn't wrong about one thing — he and the women needed Rollie and the other men more than they needed him.

A man's scream — it sounded to Charlie as though it was Rollie — jerked everyone to attention. Charlie reined up and looked for Hester, who rode Mabel-Mae close by the wagon and so, close by her sister.

"Stay here!" Charlie jumped down out of the wagon and joined the other men at the front of the train.

Just ahead of Rollie's lead wagon sat a naked man, propped against a boulder. Or what had once been a man. He wore no clothes, and he'd been slit wide and deep, from crotch to breastbone, and his intestines and other guts looked to be removed,

166

though by critter or man, Charlie couldn't tell yet. Likely a combination of both.

His left foot was mostly gone, and raw white nubs of bone stood up where his toes and foot bones had been. The flesh had likely been gnawed away by critters, in varying degrees on up to his knee on the left. The right foot was half there, and his arms had suffered similar treatment.

His torso and arms had been shot several times, as the pocked blackened holes attested. And it looked to Charlie that the poor man had also been shot with arrows, as evidenced by the ragged holes, different looking than gunshot wounds, some with nubs of wood, maybe arrows, sticking out. He saw two of those in the man's shoulders.

But it was the man's head, and his face in particular, that had suffered mightily. It looked as if he'd been scalped from the bottom of his face to the top. His eyes were missing, only bloodied holes remaining. The result was not unlike the dull, fixed expression on the head of a scalded hog ready for butchering.

Charlie guessed the man had been dead a week or so. The cold had preserved him somewhat, and kept him from stinking, thankfully. But he'd begun to blacken and pucker in spots.

Norbert staggered off beside the lead wagon and heaved up whatever booze and bits of jerky he'd taken in during the day. He wobbled, leaning against the wagon, moaning quietly as a series of heaves shook his gaunt buckskin-clad frame.

"Oh my . . ."

Hester had come up beside Charlie. He turned on her, glared down at her, his nostrils flared wide. "Go back to Delia. This ain't no thing for neither of you to see."

To his surprise and relief, she didn't argue, just nodded and walked away.

"And stick close," he said after her. "I'll be there in a minute."

The other men were still looking at the odd sight, familiarity in seeing it seeming to embolden them, and they began to make low, crude comments.

"Kind of lost his head, didn't he?" said Shiner.

"You should talk," said Bo to his bald friend.

"Ha! Why you think I keep my head free of hair? So them savages will pass me by."

"Ain't nobody getting away that easy," said Charlie, looking at them all.

"What do you mean, Big Boy?" said Rollie.

"I mean that a prize is a prize to these

168

folks. Hair or ear or nose, don't matter none. We're likely dealing with a band of Shoshoni. And it looks to me like they're doing this as a warning to us. This man didn't set himself down by the side of the only trail going in and out of the mountains. A trail that ends right at Gamble."

"What are you saying, then?" Rollie seemed almost civil to him.

"I am telling you that we best break out the guns and make camp in a spot we can protect ourselves in. We'll have to sleep in shifts from now on, keep an eye out. Might be it's only a couple of rogues, but might be a whole war party."

All that he said seemed to fall on ears of men who were doing a poor job at letting the danger of the situation sink into their booze-addled minds. Charlie sighed. "We don't have time to stand here and consider what I've said. I'll bet I ain't the only one who's fought Indians before, right?"

"I've done my share," said Norbert shakily.

"Good, then you know that I'm telling you the truth." Charlie turned to Rollie. "Look, it's time to break out those guns and ammunition your uncle has stashed on your wagon."

That seemed to break the spell over Rollie. "Me give you a gun? Are you crazy? Ha. One dead man on the trail and we're all yammering, 'Indian! Indian!' Heck." He kicked the foot bone of the dead man. "He's some old prospector got himself turned around in the hills up here and up and died, got chewed on by coyotes."

The leaning corpse flopped facedown to the ground, exposing his back, the skin on which had been peeled off in precise sections, as if by a knife.

"That's foolish and you know it, Rollie," said Charlie, stepping closer to the bruised freighter. "Now break out them guns. We can't fool around here."

"Naw, I don't think so, Big Boy. And keep your distance, else you'll end up like our new friend here. Besides, why do you think we kept you along? You are nothing more than Injun bait, Big Boy." Rollie backed away from Charlie, his hand resting on the butt of his gun. "Man size of you, why, them Indians will go for you and the women before they go for me and the boys, all armed as we are and such. Not that there are any Injuns around these parts, mind you. But don't you forget: We're the freighters, you're the freight. The sacrificial freight. Sort of like trade goods for the Injuns, if you read me."

Charlie walked back to the women. He didn't think it was possible, but he had suddenly grown even wearier of this man, of his games, and of the entire trip. It seemed everyone was either angry, drunk, or crazy. Or any combination of those traits. It had been a long time since he'd been surrounded by people who were plain happy. He wondered if he ever would be again. Would they make it to Gamble? And if they did, would the people there be any more pleased with their lot in life than this bunch? He guessed some of them might well be, given that they were sitting on the promise of great riches.

Though without supplies, who knew what they'd be like come spring? They'd likely survive, if they had ammunition enough to hunt with and wood enough to keep warm. What a hard winter it'd be without booze, flour, canned milk and fruit, even tobacco. Though not a user of tobacco himself, Charlie knew that a good many people took great comfort from it and got much enjoyment out of it.

"Was it Indians, Charlie?" Hester stood with her hand on her sister's head. The younger sister looked dazed, probably from her medicine.

"Yes, it was, no doubt. I can't be sure, but

171

I'd guess, given the region we're in, that it's Shoshoni. Maybe Bannock."

"How do you know?"

"I've had dealings with them in the past. Not bad sorts, mind you. Not quite so hard to take as the Blackfoot, but if they're riled up, you can be darn sure they won't invite us in for tea. But to do that to a man? Seems unlikely. Something about it ain't right."

"Where do you think the dead man was from?"

"Good question. Only answer that makes sense is that he's from Gamble." He rubbed a finger along his lower lip, considering the situation.

"What?" Delia struggled to rouse herself out of her stupor. "Hester, what's going on? Are we at Gamble now? Why didn't you tell me, I have to make myself pretty for Vin —"

"Shhh, honey, no. We're not there yet."

Charlie felt bad but didn't see what he could do to help. He looked back toward the front of the line of wagons and saw the men lead their teams off along the relatively wide spot in the road, then begin to unload gear. Must be they were stopping for the night. He wondered if Rollie really was afraid of the Indians and didn't dare to travel farther that night.

Charlie did the same with his team, then set to unpacking the gear they'd need. He'd like to scout the region, see if he could find some sign of the attackers, some clue to tell him who they were, how many they might be facing. But he didn't dare leave the women alone.

After long moments of silence, Charlie said, "Hester, what he said about you and your sister . . . that wasn't right. I should have knocked him down for that. I apologize for not standing up for you when Rollie said such things."

"Why, Big Charlie. That's a kind enough thing for you to say." She was actually smiling at him. Then the other shoe dropped and the hard line of her mouth leveled out, along with her eyes, gazing at him leveled and cool. "But defending us is none of your concern, do you understand?"

"You can get all puffed up and angry with me all you want, but those fellas aren't the type to ask your permission for much. I aim to be close by, so you keep your grumbling to a dull roar. We can either talk civil or not."

"I thank you, Charlie, even if my rude old sister doesn't."

The sound of Delia's voice shocked both Charlie and Hester. They regarded her a moment; then Charlie bent low in an exaggerated bow. "Glad I can be of service to at least one of you. You are most welcome, Miss Delia O'Fallon."

Her smile slumped and she looked away. Charlie figured it was her sickness grabbing hold of her again. He sure hated seeing her that way, but not even knowing what she was ill from, let alone how to help her, he reckoned he'd leave such things to her sister. Hester was as devoted to Delia as one person could be to another.

He turned back to the wagon and began unloading the night's gear from the back of his wagon.

"Don't be offended, Charlie. You couldn't know." Hester grabbed a stack of blankets.

"Know what?"

Hester sighed. "I suppose it can't hurt to tell you. She's not an O'Fallon anymore."

"What?"

"She's married. To a man in Gamble. That's why we're headed there."

"Oh, I see. But she is your sister, right?"

Hester smiled. "Yes, that's one thing that can never change."

"Kind of a rough trip for someone who's under the weather." Charlie offered it as a statement, in case Hester didn't take to questioning.

"Yes, but . . . it's what she wanted. At this point, I can't tell her no."

"Bad, then."

She nodded, turned away from him. He felt like kicking himself. *You did it again, Charlie. Always leave 'em crying.*

He tried to think of something to lighten the mood, and lifted down their carpetbags. "What in the heck do you have in this bag anyway? It's sure enough heavier than it looks."

"That one's mine. There's something in there that belonged to our father. I plan on giving it to . . . to her husband, once we reach Gamble."

"Oh, sort of a family heirloom, huh? That's nice. I once had a right fine pocket watch that belonged to my old uncle Jack."

"You don't have it anymore?"

"Naw, that got stole once in a mining camp in California. I about tore that place apart looking for it, but I never did turn it up. I reckon whoever took it needed it more than me anyway."

"Charlie, you are a curious sort of man, you know that?"

He felt himself redden again, and wondered if he would ever stop doing that around women.

"Well." He grinned. "That heirloom you

have there won't hold a candle to the surprise Delia's fella's bound to feel once you all show up."

Hester smiled. "I don't doubt that, Charlie. I don't doubt that in the least."

CHAPTER 17

Lately, Son of Cloud felt as if he was losing his power over his brother, as if Blue Dog was less and less convinced with each sun's rise of the truth of Son of Cloud's words.

He was worried that Blue Dog would give over fully to his own hotheaded ideas. And then there would be little he could do to prevent a war. He would either have to leave him, and go his own way, away from his own brother, away from his own people — even though they had cast them out. Son of Cloud still held out hope that they might one day take the brothers back in. That they might realize they were all of the same people. He hoped that day would come, but he feared it never would.

And now they had killed. Not only killed, but his brother had acted in a way Son of Cloud had never seen before. Blue Dog had not been content with taking the white's life, but he had then ripped apart the man's body, scarring, gutting, and skinning. And all because Blue Dog was confused and angry about things that could not be helped.

"If we keep killing them," said Son of Cloud, giving voice to thoughts that had been troubling him for days, "we will have nothing to bargain with."

"Why are you so bothered by such things? Is it not good enough to kill these creatures who come here and ruin our way of life?"

"No, brother, it is not enough. I am beginning to believe it is foolish to do so. For in killing them, they force us to change our way of life. We are no better than them, then. They have forced us to turn our backs on our traditions, don't you see that?"

The brothers glared at each other. Finally Blue Dog Moon said, "Yesterday you said I reminded you of an old woman. Today I tell you — and unlike you I am not trying to make you laugh when I say this — that you are the old woman. You talk first one way and then another. If you do not want to kill the whites, then you should never have left the tribe."

"We had no choice. You . . ." Son of Cloud closed his mouth, shook his head, and looked away.

"What? What were you going to say, brother? Do you think you can begin to say something and then decide not to?" Blue Dog circled his seated brother and nudged his shoulder when he passed behind him. "Out with it — you were going to say something about our people. About how we had no choice in leaving them."

He reached to nudge his brother again and Son of Cloud spun and grabbed his brother's hand, leaped to his feet, twisting Blue Dog's hand downward in a hard, sharp motion. The younger man cried out in pain and still Son of Cloud held the hand tight.

"Yes, brother," said Son of Cloud, forcing the words between nearly gritted teeth. "It is about our people. And about the fact that we had no choice but to leave." Son of Cloud bent close to his brother's pained, snarling face. "Because of you." He nodded as Blue Dog's eyes flinted wide. "Yes, it is true. The council felt that you were too much like a white man, too filled with anger. They worried for you and for the rest of our people."

"Then why did you not tell me? Or let me go away on my own while you stayed with your precious people?"

The brothers stared hard at each other, their faces inches apart, their breaths coming in fast, forced plumes. Finally Son of Cloud pushed Blue Dog Moon away from him, letting go of the younger man's hand. Blue Dog stumbled backward, caught himself against a tree, and leaned there, rubbing his sore wrist.

"Because," said Son of Cloud, his back to Blue Dog, "you are my brother and I foolishly thought I could convince you to stop causing so much trouble for yourself. For me. For others." He turned, faced his brother again, pointing with a bold hand. "It is one thing to rob whites, to steal their whiskey and horses and whatever else excites you. But, Blue Dog, if we do not stop killing, there will be a war. And it won't be between our people and us. It will be between the whites and us. And there are more whites than us. And the whites will not care if the bad things were done by one or two. If they can, they will kill all Shoshoni they meet."

Blue Dog continued to rub his sore wrist and regard his brother. Finally he said, "Why should I care? Shoshoni? White? I am both and neither. And so are you. Their problems are none of mine."

Son of Cloud could not believe what he heard. "You cannot mean that, brother."

"Do you know?" said Blue Dog. "Up until this moment, I have looked up to you. But I can see now that you are like the rest. You cannot understand that none of this matters." He walked away, leaving his older brother confused and worried.

CHAPTER 18

It only took an hour or so for the freighters to convince themselves that a quick nip of whiskey would do no harm. Charlie watched as one drink led to another, to another, and soon worry of Indians evaporated into the chill night air, replaced with the false bravado only fools and hard-drinking men feel. Charlie noted that for the second night in a row, they kept their weapons laid across their laps. If anything, they were more dangerous than they had been in previous days. But at least they were now good and worried, and for that Charlie was relieved.

He left them to it, and didn't have to work too hard at convincing Hester that she and her sister should hunker down under the wagon. He made a bulwark of gear and covered it over with a tarp. He couldn't shake the gruesome image of that corpse from his mind and knew that they were, no doubt, being watched from the surrounding hills. And there was little he could do.

But he would sure as heck get his hands on a firearm. He'd have to wait until Rollie and the boys went to sleep. Course, that might prove to be more dangerous. He should have figured this out sooner. Now he was up against it with no weapon.

If they were attacked in the night by Indians, he'd probably come out on the losing end of that stick. He sure hoped he didn't end up looking as bad as that man earlier. The thought drew his eyes to the hills again. Dark had an unnerving way of dropping down fast this time of the year, and never quicker than in the hills on an overcast afternoon.

He wished they hadn't stopped at the site where the body was found. He'd have preferred to keep on moving, but Charlie was realizing that, unlike Everett Meecher, who was hell-bent on getting to Gamble as fast as possible, they were now being led by a man who didn't seem in any particular hurry to get to the remote mine camp. That alone made him worry what Rollie's motives were.

At least the skinny drunk hadn't kicked up much of a fuss when Charlie covered the dead man with a ragged scrap of tarpaulin large enough to drape over the gory remains.

"Not going to bury him, Big Boy?" said Rollie, nudging Bo in the gut with an elbow. Bo's laughter followed hard on the heels of Rollie's.

Later, when Charlie returned from roving a few hundred feet out in several directions away from the wagons, he saw something that gave him further cause for doubt of Rollie's intentions. He and his cronies had peeled back the tarps covering the loads on the freight wagons. One had already been pillaged, as that's where they'd been getting their seemingly endless supply of whiskey.

And what Charlie saw in the opened crates were various pieces of equipment that looked an awful lot like those used in mine operations. No surprise there. He'd been around enough such operations to know these were smaller pieces of larger machines, the sort used in mine camps that had more promise than the first-blush prospecting most such camps never got beyond. Some of the pieces he knew were parts for crushers, another crate spilled pipe fittings and what looked to be rollers for conveyors, and still others contained gears of assorted sizes.

There must really be enough promising color for such expensive gear to be sent up. And it all verified what Everett had guessed at — that maybe Rafferty and the marshal, as the ones who'd bankrolled the gamble that was Gamble, were convinced enough of its future payoff. Enough so to get more sophisticated gear up there, maybe to impress a high-money outfit to come on in and do it up in a big way.

The thought both excited Charlie and sickened him, because he'd seen firsthand what the mining consortiums from back East could do to pretty places like mountainsides and river valleys. They came in and cut down all the trees, dammed the rivers, dug huge pits, killed all the critters and big game for miles around, made the water unfit to drink. He got to thinking about such things and it shamed him that he'd participated in mining in one form or another for so long.

When he'd started prospecting, it had been a clean pursuit, scrambling around creeks and rivers and hillsides, looking for promising sign of color in quartz. He'd gotten better at finding it, but never developed what one old rock hound had called "a nose" for it. Charlie reckoned his sniffer was more suited to detecting a campfire with a pot of Arbuckle's bubbling, maybe a beefsteak sizzling.

"What do you think you are up to, nosing around my freight, Big Boy?"

Charlie spun to see a grinning Rollie right beside him, looking as if the two of them were old friends from way back.

"Hey, Rollie." Charlie cast him a cautious glance, but the man appeared as casual as could be, the distinct sour smell of whiskey clouded around Rollie's head like an unseen fog. "Couldn't help noticing all this gear, the crates open and all."

"Yeah, I expect that stuff is more junk, not worth much. I'm tempted to leave it beside the trail. Heck, I don't need to haul that up there."

Charlie smiled, looked at Rollie with one squinted eye. "Aw, you're joshing me."

Rollie popped a quirly between his lips and struck a match, sucked the smoke deep, shaking his head. "No, I ain't neither."

"I don't believe they're paying you to decide what it is you're hauling, Rollie. Just that you haul whatever it is they want you to."

As he expected, as if Charlie had snapped his fingers, Rollie's sour, know-it-all mood once again immediately turned to raw anger at Charlie's comments. Charlie sighed inside and quickly said, "Look, I only mention it because . . ." He leaned close to the sputtering man and said, "All this stuff you say is useless is going to be mighty, mighty useful in pulling that gold from the ground up in Gamble. Heck, from what I understand, and I have it on good authority" — he tried to make his voice sound friendly and as if he were sharing a secret — "that Gamble is filled with gold."

"Yeah, it is, you bet," said Rollie, softening his hard edge a bit, regarding Charlie with squinted eyes through his cigarette's smoke. "And I aim to get it all without doing a lick of digging."

"Well, now, Rollie." Charlie smiled, shook his head. "If you know the answer to that secret, you are going to be a mighty rich man one day." He chuckled.

"No, I mean it, Big Boy. That gold's all settin' there in bags, waiting for ol' Rollie to roll on in." He smiled and rubbed his grubby hands together.

Charlie couldn't help it, he laughed at that. "Most all the gold in Gamble is still in the ground, Rollie, not in some warehouse up there. Why, sure, I bet they have a few sacks of dust here and there and crates of ore, bound to have some stockpiled. But look, you dump all this equipment and gear that they'll need to get lots more gold out of the ground, why, you'll be . . ." Charlie snapped his big fingers, smiling.

Rollie flinched, a confused look on his face.

"It come to me, exactly what you're saying reminds me of an old story my granny used to tell me. About a goose that laid a golden egg. Went like this: There was this goose, see, and she laid solid gold eggs. Day after day, one egg a day. Things was going along okay for the old couple who owned the goose, what with all that gold appearing, slow and steady."

"You don't make no sense at all, Big Boy," said Rollie, rolling his eyes and finishing off his quirly.

"Bear with me. One day, the man, he gets impatient. His wife's out . . . well, I don't rightly know what she's off doing, but he's alone with the goose. So he gets to looking at that goose and he figures that if he could cut to the chase, why, they'd all be better off." Charlie looked at Rollie, eyes wide, expecting the freighter to catch on. But he didn't, so Charlie plowed on ahead with his story. "So that fool of a man killed that goose, cut it open right there. And do you know what he found?"

Rollie sighed, shook his head. "Big Boy, I reckon that fool found a handful of goose guts."

"Yes!" said Charlie, poking a big finger up

at the dark night sky and smiling.

"That still don't make no sense."

"Don't you see? That goose wasn't full of gold eggs, Rollie. Just like Gamble ain't full of gold. You got to give it time, work at it to get the gold out. I aim to. But if you go up there and gut that little mine camp, why, you'll never get at all the gold that will come on out of the ground eventually."

Rollie looked at Charlie for a long moment, and Charlie thought for sure he'd gotten through. Maybe turned a corner with ol' Rollie, after all. He still didn't trust him, but maybe the man would think twice before doing stupid things like dumping all this good gear.

Rollie pushed away from the wagon and walked away, shaking his head and saying, "Hey, fellas. You will never guess what Big Boy just told me! He thinks geese lay gold eggs!"

The next few minutes were spiked with bursts of laughter and glances his way from the freighters. Charlie felt his face heat up and was relieved that at least it was nighttime so the fools wouldn't see him. All he wanted to do was pop 'em each on the nose, make them howl a bit.

He roamed the edge of the camp for a while longer until the burbling laughter ended and the men resumed their drinking. The day ended much the same as the previous day — with Rollie and his cohorts eventually flopped back in snoring heaps, the cold air not affecting them in the least. Charlie hoped they all woke up with frostbite.

The women weren't particularly talkative, not that he could blame them. It was coming off cold and they barely had enough wood to make it through the night. He did his best to keep awake, still not convinced that Rollie had forgotten his plans for dallying with Delia. Though from the looks of him, Rollie would barely be able to roll over, let alone fight off the she-cat named Hester. She was quite a perplexing creature, no doubt about that. Maybe under different circumstances he might have fancied such a willful woman, but here, on this hellish trail, and this late in his life — no, thank you, ma'am.

With such thoughts, and a last glance around the camp to ensure that everybody looked to be where they should be — all four freighters snoring, the two women huddled tight to each other and well wrapped with blankets, and the pulling beasts out of sight in the shadows — Charlie nestled his head down into his collar and figured that a few winks of shut-eye would do no one harm. He'd earned more than that, but a stolen minute here and there surely wouldn't hurt.

He awoke sometime later, though how long he had slept, he had no idea. But it was still dark and the fire had petered down to a clump of glowing coals. Something had wakened him. He remained still, with his eyes open. Several minutes passed, then to his right, the soft sound of fluttering, as if light wings taking flight, or perhaps it was a whisper. Then it was gone. But he had heard it, hadn't he?

Charlie had held his arms crossed in his sleep, and now he slowly shifted them down to his sides, the fingers of one hand resting on the hilt of his Green River knife, ready to lift it free when he stood. And he would have to stand soon, not only for the fact that he had to shake the blood back into his legs, but he felt he needed to explore the camp — something was giving him the distinct feeling that he was the object of someone, or something's staring attention. And he didn't like it.

He managed to stand and not make too much of a sound outside of cracking his knee on a wagon wheel. He grunted and bit back the pain as he ambled as quietly as he could around the outside of the camp. He stepped easily on dried leaves and twigs, and tried to take a head count of the animals. Other than the mild Mabel-Mae, who he'd tied close by, he couldn't see too many of them in the dark.

He was about to turn to the fire, quietly stoke it back to life, when he heard the fluttery sound again. And again, he held still for several minutes, but heard nothing more than the occasional rustle and blow of one of the pulling animals, a far-off small sound — a small critter, no doubt, searching for food.

Charlie made his way back to the fire. Though it was still dark, he knew it would soon be time to wake and get moving. Well, it would on a normal freighting trip. But this one had taken a number of odd turns. Still, he prodded the fire, fed twigs to the hungry coals, then blew on them until he was rewarded with smoke and small, licking flames. He nursed it along until it cracked and snapped. The huddled figures around the fire slowly began to stir at the sounds, at the tang of wood smoke, and the heat and light the fire offered.

It didn't take long for the four hungover men to stretch, scratch, and swig from their bottles in an effort to ward off the coming headaches they were surely beginning to feel.

One by one they wandered off, not too far from the fire, and relieved themselves. The ladies made sure they did what they had to do far from the men. Finally Rollie roused himself and wandered off to do his business. He was gone for some time. Then they heard him swearing and stomping in the dark over near the animals. He agitated a number of them.

Charlie could hear slaps and he knew Rollie was smacking the animals, maybe to get them to move for him. It was obvious to Charlie that Meecher had no love for animals. The big man stood, looked for Rollie, and saw him storming back toward the fire.

"We been robbed!" He strode into the light and swept them all with a glaring look from his still-puffy, bruised face.

"What are you talking about?" said Charlie.

Rollie poked a finger at Charlie, coming as close as any man had in a long time to actually poking the big man in the chest with the finger. "We lost two horses."

"What do you mean . . . 'lost'?" said Bo, rubbing his temples with two shaking hands.

"I mean," said Rollie, not shifting his eyes from Charlie's face. "They've been stolen."

"What? That's impossible," said Charlie, even though he knew it was quite possible. Especially with all those animals and with Indians loose in the hills all around them.

"You know what I think?" Rollie took another step closer to Charlie. "I think you took them."

Charlie and the women, even a couple of the freighters, laughed. "You're joshing me, right, Rollie?"

But the hungover freighter shook his head slightly. "You were the one tending the fire, the one who stayed up all night, the one who suggested yesterday that we all should sleep in shifts, stand watch, all that foolishness. Wonder why that is. And why in blazes is your nasty mule still here?"

For a moment, all eyes turned toward Mabel-Mae, who, it seemed, had far less interest in them than they did in her. She stood still, as always, one ear flicking occasionally.

"My mule is here because, well, because that's where I tied her last night. And I suggested what I did for one simple reason: There are Indians around us, Rollie. Heck, that dead man we come upon yesterday should have been reason enough. How dumb does one man get anyway?"

"Don't you dare call me dumb."

"Fine, then stop acting that way."

"You took them horses, I know it."

"Okay, Rollie, say I did." Charlie crossed his arms, beginning to warm to the tall tale that was unspooling before him. "What did I do with them?"

"You tell me, you're the one who took them!"

Charlie noticed that beneath the bruising and bloodshot eyes, Rollie Meecher was working up a fit of rage not unlike what his uncle Everett had done a few times in the short amount of time Charlie had known him.

"Aw, Rollie." It was Norbert. As with Shiner and Bo, he too sat on the ground before the fire, his long, bony hands cradling his head. He spoke without looking up. "Let off that crazy talk. Ol' Charlie wouldn't have no reason to take no horses, no matter which way you come at this problem."

Charlie was impressed. For once, one of the men didn't back down to Rollie, and what's more, it was Norbert, with whom Charlie felt some bond, however thin and stretched it might be.

Charlie decided to intervene before Rollie decided to shoot Norbert for standing up to him. "Look, Rollie, as soon as it's light a couple of us can go off and look for the horses. Maybe they got loose and wandered off. Can't be they've gone far. In the meantime, if we can't find them, then we should give thought to rerigging a wagon or two."

Oddly, Rollie said nothing, just glared at everyone and kept to himself. They all went about their business of making coffee and preparing a bit of food — eggs and biscuits. Turned out that Bo was a pretty good hand at cooking.

"Biscuits is about all I can do, though."

But he seemed pleased that Charlie tucked right into the stack of them. In truth, Charlie could eat the bark off a tree and it would have tasted as good to him, he was that hungry. Instead he smiled and nodded and kept right on chewing.

Once light came, they never did find the horses. But they found two spots on the picket line where their ropes had been sliced by a knife. Whoever did it had not gone to any pains to conceal the cuts. As Charlie searched farther out in a direction he hoped might provide clues, he thought back to when he'd awakened before the others. He felt guilty now, as he'd promised himself he'd stay awake, then didn't. And he'd also heard those mysterious fluttery, whispery sounds. Now he wondered if maybe they had been Indians.

He found no clues, though plenty of broken branches and scuffed leaves. He felt sure that a trained tracker could follow the trail, wherever it was. None of the freighters had any decent skill or experience tracking, and soon they all met up at the fire and drank the last of the coffee. They finished cleaning up camp, then moved out, everyone looking in every direction they could. Charlie even caught sight of Rollie craning his neck left and right for sign of Indians.

CHAPTER 19

The day began cold and soon became a long, wet one. The snow increased within hours after their midday break. Soon the rough trail was covered with a thickening layer of white. The frozen stuff pelted at them nearly horizontal to the ground, gusting at times until it felt as though they were being blasted with sand.

Charlie tied Mabel-Mae's lead rope to the wagon and made Hester climb in beside Delia. He wasn't worried about the mule, but he was worried that Hester might wander off the trail and somehow lose sight of the wagons. The wind increased throughout the day and took on a nasty habit of buffeting them with squalls whenever they passed between trees and into the open.

A number of times, Charlie heard shouts from wagons up ahead, but could not make out what they said. Soon they passed into a thickly treed clearing that looked to hold promise for a campsite. The wind was cut well by the trees and a series of jutting, rocky outcrops. The spot was wide enough for them to position most of the wagons in such a way that they helped block even more of the wind and snow. Charlie's wagon was the only one that couldn't easily be wedged into the configuration, but they managed to snug it up to the rest to be of some use.

They all kept their heads down, wrapped in scarves, hats pulled low, and went about their camp tasks, even the mildly drunk freighters, with a vigor that surprised Charlie. He had amassed a sizable pile of firewood and it was matched by Bo's and Shiner's combined efforts.

"Maybe have some more of those fine biscuits of yours, Bo?" said Charlie, hoping to break the ice with the man, but Bo shot him a surly look, mumbled something, and ambled off to find more wood.

"Don't pay any attention to them, Charlie." Hester stood beside him, shaking her head. "They're idiots and they'll never change. I've seen their kind before."

"Me too. World's filled with them and it's downright depressing at times. Heck." He smiled. "Sometimes I'm one of them. And it don't get more depressing than to wake up one day and find you've been acting like one of the people you swore you'd never be like."

Hester stared at him for a moment, then said, "I swear, Charlie, sometimes you are almost a poet." Then she walked away.

"What'd I say?"

"And I'd advise you, Charlie, to not pay any attention to my cantankerous sister." Delia moved slowly, carrying a small armload of branches and twigs. Her smile told Charlie she was in the midst of one of her good spells. They seemed to happen infrequently, but when they did, she was downright chatty and a little firecracker of good humor, something that her sister wasn't.

All Charlie could do was try not to laugh at Hester's obvious displeasure at her sister's assessment of her.

By the time the fire was blazing, the animals tended, and the tarpaulins tacked up, dark had crept upon them and with it, the wind had dwindled. The snow continued to fall and the temperature inched downward. Once again, Charlie, Hester, and Delia had hunkered down on one side of the fire, the freighters on the other, drinking and growing increasingly loud.

Hester prepared a decent feed of biscuits and beans for them, using some of Charlie's own supplies, some of their own, and followed it up with a tin of syrup-soaked pears from a crate in the wagon. She prepared enough for all, and dished up plates for the freighters before herself, her sister, and Charlie.

"Let me lend a hand. I'll take them over," said Charlie, scooping up the plates.

"No," said Hester, staying his hand. "I cooked it, I'll pass it around." She brought four around and went down the line, handing out the high-sided pie tins piled with steaming food. As they sat facing the fire, Norbert, Bo, and Shiner all nodded, grunted their thanks, and tucked in with gusto.

Rollie was the last one she came to. He had been fiddling with his pistol and sat with that resting loosely in one hand in his lap, the neck of a well-tended whiskey bottle in the other. He'd stretched his legs out fully toward the fire, forcing Hester to step over them. She was in the act of doing so quickly. Rollie reached up with one leg in between hers, raising her skirts to reveal the long-handles she wore underneath. He laughed, inciting giggles from the other men, who all had their eyes on the scant bit of covered leg revealed above her boots.

Without pause, Hester tipped the scalding hot beans and biscuits onto Rollie's lap, drizzled them onto his Colt, his hand, and his crotch. "Oh dear!" she said, jumping over his legs and retreating around the side of the fire. "I am so clumsy."

Rollie's initial howl of surprise soon turned into cries of pain as the heat of the beans bubbled up blisters on his hand, and the juice oozed into his gun, and soaked into his grimy denims. He danced in a circle, wiping the sticky bean juice from his hand and howling blue oaths. He squared off at Hester and leveled his Colt at her, his gun hand red and already blistered. "You! You stupid cow! Look what you did!"

"Hardly my fault, Rollie. You knocked me off balance. . . ."

Charlie had known as soon as Rollie began his shenanigans what the outcome might be, and he wedged his bulk in between the shaky gun and Hester, who, not unexpectedly, had shown no sign of backing down.

"Now, look here, Rollie. You had no call to go doing what you did, and if she says you're the one who made her lose her balance, why, it's your word against hers. But I'm siding with her. You fellas?" He looked to the other three freighters, who sat with their eyes wide and mouths agape, full of half-chewed food, their fingertips dripping bean juice.

A couple of them nodded, having seen what this huge man had done to Rollie a few nights before, and wondering what he might do to them.

The entire time he spoke, Charlie worked his way toward the shaky, seething Rollie, in hopes of catching hold of the revolver. He didn't want to catch a bullet instead. He opened a hand, extended toward Rollie. "Give me the gun, Rollie. Give it up. You ain't in no fit state to be wagging that thing around. You been drinking steady for days. That ain't no way to live, Rollie. . . ." Charlie edged closer, keeping his gaze on Rollie's wide eyes, on his wide-stretched mouth, spittle flecking his beard.

A few more inches and Charlie felt sure he could bat that Colt out of the fool's hand, away from the others. Then he'd close in, button up the crazy man's eyes, tie him up if he had to, and call it a night.

But Rollie had other ideas in mind. Charlie reached his big hand one inch closer and the next instant the campsite exploded in sound. Charlie felt a hot lance of pain stab low on his right side, smelled smoke as if from burned wool and leather. He clutched at his side, felt wetness, and raised a hand. Sound seemed to dull, become a wash of noise, low and blurry, as if he had been dunked in water. In the flickering firelight, he saw what looked like blood on his hand. *Couldn't be, though. Have to be hurt to bleed. . . .*

"You all saw him! He come at me! Come at me with that knife of his! He was fixing to kill me!"

Slowly it came to him that he'd been hurt, shot, by Rollie. And then as if his head had been lifted out from being held underwater, sound, glass-sharp and sights of faces, fire, the wagons, these visions keen-edged and crisp, sliced at him from all around.

None of it made sense to him. Charlie smelled wood smoke, then felt a new pain on the side of his head. He turned to see the butt of Rollie's Colt swinging at him, the madman of a freighter leering, the thrill of excitement painted on his face, and Charlie tried to dodge it, but too late.

He spun, then, saw the campsite go around and around him, grow bigger and bigger, blurrier and darker all the time. All that sound — screaming, might be it was a woman screaming, "What have you done? What have you done?" He heard more shouting and horses and mules — slowly pinched out too. And then Big Charlie Chilton knew no more.

CHAPTER 20

"What have you done, you murderer!" Hester O'Fallon dropped to her knees by the big man. She couldn't believe what she'd seen, couldn't believe that the worthless drunken bum freighter would shoot mild Big Charlie for standing up for her.

She tried to see in the fading light, but between that and the snow that had begun falling harder, as if making up for lost time, tending Charlie was taking some doing.

"Somebody check on that other one, the sickly, pretty girl." Rollie gestured toward the spot under the wagon where Hester had set up Delia in a protected spot out of the wind.

"No! No, you leave her alone!" Hester ran to her sister's side, but found the girl sound asleep, seemingly at peace. She'd dosed her with laudanum earlier, hoping Delia would get a good night's rest. The girl had awakened to the sounds of gunfire, but in her stupor hadn't been able to rouse herself beyond a wobbly, questioning glance.

"Someone shut her up and tie her up to that tree yonder!" Rollie waved his pistol at her and said, "Or I will, permanent-like."

Norbert hobbled over to the girl beneath the wagon and bent to her. Hester tried to kick at him, but Shiner grabbed her arms from behind and dragged her, screaming and kicking, backward toward Rollie. "Shut up, woman!"

Norbert seemed rattled by the entire affair, but felt Delia's neck for signs of life, bent to feel her breath on his face. He rose, shaking his head slowly. "She ain't with us no more, boss." He bent back to her and covered her face with her blanket.

"What?" said Rollie, lurching toward the wagon. Before he got far from her, the now-crazed Hester lashed out wildly with her legs and landed a hard kick square on the side of his leg, half collapsing him sideways. He spun and seemed about to backhand her across the face when Norbert came up behind him and held Rollie's arms.

"Let her be, boss," he said close by Rollie's ear. "She lost her sister, for Pete's sake. Leave her be for a few minutes."

Rollie stopped struggling against the tall man, then shrugged hard out of his grasp.

"You ever touch me again, Norbert, and you're done. You used up all your chances with me. Now tie her up."

Shiner held the now-sobbing Hester tight, too tight for her to break free, her struggles becoming less frenzied as Norbert cinched the ropes about her wrists behind her. "I got it," he said to Shiner, who roughly thrust her to the ground.

Norbert waited until Shiner was out of earshot, then lashed another rope tightly about her ankles. "Listen to me," he said, looking up at her as he tied, without raising his head or moving his lips much. "Your little sister's alive."

Hester stopped crying and stared, red-faced and trembling, at Norbert's rough cob of a face.

"I did that so they wouldn't bother her . . . in the way they want to." He double-knotted the rope to buy himself more talking time. "But you got to worry about yourself now. I don't know as I can protect you much more."

CHAPTER 21

Movement and sound, like rocks rattling in a can, woke Charlie. He was walking. No, that wasn't quite right. He was moving, but he didn't think he was doing the work of it. Someone was moving him. That must be it. He couldn't call what he felt awake, since he couldn't seem to open his eyes. But soon the sounds he heard became words, people's voices, and he recognized the voices as Rollie's and one of the other men's, which one he couldn't tell at first, but it soon enough sounded like Shiner.

"Yeah, well, you and the others go along with me and I'll make you all rich men."

"Just how rich we talkin'?"

"Rich, I'm telling you, beyond your grandest imaginings."

Charlie could tell it was Shiner, or maybe Bo, that Rollie was talking to. Charlie didn't much care. He tried to speak, but nothing came out.

"How you going to pull off such a miracle?"

"Heck," said Rollie, "it's simple as simple can be, boy. What we do is we'll wait 'em out, let 'em starve, and then take all these here goods and their gold too."

"What if they won't give up their gold?"

"They will, when they're starvin' for flour and whiskey. And if they ain't dead, they soon will be," cackled Rollie.

"What if they head on out, hunting and whatnot?"

"We pick 'em off, boy. Use your head."

"But how we gonna live until then?"

Rollie sighed, then said, "We have wagons full of food and supplies, don't we?"

"Yeah," said Shiner. "Hey, that's right. So when the town's empty, we head on in, take the gold —"

"And anything else worth taking," interrupted Rollie. "And then we head west over the mountains, drop down to California. I figure we can make it by spring."

"What do we do there?"

"I don't know about you, but I'm fixing to live like a king. You, on the other hand, are probably too stupid. I doubt they will let you in."

Rollie's laugh accompanied a sharp pain in Charlie's side. Felt as if he was moving somehow. Maybe they were hefting him, helping him to his feet. *No, no, Charlie,* he told himself. *That isn't possible. The man shot you. . . .*

Despite his pain, Charlie couldn't believe what he was hearing. Rollie was fixing to starve out and kill off the people of Gamble? He had to stop him, had to do something, but how? Then he heard the men's voices straining, heard them grunting. They were lifting him, that much he was sure of, and then they let go of him, dropped him on something hard.

His head hit, and it felt like thunder cracking in his skull. Hot rivers of pain flowered up his side, down from his head, then met in the middle, and lit his chest on fire. It felt as though he were about to explode.

Charlie tried harder to speak, to make some sound, some movement at all. But he didn't think he was too successful at it. The men had been talking the entire time they flopped him wherever it was they did, but he couldn't make out any more than the blurred sounds of their voices.

"You can't leave them here!"

Rollie raised the snout of the Colt's barrel to Hester's forehead, dead between her eyes. His mouth smiled at her. His eyes did not.

She trembled, but her gaze locked hard on his. "Do it, you . . . worm."

Hester saw a nerve jump and jounce at the corner of Rollie's left eye, dirt smudged in the little wrinkles there. His thumb peeled back the hammer all the way, and he pressed the barrel harder into her head.

"Do it, curse your worthless hide." She said it low but clear.

"That's what you'd like, isn't it?"

"Yes," said Hester, without hesitation.

Rollie smiled again, revealing stained teeth in his stubbled face. He eased off the hammer. "Then that is exactly what you will not get. Not yet anyway. We'll see about later . . . later."

Rollie turned away and the tied-up woman's face sagged in confusion and despair. "No, that's not right! You can't do this to me! You animal! You filthy animal!"

Rollie turned to face her, his face becoming a mask of slow rage as she screamed on and on. Finally he could take it no longer and two long strides brought him beside her. Quick as a lightning strike, he lashed out with the butt of the Colt and hit her above her left ear. Her eyes rolled back and she sagged against the ropes lashing her to a tree.

Rollie stalked back to his wagon, then

stopped. "Put her in my wagon," he said to Bo. "But you make sure she's still tied, hands behind her and feet together. And gag her too, you got that? But not permanent." He smiled. "I expect I'll have need of her before too long."

The rotten-toothed man nodded and Shiner moved to help him cut down the unconscious woman. Shiner had hold of the older sister's feet, her skirts hanging halfway up her legs, but all the men saw were faded pink long-handles. Still, they were almost revealing her naked leg, and that was enough to get them to thinking about the fun they were going to have once they got to California with their gold. Yes, sir, it was working out as Rollie said it would.

First he got rid of that nasty old uncle of his; then he got hold of the freighting business for himself; then they were headed next to that gold town up ahead in the mountains. Just as Rollie said. Except for Big Boy and the women. Shiner looked up at Bo. "Where'd this one's sister get to?"

Bo flashed a frown. "Didn't make it. Started scratching at me a while ago when I tried to get to know her, you know, and she scratched me right on the face." He turned his head to show Shiner two deep welts down the side of his cheek.

"Lucky you didn't lose an eye."

"You darn right."

"So where's she at?" Shiner asked again, lugging the unconscious woman and walking backward toward Rollie's wagon. He was having a hard time walking and keeping an eye on the woman's legs at the same time.

"Had to pop her one with a stick of firewood. Could be I hit her too hard. She ain't moving and I felt no heartbeat."

"No big loss," said Shiner. "Rollie said she was sick anyway. Ain't nothing we should have to deal with."

"You said that right. This one, though. She's a spitfire. I reckon she'll be some peeved when she wakes up, finds her sister and Big Boy are no longer with us, as the preacher says at funerals."

They reached the wagon and Shiner propped the unconscious woman's boots on the flopped-open tailgate of the wagon. He climbed up into the wagon as Rollie walked up. "Yep, set her right there in that spot I got ready. Now tie her up." The two men did as he said; then he said, "And the other one, she's for-sure dead?"

"The girl?"

Rollie rolled his eyes. "Of course, the girl. I know Big Boy ain't getting up again. I'm

the one who drilled him and hit him, ain't
I?"

"Yeah, well." Bo didn't look up.

"Bo," said Rollie. "Bo, what'd you do?"

The greasy man spread his lips wide,
exposing his blackened nubby teeth. "I'm
sorry, Rollie, but she attacked me." He
showed Rollie his bleeding cheek. "Wasn't
nothing I could do. Had to do it. Clunked
her with a piece of wood."

Rollie sighed. "Then Norbert really was
right? She done for?"

"Yeah, I reckon she's not drawing breath
no more."

Rollie rubbed his chin. "Okay, then, you
probably did us a favor. She was sick anyway. Not looking too healthy. I reckon she
wouldn't have lasted all that long anyway.
But tie that one up tight. She's going to be
all worked up when she finds out. Now let's
go. We only have a few hours of light left,
and I want to make use of them."

"You sure we won't need any of that gear
we're leaving behind?"

"Norbert, what did I say about asking me
about my decisions?"

The thin man nodded, wished he hadn't
said a thing.

"Besides, it's junk. The only things them
people from Gamble are going to want will

be food and booze, tobacco, you name it. Anything but that equipment."

"Charlie said they was going to use that stuff for digging the gold. Equipment and such."

Rollie shut his eyes tight, then leaned back and drove a scar-knuckled fist right into Norbert's rangy jaw. The buckskinned man flew backward, piled into the side of the second wagon, and lay still for a moment. He came around quickly, shook his head as if to shake off a fly. He focused his eyes on the man staring down at him, arms crossed and a ticked-off look on his face. Norbert rasped his hand along his tender jaw.

"What all you do that for, Rollie?"

"If I have to tell you, then I might as well shoot you now. Get up and get busy." Rollie walked off, leaving Norbert struggling to stand, still dizzy and wondering what it was he'd said that riled Rollie so.

"I can drive a team now, boss."

"No, you can't. You ain't been right since you went swimming. Shut your piehole and ride shotgun." Rollie turned and shouted to the others. "I'm moving out soon. You all can do as you please. Make sure those two wagons of mine come with me and don't stay with you."

Shiner and Bo traded looks.

"Boss ain't making sense," said Bo.

"That's his way of telling us that we're in it with him all the way." Shiner rubbed his hands together. "And if that means money, then you bet I'm in. I can almost smell that gold from here."

Bo walked back to his own wagon. "How far we got to go anyway?"

"Boss said a few more days."

"Good," said Bo. "With them Injuns about, I fear for my topknot."

"I don't have that worry," said Shiner, running a callused hand over his stubbled head.

Not long after, Rollie and Norbert had finished lashing down a tarp on the lead wagon when Rollie said, "Norbert, I want you to make yourself useful and set fire to that wagon." He nodded toward the wagon on which lay Big Charlie Chilton, and under which lay Delia, the sickly sister.

"Burn them?"

"But . . . she's alive. I mean, I ain't no doc, but she might well be alive. And the big fella, he's still kickin' too."

"Not by much." Rollie pointed the Colt at Norbert. "Besides, if you don't do it, I'll be more than happy to plug you one right here, leave you to burn with them. Or did you forget what I told you about your chances with me being all used up?"

Norbert raised his long, bony hands, let them drop.

"Good, now do like I said and burn them, the wagon, the whole thing." Rollie saw the horror on the buckskin-clad man's face. "Heck, they'll never know a thing. Be a good way to go — they was both on their way out anyway. This here is the right thing to do, mark my words. Think of it as us doing their dear, departed souls a favor. We don't burn 'em up, they'll be lion bait. You want that on your conscience?"

Norbert shook his head. "I still dunno about this, Rollie. Seems to me we'd be better off if we'd have kept that big boy alive." The thin man stood hunched by the blazing campfire, shivering. Ever since his fall in the river, he'd not been able to get himself warm. There had been times during the past few days that he wondered if he even caught fire, would he be heated enough inside?

Rollie tilted his head so far to one side it seemed to Norbert as if the young boss man was going to break his neck. "I say you could give me advice? I ask for anything from you other than to do what I told you to do?"

"No, I heard you, Rollie. It's just that . . ."

"Look." Rollie's features softened. "I

217

already told you. That big boy knew too much about Gamble. I expect he even had an idea of what we're going to get up to. Besides, I happen to know that he is an old outlaw. So that makes us having kilt him the right thing."

Norbert's eyes narrowed. "I ain't heard about him being an outlaw, and I ain't never heard nothing about killing being okay, except in war, maybe."

"Yeah, well, I have, and when it's time to tell you, I'll tell you. But for now, do as I say, okay? I got enough troubles on my plate without you chucking on another helping of them. Now get busy. I got canvas to tie down before more snow comes. We got to put some miles under the wheels today if we want to beat the snow."

Norbert tried to take his time, but it looked to him as if Rollie was onto him, because the boss man eyed his progress toward the fire to set alight a torch, then carry it to the wagon where Charlie was laid out in the back.

Norbert swallowed hard, then lit three spots of the wagon on fire. He hoped that would do the trick — enough to satisfy Rollie anyway. He also hoped that the falling snow would quench the flames before they could do any damage.

He looked toward Rollie, but the man must have been satisfied with Norbert's efforts, because he had turned back to readying his own wagon to move on out of the camp. Snow had begun falling and Rollie was doubly determined to head up-trail as soon as possible.

Norbert mumbled an apology without looking at the wagon. He winced when he heard flames crackle as they sank their flickering fangs into the wagon's wood.

"Move it out!" Rollie's voice trailed back to them and soon three wagons, repacked and retarped, rolled forward. The extra animals were tied behind the middle and last wagons and the slow, steady procession headed deeper into the mountains along the rough-cut road toward Gamble.

In the back of the first wagon, the unconscious woman flopped and clunked with every rut and rock and hole the squeaking steel-banded wheels passed over. Norbert sat sideways in the seat, kept one eye on her.

"You staring at her ain't going to make her like you."

"I know it." Norbert shifted, rubbed his knees, still so stiff and sore from the river. "Wanted to make sure she didn't bounce outta the wagon. Bo and Shiner can't tie a knot to save their hides."

Rollie laughed. It was a relief to Norbert to see him happy. He'd known Rollie for quite some time, and he'd never seen him so belligerent and quarrelsome as lately. Might be the drink. Rollie had been hitting the bottle hard of late.

"I wish you'd spend some of your eyeballin' time looking out for savages, Norbert. Between you and me, I will tell you that I didn't like seeing that gutted, skun-faced man back on the trail. That was raw, that was."

Norbert nodded in agreement. "No mistake." He sat upright and double-checked the chamber on his battle-scarred Henry rifle.

CHAPTER 22

It was the cold wetness that Charlie Chilton felt first. Something touched his face, like light tears, or drops of dew lifting off a flower's petals when you touch a fingertip to it — *just like that,* he thought. But no, that wasn't it. And soon the sweet sensation passed, clouded over by something bigger, like a whole-body headache. Its twinges stabbed at odd intervals, enough that you couldn't prepare for them, couldn't suck in a breath to steel yourself before they hit.

And then rough, ragged hunks of memory of the previous night came back to him, and he knew more with each passing second what had happened. *Is this what it's like to be dead? No, Charlie, no, it ain't. Not by a long shot,* he told himself. *You got a whole lot to work through yet, boy. Like all this pain.*

And how do you account for the white light trying to force open your eyes? Should you even let it in? Now, that's a decision you best make soon, boy. All this and more Charlie told himself in the first few seconds of waking.

He tried again to open his eyes, still not sure if he was alive. It didn't take him long to figure out that he was alive, had to be, because being dead, as far as he could guess, what with heaven and all, couldn't possibly hurt this much. And by gum, did he ache all over!

The stink of burned, wet wood filled his nostrils, and fought with the bitter, metal-tinged scent of blood and the cloying, sopping smell of wet wool. His ears pulsed with what sounded like echoes from a battlefield — were they screams? And another sound beneath, almost constant, deeper in tone . . . wind maybe? But no, not so haunted as that. More human, and then he knew what the sound was — it was moaning.

Charlie worked to pull in breath, and the moaning stopped. He coughed, let out what air he could, and the moaning commenced. He did this twice more before it occurred to him, as the fuzz-packed edges of his brain began to clear, that the moaning sound came from within himself.

If he could hear that, however muddy and far off it sounded, maybe he really was still alive. He tried to speak, coughed, barely heard it, but was rewarded instead with sharp lancing pains from three directions at once. It was as if he were being shot at over and over again, or burned with red-hot sharpened steel rods. His shoulder, the left, and his side, maybe his gut. But the worst pain came from his head.

Open your eyes, Charlie, he willed himself over and over again. Finally he felt his eyelids begin to crack upward. They were the heaviest things he had ever lifted. In a lifetime of being the one everybody called to help lift a wagon to change a fouled hub, or to drag on a swamp-bogged horse, these eyelids were far and away the most difficult, heaviest things he'd ever had to lift.

While he worked to at least flutter them, he moved his tongue inside his mouth, felt something odd there, maybe a chipped tooth. What could have caused all of this? None of it made sense. And yet there was a spot of promise that he knew if he could keep on worrying it, somehow he would get answers. If only it didn't hurt so much to think, to move, to open his eyes, to lie still, to breathe. But he knew he had to keep trying. That was the only way anything ever happened in life, keep on trying.

He concentrated on the blood taste in his mouth. If he was bleeding, that must mean without a doubt that he was alive. *Now open the eyes, Charlie, boy.* And slowly, a gray haze, like a film on an ice-crusted stream, let light in. He opened them wider, and he saw brighter light. One eye finally popped open and didn't reveal all that much, but it did prove that he was alive.

He pulled in more air through his nose, found one nostril was plugged, as if he'd been clubbed in the face hard by something . . . there it was again, a glimmer of a memory. He chased it, but the pain in his head was too great to allow his mind to roam far.

And so it went for him. Charlie spent how long he knew not willing each little piece of himself into movement. He wasn't certain, but he felt as though he had somehow managed to make his fingers move, maybe his toes. Then he was sure of his success because his second eye opened and more bright light came to him.

Something pressed on him, stiff and cold. Wood of some sort, a board, maybe. It felt close to his face and it smelled . . . charred. So that was what he'd been smelling all this time, burned wood. He lifted his head and an ache joined forces with dizziness to conspire against him. He didn't care. He had to keep moving, keep trying, and he did, working harder as each second brought fresh waves of throbbing pain thundering like runaway horses deep in his skull.

He tried his voice again, found that he had still been pushing out that same low-level moan, a sound he could scarcely hear, as if through layers of quilts.

Oh, quilts, now, that was a thought he could easily give over to — a big, plush feather bed in a fine hotel, piled high with pretty quilts of scraps in all shapes and sizes, each piece meaning something to someone. To sleep under all those memories. It felt as though it was bringing a smile to his face, though he wasn't so sure he could even make one of those anymore.

With the suddenness of a slap, cold wind stung his face, whistled into his nose and half-open mouth and chilled him from the inside out. It also cleared his head when nothing he tried had worked.

One more bit of effort, one more, then another . . . and Charlie Chilton felt himself pushing upward. Where was he? What way was he facing? He'd read of people in an avalanche who didn't know which way to tunnel once they came to, so they commenced to digging and wound up dead, found by rescuers later as having gone in the wrong direction, having dug downward even farther.

Wait, Charlie. Why are you even telling yourself this? You are not in an avalanche — else-wise, how come you feel wood pressing on you and stinking your nostrils and clouding your mind?

One last try, he had one of his hands partially wedged beneath him now, and he pushed with the effort a man might only use in his last desperate moments. Who's to say they weren't?

The wood began to move and he pushed with his head, felt his pain, and worked through it. Something pressed on his head, eventually moved as he continued shoving, and brighter light cracked through as the wood over his face parted. Daylight! With it came strafing cold, and he didn't care. It felt so very good to be reminded that he wasn't dead.

Whatever had happened, this was one accident that he felt sure he had lived through. A sudden thought paused him. Had there been others with him? Charlie recalled that yes, he had been with other people — faces skittered into view in his mind's eye. Angry faces, scruffy men, bald, bad teeth, bearded, one of them young and perhaps had once been handsome but now was a boozy mess. Rollie! That was his name, Rollie Meecher.

The nephew of the man who owned the freighting outfit.

But there was someone else, someone important he had to remember — and another face hove into view, as if in a photograph. This face also was not smiling, but unlike the others, it was a woman, and she was smiling with her eyes. Or maybe it was concern. Genuine concern. But for him or for someone else, he did not know.

And her name came to him, Hester O'Fallon. And she had a sister, Delia. A sickly girl. And they had all been traveling to . . . the mining town. What was its name? Gamble. Yes, that was it. But something had happened and an accident perhaps. He had no idea what had happened or where he was. Somewhere on the trail, then. On the way to that town.

Cold wind snapped him from his musing reverie. Cold, biting wind that stiffened his half-opened eyes and made them tear at the same time. He opened his mouth and forced out sound, heard it come out as another moan, raw and weak, not at all a sound he was proud of. But at least he was still able to make sound.

Something gripped him deep inside. It felt as if a long-fingered hand, icy cold, crawled upward from his guts right up through his windpipe, wrapping itself around everything in there at the same time, curling like snaky green weeds trailing and whipping in a low-water creek. Charlie's only thought was that somehow, after all this work since he'd come awake, now he was finally dying. His eyes snapped open wide and he pulled in a deep draught of air and bellowed. That last face he'd seen in his mind's eye, the one that now floated in his vision, urged him to not give up.

Charlie bellowed loud, a harsh, guttural sound, a howl of rage and fear and confusion and anger and hate all at once. The sound of his own mighty voice in his ears gave him tremendous power and he pitched forward, thrusting off himself what felt like timbers, great charred things, as if he'd been buried under a collapsed, burned building.

He sat up, his chest working hard and fast like a blacksmith's bellows pumped by a frantic man. Runnels of bloody snot and spittle stringed from his nose and mouth. His head pounded like massive steel hammers ringing on the world's biggest black anvils, *pound, pound, pound,* until it felt as if all the cotton batting had been peeled back from his brain and all was clear again.

His hearing too had become restored. No more was it a dull ringing sound, as if heard underwater. His voice slowed but still rasped in and out, that of a desperate boar grizzly running full out after a last-hope meal. It was a ragged, blasting thing like air shot through shredded paper. The sound slowed and with it Charlie's raging roar, now dwindling to a grunting moan.

He was sitting upright, his chest still working with hard-earned breaths, his left arm hung limp, difficult to move. His face felt tight. He touched gentle fingertips to it and felt a crust of something there that had dried, tightening. He scratched at it, looked at his begrimed fingernails, found it to be dark, flaky — blood, dried blood. He didn't dare dig at it more for fear of opening up some unseen wound that would only bleed anew.

There was something else that he felt, through the blood, through the harsh new light, as if seeing it for the first time. It was as if he had truly been reborn, as if he had crawled on his belly through an unseen landscape of red-hot steel, through darkness, raw, hot pain, muffled sounds, and the stagnant stench of rot and blood and burned things and the faces of people lost to him.

But at the end of it, instead of all those stamped-down things pinching out until the last things that made up Charlie Chilton were no more . . . they opened up. Maybe he opened them up. Maybe it was this new and glorious thing touching his face. He opened his eyes even wider in the blinding bright light and saw small somethings falling down on him. Bright things, slow, but many of them. Cold, touching, kissing his burned, battered features. Each by itself did little, but together they felt so good.

And then the word for them came to his mind and he suddenly remembered everything that had happened to him the days before, the night before. Snow. Snow was falling on him, and though it felt good, it would do little to wipe away the memories of the man who had shot him, who had clubbed him the night before and left him for dead. Rollie, Bo, Shiner, and Norbert. They were all guilty, killers all.

And what of Hester and Delia? And Mabel-Mae? Of the goods for the waiting people of Gamble? What of them? Wronged to the ultimate degree too? Killed by the bad men?

Charlie shook his head slowly side to side, as if he truly were that boar grizz he had envisioned himself to be, grunting and relishing the throbbing washes of pain that now had the power to make him feel alive again. And he felt angrier than he had been in a long, long time. The last time had been years before, with the little girl's death.

Then he had been angry with himself. Had thrown away the ownership of a gun, his gun of choice the sawed-off, pig-nosed killing steel that he had relied on for so long to scare people, innocent people. To intimidate them. To take from them. Then the little girl had died . . . and that's when he became angry. He'd worked himself like the lowliest slave he could imagine, someone who was seen as having no worth, but who could not ever escape the stirred rage by dying. He forced himself to be subjected to the long, scar-covered pain of heavy daily labor. He drove himself for years beyond the endurance that most men could take.

And it helped. Or maybe time was the thing that helped the most. Because after so many years, he was no longer as angry with himself. The anger had not washed away completely, but it had become so covered with scars that he felt, for the first time in a long while, as though he might be able to live with himself, might be able to tolerate himself, even a little bit.

And that's when he also began to dream that he might find a place where he could be alone with himself, perhaps with a dog or a mule. If he were lucky, both. Maybe in a valley somewhere deep in the mountains, in a place where he could never again hurt anybody. A place where he would be a menace only to himself, because that's what he knew how to deal with.

That's when he became angry with himself, the angriest he'd ever been with anybody. Until now. Now those bastards had earned his mightiest of rages. He rocked forward, trying to raise himself up, and stopped. What he saw couldn't be.

Wrecked, half-burned wagons and crates jutted, smoking, from a foot of snow, and more was dropping down. He turned, looked around. He appeared to be half-buried in the wreck of a wagon. They must have set the wagon ablaze. But who? Rollie and his boys or the Shoshoni?

Maybe he'd been wrong; maybe they all had been caught, trapped by the Indians? Then what of the women? Had they all been left for dead? He scooped up a paw full of snow and pressed it to his throbbing face. It came away smudged with red and black. He tried to put weight on his left arm, felt a sting, saw his hand knuckle under, but he kept going. No way was a little wound going to slow him down.

It took long moments, but he finally made it to his feet. Much had been burned, and other hunks were still smoking. Charlie didn't see the soft rise of any animal bodies buried under the snow, which might mean that the Indians drove them all off — unlikely since that many animals would be too great a burden in the mountains and tricky to make off with, especially in the snow. He saw no tracks leading away, so he had to assume that whoever did this left before the heaviest snow came. Otherwise he'd see indents and depressions where the tracks were buried.

The snow that had fallen in the night must have been one heck of a big dumping. It was still snowing, and felt good on Charlie's hot face and hands, but it had slowed.

Charlie stepped forward, beginning to shiver uncontrollably. He took that as a good sign, knowing that if he felt something, anything, then he was alive.

"Where to now, Charlie?" he asked himself, surveying the remnants of the camp. His right hand instinctively probed the side and back of his head. It touched crusted blood and above that, the still-raw wound. He must have taken quite a knock to the bean.

How did he get overlooked? So many questions bothered him as he stumbled about the mess that had been their campsite.

His boots caught a number of times on hunks of wood and what sounded like metal, but his primary focus was on trying to find anyone else — bodies, most likely — but so far he was relieved that he'd found no one.

He resisted the urge to shout to them yet. Even though he'd been shouting earlier, now that he'd somewhat recovered his senses, he realized there was still the possibility that whoever had done this could still be around, possibly watching the camp, or had heard him and decided to return. Or they might show once the snow let up, in hopes of finding something of value.

He was guessing. He had no idea what had happened or what would happen. He only knew that he was probably alone, probably had been left for dead. All around him Charlie saw smoking wreckage and for the first time in a long while he wasn't quite sure what to do.

CHAPTER 23

Soon the cold seeped even deeper into Charlie's core and he knew that if he didn't get a fire going soon he was sure to die. And that would be foolish, considering how much he had lived through.

While there were still smoking boards, there must still be embers, and where there were embers, there would be easy fire. Easier than trying to make fire. He realized that since he still wore his big sheepskin-lined mackinaw, chances of his gear still being in his pockets — including his flint and steel and the box of matches he kept handy for lighting a fire, would still be there. Save them for when he really needed them.

For now he would work to get a blaze kindled from what still lay smoldering around him. He kicked at the snow, grateful that it hadn't turned to sleet and skinned over the top with a layer of ice.

He would get a blaze going and then he

would rummage for anything that might have made it through the fire, anything that might be useful to him, particularly if it was made of cloth. He sorely needed to cover his hands. His own fur-lined mittens were nowhere in sight.

The blaze took less time than he expected it to. He hunched over it, feeling the life-giving heat force its way into his hands, his face. With the heat came the ache, dull and throbbing and persistent. He knew the warmer he got the more he would hurt. He would worry about tending to his wounds later. Right now he needed to be warm. The need for warmth overcame him quickly once he began moving around the devastated campsite.

He looked up, squinting into the lead-colored sky, but could see no trace of the sun. He was usually pretty good about judging the time of day by shadows and the angle of the sun, and his own internal way of knowing such things. But now he had no idea what time it was.

He was thirsty, that much he knew, so it was time for a drink. He scooped snow and managed to stave off the pangs of thirst for a little while. He'd warm his feet and knees before exploring more of the camp. Might be they left useful items behind. Maybe a tin can or a cup to melt snow in. Maybe even a sack of meal, flour . . . something.

He made his way back to the spot on the wagon wreck where he'd awakened and cuffed at the snow. More burned boards, the charred turnbuckle and rope for cinching down loads. But there was something more there, back in what had once been the bed of the wagon, the very one he'd driven. It looked dark, of rough, thick-woven material. Where had he seen something like that before? He lobbed a short hunk of wood at it, knocked more snow from it. Yes, it was cloth, but it was too far out of reach.

He eased his way back into the wreck, on his knees, his side aching. He'd have to look at that soon, tend to it somehow, and hope the wound didn't become infected.

"Better be something useful," he mumbled. After a painful minute of grunting and inching himself forward, Charlie laid a hand on it, and the thick fabric under his hands, though charred, was recognizable to him. It was one of the carpetbags belonging to the sisters. He felt bad about rummaging in someone else's goods, but the odds of them being anywhere nearby were slim to none.

The brass clasps along the top of the case were blackened and the leather loop handles had been mostly chewed away by fire, but he dug at the clasps with his thumb and one of them popped open. It didn't take him long to spread the bag's jaws wide. Inside he found clothes, a small framed photograph of a man and woman, the glass covering it cracked from corner to corner. From the fashions it looked maybe to be a portrait of the girls' parents. He could almost see something of Delia and Hester in each of the faces. Were they still alive, these people? He'd never asked.

He reached into the bag again and pawed through. It would be asking too much to find a pair of mittens. Heck, he'd even settle for a pair of socks he might wear as mittens. So far, just women's thin undergarments. Not many, and of sturdy cotton, but they would have to do. Then his fingers brushed something that didn't feel like wood. It also had a bit of give to it. But it was hard, like a box. He dragged the bag closer to himself and peered in.

Leather? A leather case, and with buckles on top. Charlie drew it out, and it required both hands. His left still troubled him, but he could flex it now and felt the necessity of exercising the hand. With every movement he was reminded of what felt like a wound in his shoulder. The case was longer than his forearm, and as wide as he could stretch his fingers apart. The depth looked to be four or five inches. And weightwise, it was a hefty thing.

The heat had puckered the leather, changed the color from what looked to be a rich brown to the darker hue of a wad of used tobacco. "What could it be?" his deep voice rumbled in the dead-calm camp. Even the low crackle of the fire behind him had decided to pay attention, it seemed.

Charlie slid his blackened, bleeding hand along the case top, then pried the buckles apart and pawed the top of the case open. Seated in custom compartments of rich green felted material was a handsome, well-tended, double-barrel shotgun, broken down into two sections, the butt and trigger mechanisms — all richly engraved with a dog-and-pheasant hunting scene and plenty of detailed scrollwork — and the side-by-side barrels, both gleaming in their obvious elegance. A snowflake touched the blued metal.

Rarely had Charlie seen anything so finely made in his entire life. And never had it been so close to his own hands. It was a work of art, to be sure. And it occurred to him that it must be the family heirloom Hester had said she was going to give to

Delia's man once they got to Gamble.

Charlie peered for long moments into the leather case. "Well, I'll be damned all to hell. . . ."

A thin, raspy voice from somewhere close said, "You'll get there right quick —" The voice coughed. "If Hester catches you talking like that."

Charlie spun, the gun and case forgotten for the moment. He held up his two bloodied, grime-covered ham hands before him, ready to swing. "Who's there?" he said, peering from the collapsed wagon into the snowy gray light. But there was no one to be seen. Just the smoking, wrecked camp. He heard a cough, sounded as if it came from below him. He looked down between his knees . . . and saw an eye staring up at him!

"It's me, Mr. Chilton . . . Delia."

Charlie shook his big bull head, but that only made the headache and spinning feel worse. "Delia? No, no, I'm imagining things."

"No, you aren't," came the voice, more frantic and pinched now. "But I can't take much more of you kneeling on me."

CHAPTER 24

"Did you see them?"

"Yes," said Blue Dog, nodding to his brother. "Whites are strange. I cannot figure out why they are so determined to work so hard to get to their deaths faster than ever. It seems that they cannot wait to die."

"Ah," said Son of Cloud. "But they believe they are soon to be rich. They are hurrying to their beloved money. It is all to the whites."

Blue Dog stood and stretched his back. "I do not care about anything they care about. I will kill them all as soon as they are close enough."

"Close enough to what, brother?" Son of Cloud paused in tying his blanket behind his cantle. He knew he would not receive anything but an arrogant smile from his brother.

Son of Cloud rested a hand on the leather saddle, musing on the fact that it once belonged to a U.S. Army captain, a man who had thought their father, Fights With Storms, was an ignorant, friendly savage. That is what the man had said out the side of his mouth to his fellows, all the while smiling and nodding and holding up his hand in a friendly gesture. As the six white soldiers rode forward, the captain in the lead, all offering forced wide smiles, Fights With Storms had offered one in return and at the same time watched two dozen of his fellow warriors closing in on them from the sides, from behind, none of them smiling.

Their father had kept the saddle and a few other pieces of the man's gear and personal possessions. There was a photograph in the captain's saddlebags of a woman with light hair, perhaps the gold color of dried grass. She had been pretty, their father had said, staring straight at him from the image, almost as if she knew what he had done to her man, daring him to find her and do the same to her.

Instead he had been surprised to find her at the soldiers' camp some miles away, and he had taken her for his own. He had said that he believed she had come to love him, but she had died within days after Blue Dog Moon was born. No one had known how she really felt, if she had loved the man who had killed her husband, the white soldier. Son of Cloud liked to think that he remembered her, but he knew that was impossible. He had been too young when she died. And now none of it mattered anyway.

Son of Cloud shook his head and slapped the seat of the saddle. Such foolish thinking would get him nowhere but dead. And he could not let that happen before his brother. He had too much to do. He had to lure his hot-tempered younger brother from the road he had been traveling. The man was too much like their father, Fights With Storms.

He also had died too young, and though the old men said he had been a mighty warrior to the end, in truth he had wasted his life attacking a mining camp alone. Fights With Storms had believed what the other warriors told him, that he bore the spirit of many dead great warriors.

Son of Cloud knew the truth behind such things, knew such boasts and praise to be hollow. But his brother did not. Killing whites was a bad enough thing. Killing too many whites at once, such as he wanted to do in the mine camp of Gamble, was something else, something that would result in one thing — early death and wasted life. But how to convince his hot-tempered young brother?

Son of Cloud looked across at the younger man who stared back at him, studying him, not smiling now. His blood, his brother, they of the same mother and the same father, and who shared so many traits and yet could be so different in so much of their shared lives. It was a puzzling thing.

"Big brother," said Blue Dog Moon. "You worry too much. I see it on your face. You seek to change me. You have said as much. I tell you now as I have told you in the past and I will no doubt tell you in the future — you cannot change me. I am formed and whole. And no person, white or brother" — his eyebrows rose — "will alter my path."

Son of Cloud turned to urinate on a tree. Over his shoulder he said, "That is true, Blue Dog. And that is also what makes you the man you are and what makes me worry. And so we travel in circles in our heads. You see?" He turned and smiled at the young man before climbing into the saddle. Blue Dog Moon was at once infuriating, yet, as no other person, he knew how to make him laugh. He was also a killer who seemed to enjoy the act, and that was the most troubling part of all.

CHAPTER 25

Despite his pained head and body, Charlie couldn't seem to move fast enough to get off whoever it was who said he'd been kneeling on her. Could it really be Delia? Even as he lunged backward off the busted, charred wagon, snow and soot spraying in all directions, his mind fixed on the notion that he must surely be hearing things. Couldn't be real — but whoever it was, whatever it was, knew his name, mentioned Hester! Said she was Delia. . . .

He stood crouched by the end of the wagon. "Delia . . . is that really . . . you?"

A thin white hand, grimy with soot, shot up between two charred boards, the fingers clawed and grasping.

Charlie stumbled backward, his hoarse scream sounding animal-like.

"Course it's me," came the voice, strained and grunting. "Now help me out of here."

It didn't take Charlie but a moment to realize he hadn't been hearing things, but the sight of that hand had nearly sent him howling and limping off down the snowy mountainside. But the voice, too . . .

He lunged back to the wagon, pawing boards and snow aside, then a layer of scorched blanket, and there she was, the sickly young woman he'd scarcely exchanged but a few dozen words with the entire trip. "But . . . how?" he said, even as he tried to figure out how to lift her out of there.

She didn't wait for him as she worked to get a hand underneath herself, then pushed upward. "Don't just stand there, Charlie. Help me!"

He hauled her up out of the burned-out nest she'd been stuck in. "How?" he asked again.

She stood wobbling before him, her hair singed to a frazzled fringe on one side of her head, her face, where it wasn't smeared with greasy soot, red and shiny with blisters through the soot. She moved her arms slowly, saying, "Good thing you know who I am, otherwise you'd sound like a big old owl right about now."

"Huh?"

"No, you'd be asking, 'Who? Who?' " She

seemed to find this amusing, because she smiled.

"Delia." Charlie bent low, and leaned close to her. "Can it really be you?"

"It can and it is, Charlie."

He held her gently by the shoulders, still not sure what to think about all this. If he didn't know better, he'd swear he was dead and this was some sort of odd combination of heaven and hell.

"Now I'd appreciate it if you'd peel up those blankets I was in. I'm getting so cold I can hardly stand it."

He did as she asked, but kept shaking his head. "I don't understand this at all, Delia." He looked at her again, hoping somehow to verify that it really was her.

"You don't? How do you think I feel? Hester had me half knocked out with laudanum. Then that buffoon, Shiner, I think it was, started groping me. I tried to fight him, but I think he hit me." She touched the side of her head.

"Next thing I know I heard shouts and screaming or laughing, I don't know which, and then I saw flames. I tried to get up, but between the laudanum and getting hit . . ." Delia touched her head again, and it was then that Charlie saw beneath the soot what appeared to be a big, welted bruise. "The last thing I recall, I was in an oven and I felt like I was burning alive."

"The snow," said Charlie, nodding at the ground, as if that would explain everything.

"What?"

"Near as I can figure it, the snow is what saved us. Those boys set fire to the wagons and lit a shuck out of here. But the storm came on quick and helped douse the flames. Else-wise I figure our goose would have been cooked."

Delia didn't speak, merely nodded and drew the damp wool blankets around her. In a small voice, she said, "Charlie, I . . ." Then her knees bent forward and she crumpled to the snowy ground.

"Delia!" He rushed forward, ignoring the lancing pains in his side, shoulder, and head, all screaming for rest, for washing, for medicine and attention. None of that mattered at the moment.

With the limp, featherlight girl cradled in his arms, Charlie looked around the mess that had been the outfit's camp. He realized he had been wasting time in not kindling a bigger roaring blaze. He balanced her as gently as he could on one knee and in the crook of his sore left arm. With his right, he snagged the blankets that had slipped from Delia's shoulders when she fell. "Gonna be all right, girl. Hang in there for me." He resisted the urge to slap her face, despite the fact that it was the only sort of doctoring he knew how to do.

Charlie carried her to the remnants of the fire ring, her head and shoulders propped against a snow-slick log. He hurried to gather more still-smoking planks from the half-burned wagons, ignoring the blisters the hot boards raised on his hands.

He piled them into a rough teepee shape and as gently as he could lowered himself down onto his knees. He was sorer than he'd been in a long, long time. What sort of beating had those boys doled out on him? Time enough to find out later. Right now he had to get this blaze really crackling. And within a couple of minutes, Charlie was pleased to see he had even more flames licking up into those boards.

He chose the driest wood he could find, but it still spit and hissed, telltale signs of damp burning materials. A couple more trips to the burned-where-it-sat wagon and he had drier materials to work with. Then he concentrated on clearing away the biggest amount of snow from the side of the fire and slid the girl over as close to the warming blaze as he dared.

She started to come around, but then

dropped off again. He hoped it was only the hard experiences she'd lived through and not her illness, whatever that was. Hester had been cagey about it, but from what he could see and what he overheard, the girl had bouts of crippling pain that left her weak as a mewling babe. At other times, like when she'd nearly clawed her way out of the wagon wreck, she'd seemed nearly normal. Though anyone looking at her could tell Delia was far from normal.

Before she'd been burned and blistered and smudged up with ash and soot, she had been skinny as a dancer in a painting, and pale as a parsnip, too much so. Looked like one of those girls who always stayed indoors. Except Charlie knew better. Heck, he reasoned, being sister to Hester, she knew she had to stay active and on her toes.

As if she'd read his thoughts, Delia shouted, "Hester! Hester? Where are you?"

Charlie kneeled down beside her. "Everything's gonna be all right, girly. Don't you worry none. Ol' Charlie's got things all taken care of, you wait and see if he don't."

He gently patted her dirty, small hand. So light and pale, how could a body be so frail seeming and still get around?

And what was he going to tell her about Hester? What was there to tell? He didn't know where she was. He'd stomped all over this campsite and nudged everything that made a hump under the snow, but found no bodies. Not even an ox or a mule or horse. He was relieved at that. He'd half thought that those bastards would have killed Mabel-Mae because she was his. He reasoned that if he couldn't find her, and if they were in a killing mood, they'd kill Mabel-Mae before they'd turn a gun on Hester. So he took not finding his mule as a good sign.

"Night'll be coming soon," he said in a low voice, almost a whisper, to no one. The snow still fell in slow flakes, more clumped than usual and straight down, which boded well for them. It meant no wind. Didn't mean it wouldn't change, but for now, he'd take whatever little help nature offered.

He made his way slowly back to the wagon and brushing off the boards and seat, the wheels and traces, he managed to investigate much of what the freighters had left. Charlie had earlier toed what sounded like metal, and when he rediscovered it, he found it was indeed one of a number of pieces of the gear he'd tried to tell Rollie about, mining equipment that he knew the folks in Gamble would need come spring. But Rollie still hadn't seen the use in it.

Now it all came flooding back to Charlie's mind. Rollie had revealed his plan to his boys, unaware that Charlie had overheard. It all seemed as if he were recalling a dream, but somehow he knew he had really heard it. Rollie's plan called for them to draw close to the town, then set up camp and wait out the folks from Gamble, lure them out if need be, and shoot them as if they were trapped swimming in a shallow puddle. It was downright inhuman, murderous, and treacherous. And Charlie knew he couldn't live with himself if he didn't try to stop them.

He looked round, aware that his chest felt tight, his throat choked with pent rage. *Fight it down, Charlie,* he told himself. *Even if you did want to go after them, you have a sickly young woman, and your own self is wounded, who knows how bad?* Judging from the pains in his side and the blurriness of his vision, he didn't think he was in very good shape.

He'd been hurt plenty of times before. Shot once, in the meat of the leg, though the slug passed through. That wound only ached in the cold and damp — both of which he reckoned the weather was giving him in double doses right about now.

Charlie tried to occupy his mind with the task at hand. He kept on flipping over boards and rummaging, and soon enough he let out a yelp of joy. He'd found a few overlooked tins of milk and meat, and even one tin without markings. Could be anything. He'd save that one for last. With all those cans, plus snow, which he could melt in the can, he reckoned they'd make out, for a time anyway.

On his way back to the fire, he passed the back of the wagon and saw the leather case, closed, with the gun inside. He'd forgotten about that.

He grabbed and slid it back in the carpetbag. When he hefted the bag out of the wagon, it revealed the scorched bulk of the second bag. They were bound to have clothes in there for Delia to wear. Maybe if he got her to put on enough of them, she'd feel better. He also knew he had to find her medicine.

"I was waiting for you to come back. I thought maybe you'd left me here."

"Are you joshing me?" Charlie tried to sound happy and carefree, not an easy task, considering their predicament. "I'm way too afraid of wolves and bears to go off on my own out there."

He saw the flash of worry on her face and realized he probably should not have talked about such creatures to her. "I meant —"

"I know what you meant, Charlie. It's fine. I'm not a baby. Just a little under the weather. You didn't happen to find my bag in there, did you?"

He smiled and held up a blackened bulky object. She smiled. "Oh, thank you. Could you bring it here? I'm so tired and I think I need a little of that medicine."

"You sure it's still here?"

She shook her head slowly. "No, I'm not sure. But I have to look. I saw Hester slip the last bottle in there. She's been rationing me. It's laudanum, you see, and she didn't want me to make a habit of it." Delia smiled, her eyebrows raised high. "Can you believe that? As if I have to worry —" She didn't finish the statement, but let it hang in the air between them.

Charlie guessed at what she meant, but hoped maybe he'd got it wrong. He set to pawing around in the other bag. "I don't suppose there are slugs for the shotgun in this bag?"

"Should be," said Delia, smiling wide and pulling free a half-filled bottle. "Hester always kept charge of that. She was going to give it to Vin. Said it was a way to welcome him into the family. Which I thought was very nice of her, considering how she really felt about him. But no matter. Love is love is love, right, Charlie?"

She'd swigged and Charlie knew very soon she would begin to feel the effects of the drug. Mild at first, but she'd soon be smiling and relaxed. For that he was glad.

"You don't know where my sister is, do you, Charlie?"

He'd been afraid to bring it up. He cleared his throat. "No, ma'am, that's a fact, I do not. But I have a feeling she's fine." *Fine as she can be with those bums,* he thought, but didn't say anything of the sort out loud.

"Charlie, promise me you'll get me to Gamble. Hester will be there, I know it. She's never let me down before. She has to be alive. I would miss her so, Charlie. She is my world, you know." A single tear slid down her cheek.

Charlie knew he and Hester were two peas in a pod — both caring for this girl, both stuck in situations not of their making, both determined to get to Gamble, though for entirely different reasons.

While he still had daylight, Charlie dragged more wood over, not taking much care to keep down the noise, since the girl appeared to be sleeping soundly. He was going to heat up food for her, but she didn't stay awake.

As he sat down he felt another pain, one

255

he hadn't felt before. Down below his waist. He reached down there and felt the familiar thickness of his sheath knife beneath his swollen fingers. So they hadn't taken that from him.

How far did they get with three wagons and all those animals, in what would soon be a foot of snow and being led by a drunken, murdering madman?

Charlie used the knife to pry open a tin of meat, then pawed around in the carpetbag and pulled out a couple of garments that looked as though they might be warmer than what he had on his hands, which was nothing. His feet throbbed with the cold, but he didn't dare slip off his boots, as he suspected he'd find a swollen, black-and-blue mess, and he'd never get the blamed boot back on over it.

Then his hand once again brushed against the leather case. He slipped it out of the bag and stared at it for a minute or so. Then shook his head. A pity, as odds of finding shells were slim to none.

Still, there was always the possibility. He felt around in the bag, and then his hand closed around a fist-sized box of shells. He guessed that would be a box of two dozen. That made his night. With the gun and his knife, there was little they could not do.

Then he stopped short. He'd thought "they," and then fought down the bile rising in his throat. There was no way he could track those scoundrels with a sickly girl in tow. Heck, he was gimped up himself and the girl was in bad shape at the best of times.

Soon sleep tugged at his eyelids. He'd worry about tomorrow tomorrow. Just now he didn't give a fiddle about anything else but covering up the gun, slipping it back in the carpetbag, and laying more wood on the fire. It was a bold, powerful blaze now, and as Charlie sat back to admire and enjoy it, he almost smiled. If they had died, they'd never be enjoying these splendors now, would they?

With that bit of logic puzzled out, Charlie slipped into a deep sleep.

CHAPTER 26

The oxen's eyes bulged wide, white and veined, as if to stand too much more torment they would pop. Their pink-black tongues, flecked with foam, stuck out rigid from their mouths as if carved of wood, and their labored exhalations drove clouds into the air. Their great tree-trunk legs strained, desperate in their efforts to move forward. The only thing they knew how to do, the only thing they had been trained to do, was to pull the mighty load. And yet, try as they might, the oxen barely budged it, the stout limbs stomping in place, snow churned into a dirt-flecked grime beginning to soften into a muddy sop, still well above their knees.

Hester forced herself to watch, to really see the full attack on the poor beasts that Rollie laid the lash to. Raised welts and weals now running red with gore criss-crossed the panting animals' backs. Rollie seemed to enjoy giving vent to his full rage.

He barked and spittle flew out of his mouth much as it did those of his victims. By now there wasn't a pulling beast within range of his bullwhip that had not suffered under his savage attack.

"Pull! Pull, dang your hide!"

Rage bubbled up in Hester until she could no longer stand it. "Stop it, you idiot! You kill those animals and we'll never get anywhere!"

Despite her anger at the foolish man with the whip, as soon as she said it she felt a twinge of innate regret. Something she could not prevent had welled in her like fresh blood from an unhealing wound. She didn't want to care what he did to her, but she was ashamed to admit that she did care. He had singlehandedly taken from her the only thing that mattered anymore. He had killed Delia, left poor Big Charlie dead too. Why should she care what this jackass did to her?

Rollie's whip arm jerked as if convulsing. His chest rose and fell with his efforts, and he stood still, closed his eyes, the hand that gripped the whip white-knuckled and trembling.

"Did I hear someone telling me to do something? Me? Telling me?" Rollie spun, staggered, fixed her with his red-eyed gaze.

259

"And it darn sure couldn't have been a woman. Someone who would be dead now if it wasn't for me."

He thrust the uncoiled whip in her direction. She couldn't help flinching, and hated that she did even as she did it again, causing him to smile at her fear.

He reared back and made to swing it at her. Still bound at the ankles and wrists with her hands behind her back, Hester could only lie flat in the wagon and turn her head away. She curled up as small as she was able and waited for the stinging lash, knowing that in his eyes, she was no better, regarded no more highly, than the pulling animals.

"Hold there!" Norbert shouted, standing away from the rear of the wagon.

Rollie pivoted slightly in midstrike and with a wide smile and a hissing sound from his mouth, he unfurled the whip in a hard strike, laying it out right at Norbert. The man didn't have time to do much more than cover his face with his hands and begin to turn away before the split-tailed, steel-studded whip lashed into him.

It wrapped itself around his bent arms and chest like the long, slapping fingers of a demon lover. He gritted his teeth, barked an oath more animal sound than word, but didn't cry out.

When the whip slipped free of the stained, rank buckskins, it left behind uneven slices, blood already welling through in spots. Rollie yanked it back to him, looking at each of his four traveling companions in turn, ending with a long, sneering look at Hester. "It appears you have a champion, woman. A champion who is too stupid to keep his mouth shut, a champion who will likely end up dead if he continues on with his mouthy ways." Rollie cut his gaze to Norbert, whose thin face under the shaggy beard had paled even more than it had been.

Rollie rested a hand on his revolver. "Let me make this plain to each of you. This plan of mine will work, but don't think that these here wagons" — he gestured with his whip hand, the implement still gripped firmly, the long, loose end swaying and cutting furrows in the snow — "and all the junk in them are all that important for my plan to succeed. And neither are any of you. I am the only important thing here. You got that? You are each here because you can be useful to me. But I will make you all rich only if you shut your faces and do what I say."

He stalked over to the wagon and stared down at Hester. "Except for you. You ain't getting rich at all. You are along for one reason only. And we'll get to that later." He turned to the rest. "But you all, you will die as sure as I am standing here if you so much as try to stop me again."

Rollie tossed the whip under the wagon seat and reached in, rummaged for a moment, then pulled out a nearly full whiskey bottle. He grabbed the cork with his teeth, held it, and swigged, then dragged the back of one gloved hand across his stubble-bearded face. "It's early enough in the day." He swigged again. "The snow appears to have stopped. Heck, I don't know what in the world these animals could want."

Bo cleared his throat, scuffed his boot in the snow before him.

"You got something to add, Bo?"

The man spread his lips wide, revealing his rotten teeth. It was an unnerving habit, not quite a smile, yet not a frown. His voice was low, with a wavery, uneven edge. "I don't like to say so, if'n you plan on whipping on me for it."

Rollie sighed, shook his head. The gesture looked to Hester as if he made it to further belittle them all. It worked.

"Go ahead, Bo."

Bo cleared his throat again. "It's just that, well, them animals is all played out. We ain't given them much of a rest since we started."

Rollie tilted his head to the side. "Bo, they

are dumb animals born to the task of pulling these wagons. If the snow slows 'em down, it's because they are too weak, should have been killed as babies." He pulled again on his bottle. "Just like you, Bo." He laughed alone. "Am I the only one thinks that's funny?"

"I worked for your uncle for quite a while, Rollie, and he might have been a tough nut to deal with, but he could get his animals to do most anything."

Rollie bent forward. "Oh, really? Tell us how that happened, Bo. I think we'd all like to hear that."

Though she despised Bo nearly as much as she did Rollie, Hester still wanted to warn him that he was stumbling right into a silly little trap laid by Rollie. But if he was too dumb to know it, she wasn't about to say a thing.

Bo pulled himself up to his full height, spat a stream of chaw juice, staining the snow by his feet. "Well, it's simple, really, Rollie. Them animals are like people. Need rest and feed."

The group fell silent while they all waited for Rollie to take in this pearl of wisdom. The only sound was the continued rasping breathing of the oxen. Most of the other horses and mules of the other teams were also breathing heavily, but it had been the steady but slow-moving oxen who had attracted Meecher's anger that morning. He'd laid into them all day until, exhausted, they finally ground to a weary halt at the base of a slight rise.

He'd kept at them, whipping and whipping, their legs churning the snow to muck, but to no avail. And now here they were, stuck behind the front wagon, dragged by the offending oxen, the wagon he'd insisted on driving that morning. They had had a solid beginning and the oxen plodded on with impressive, steady reliability. But it had not been enough, would never be enough for a man like Rollie Meecher, and he'd driven them far too hard and fast.

Rollie walked backward until he stood by the heads of the lead oxen. "Oh, you mean they need sleep?" He skinned his Colt and peeled the hammer back with one motion, placed it on the temple of the nearest ox, and pulled the trigger. The great beast shuddered, its eyes pulsed out even more, and then it grunted and dropped, knocking into the ox beside it.

The three men and Hester all gasped, their eyes wide, as Rollie repeated the treatment to each of the four great, bloody-backed beasts of burden. Each, in turn, toppled. None of them died immediately.

This can't be happening, thought Hester. *Will he keep on doing this to . . . all of us?*

All the oxen were down, pawing at the snow with their hooves and flailing their last, hot red-black blood pooling and steaming all about them. Their grunts and breaths, wild eyes, and snotting noses crushed what was left of Hester's ragged feelings and she closed her eyes and tried not to cry. She gritted her teeth and wished for a whip of her own to shred Rollie's skin. She would dearly love to see how he liked it.

"Now, anybody else wanna talk about that nasty old uncle of mine? Go right ahead." No one said anything. "Good. Now help me sort this junk. We're going to move even faster now with less wagons, and we'll still have extra critters towing 'em. And before we head out, set fire to that wagon too. I'll be hanged if I'm going to let any Injuns have anything, even if it's junk."

CHAPTER 27

Sheila Trudeaux poured out the last of her cornmeal and poked the little dry pile with her finger. It didn't look like much, and in truth it wasn't much. She doubted there was any more of it left in all of Gamble. It had been nearly two weeks since Samuel Proudhorn had left for Monkton.

She missed his big, bearded face, his bald head, and his funny English way of talking. Everything he said sounded so elegant. Even though she made her way as a dove, Samuel always made her feel like a lady with his manners and fancy talk. And now he was probably living it up with sporting ladies back down in Monkton, raising a glass with that foul Marshal Watt.

How she ever let herself get roped into moving up here, she didn't know. Like with all the other falls and winters she'd spent in mountain country, at all those other mine camps, she felt the cabin fever already working at her. Always came on her faster than other folks, and it seemed to come on earlier every year. She knew the snow would be coming soon, but she didn't think it would have happened so soon and so much all at once.

Old Mose had agreed, and said that from his rheumatics, it was liable to keep up for a long spell to come. Heck, she could have told him that. It was winter in the mountains.

"Wouldn't be so bad, but that blasted Rafferty promised to have all our winter supplies here by now."

She turned to see who had sneaked up on her. It was Clayton Eldridge, self-appointed mayor.

"Yeah, well," she said, "tell me something that will surprise me. We are going to be in one big ol' fix, you know. Ain't a man in this little mine camp who can shoot game to save his ass. We're about down to the bottom of the barrel all over town where flour and meal are concerned." She turned to face Eldridge. "I honestly don't know how we're going to make it through until spring."

"Oh, have some faith in Samuel, Sheila. He's bound to show up any time now with good news, telling us the freighters are on their way. And then won't you feel bad for thinking dark thoughts about them all?"

"No, I won't, Clayton. I want to make a loaf of bread, and I bet between us all in this town there ain't enough flour to make the countertop powdery."

"We can live without bread, Sheila. And as far as hunting goes, why, this town's right full of men with guns who have all hunted before. I daresay we'll get a deer soon."

Sheila wetted her fingertip and stuck it in the little pile of cornmeal, then licked it off. "A deer? A single deer? Clayton, last time I counted we had a whole pile of people in Gamble who are supposed to magically survive until spring, and keep digging up a fortune in gold at the same time. We are going to need more than one deer, Mr. Eldridge. More likely we'll need one every couple of days. No less than that, though."

He opened the door, pulled his hat tight. "There's always rabbit, Sheila." He smiled at her and, wonder of wonders, she smiled back.

Clayton stepped outside and clunked the door shut behind him. He wished he'd never stopped in to see her. Or any of them. Everybody was feeling the same way. And as unofficial mayor of Gamble, he'd felt it was his duty to visit each person after the first big storm of the coming winter season, see how everyone was doing.

Now he wasn't so sure it had been a good idea. They were all bitter, low on food and booze, and worst of all, they were becoming convinced that Samuel Proudhorn was dead. Several, including Fancy and Luther, believed that he never even made it to Monkton. Clayton had secretly wondered that too. Maybe the Indians had gotten to him. And that line of thinking had stirred up all sorts of worrisome thoughts and questions about Indians. As if Gamble needed any more to worry about.

CHAPTER 28

Jasper Rafferty left his wife, Edna, in charge of the store, half hoping she wouldn't get to worrying about the children and forget to keep a hawk's eye on the merchandise. He knew that if given half a chance, the rascally public would rob him blind.

"How do you know that?" she always asked him.

"Because it's what I would do," he'd say, with a wink. Edna always gave him such an odd look, as if she couldn't believe he'd say such a thing. But it was that attitude that made him such a keen businessman.

Why, last week he'd even opined on that very thought to Marshal Watt when they were going over their plans for Gamble, but the man had merely shaken his head as if Jasper had said something foolish. He'd show them all, business was business and nothing less than death at the hands of a wayward savage Indian would stop him from becoming a wealthy man. He'd trump that silly silver baron in Colorado. He'd have mansions built, one on each coast and one here, to oversee his empire. Nothing would stop him now.

As Rafferty swung open the door to Skunk's stable, his nose wrinkled at the cloying animal aromas that assaulted it. Why had Watt wanted to meet him here? What was wrong with the clean, warm environs of the marshal's office?

"Jasper? Good, I've been waiting for you. C'mon over here. Look at this horse. Pawnee Joe brought her in." The marshal nodded toward the horse. "You recognize her?"

Rafferty squinted at the horse in the half-darkened stall. The only thing he recognized was the need for him to get out of there soon, lest his clothes begin to harbor the stink of barns and the animals who dwelt in them.

He fought down the urge to cover his mouth with a handkerchief. He'd seen a gentleman from St. Louis do so last year when walking Monkton's dusty main street. Jasper had determined then, given the cut of the man's clothes and finely made brogans, that he too would protect his delicate sinuses in such a manner, should the need arise. But somehow, here in front of his brother-in-law, Marshal Watt, it did not feel like the right time. "No, why should I?"

"Oh, that's right. I keep forgetting that you spend your days tending bolts of cheese-cloth and muslin, sorting beans, and weighing coffee. No time for livestock in your day, is there, Jasper?"

"Mock me all you like, Marshal, but it's due as much to my efforts as yours" — at this, Rafferty smirked enough to show Watt that he thought less of his efforts than his own — "that we are poised on the cusp of tremendous wealth."

The lawman leaned closer. "Why don't you say it a little louder, Jasper? I don't believe Skunk heard you."

"Well, never mind all that," he hissed, looking around the stable's interior. "What about this confounded horse is so vitally important that you drag me from my place of business to see it?"

Marshal Watt sighed. "The horse belongs to Samuel Proudhorn. You remember him, don't you? One of the most capable miners we put in place up in Gamble."

Rafferty looked again at the horse, then back to the marshal. "What are you saying? Is he here, in town?" Rafferty craned his neck, looking around him in the dim stable, as if the great-bearded man might be lurking in a nearby stall.

"No, he's not in Monkton, not as far as I can make out anyway."

"You sound so certain."

"I am pretty sure. As I said, Pawnee brought it in. Claims he found the horse more or less headed this way, looking tired, sore, bewildered. She threw a shoe somewhere along the way."

"I fail to see what this has to do with me."

"I figured you'd say that. Never change, do you, Jasper? And you never pay attention to anyone but yourself."

"I don't know what you mean."

"Course you don't, otherwise you'd know that Proudhorn would never ever, *ever* let this horse out of his sight. Unless something's gone wrong."

"Like what?" Jasper could feel the color draining from his face.

"I don't know yet." Marshal Watt beckoned Jasper closer, held the lantern nearer to the horse. "See here? And here?"

Jasper nodded. The horse whickered, unsure of these strangers crowding her.

"She's been cut, intentionally."

"It looks like a . . . design, some sort of symbol?"

"Yeah," said Watt, "that's what I wanted you to say. Helps verify it to me." He nudged his hat back on his head and lowered his voice. "It's a Shoshoni mark. I haven't seen one in a few years, not since those troubles we had. You remember, back when those miners tangled with that rogue band?"

Jasper nodded, a cold fist tightening in his gut. "What are you telling me, Marshal?"

"I can't be sure yet, but if it is Shoshoni, and they are up in those hills, and this" — he gestured at the horse's scabbed cuts — "would leave me to believe it is, then Proudhorn was probably taken prisoner or, more likely, killed by them. And the only reasons he'd have to be out on his horse would be that he was out hunting or that he was on his way down here. Or it could mean that Gamble's been raided and its occupants . . . dealt with by the Indians."

"What?"

"I don't quite think it's come to that, since the Shoshoni are all pretty well dealt with. What I guess is that we're dealing with another rogue band. That means it'll be a small group, not many of them."

"But why would he . . . ?" The cold fist in Jasper's gut grew colder. "Oh no, that means the freighters didn't make it to Gamble?"

"Not necessarily, Jasper. It might mean

that he was on his way down to see about them, since you, okay, we, sent them north so late in the season. I doubt they got lost. It's a well-cut trail up there."

"It should have only taken a week."

"Yeah, but we got snow, don't forget."

"Okay, allow for a few more days. But they really should be there by now." Rafferty spun in the stall, looking up at the rafters, wondering about the dark possibilities of losing all that freight to . . . Indians? It was unimaginable.

"Get a hold of yourself, Jasper. Nothing's been proven yet, but it does mean we have to get up there."

"We? No, no. Not 'we,' Watt. You. You and a . . . a posse. That's it — form a posse. You're the lawman, after all. Right?"

"That really what you want, Jasper?" The marshal stared hard at Jasper. "Seems to me we'd want to still keep this quiet. Aside from the fact that as this town's lawman, I have little interest in explaining a potential Indian attack that might not have happened. But then you toss Gamble into the stewpot, and we have a recipe for a lot of people snooping around into our business before we have a chance to prove up on it all come spring. You follow me?"

Rafferty stared wide-eyed at the horse.

"Jasper, hey. You understand what I said?"

The merchant nodded, suddenly not feeling so well. "What do we do now?" he whispered.

"First things first. I made Pawnee Joe a little business proposition in order to keep his mouth shut."

"What? Marshal Watt, what did you promise that foul-smelling trapper?"

"Careful what you call your new junior partner, Jasper. Else he's liable to blab all over town what he thinks might be in the works. Don't forget he's been throughout those hills. He's even been to Gamble. A regular visitor up there, if I understand him correctly. He's nobody's fool, Jasper. But for a cut of the action, he'll keep his yap shut tight."

Rafferty exhaled long and low. "How much?" he said weakly.

"That's yet to be determined. But he's waiting for us at my office. I set him up there with a bottle. But that won't last him long. Let's go."

Chapter 29

"Charlie, let me down. I can walk on my own now."

"You wait until we get back to a level spot in the trail. Bound to be one ahead."

"Charlie, we are in the mountains. There aren't any level spots, unless you look at them from an angle."

"Huh? Delia, that don't make no sense. Besides, you have to save your strength. I expect later in the afternoon I'll be spent and you'll have to carry me. That sound like a fair trade?" Charlie heard a sound he hadn't heard before from her, hadn't heard from anyone in what seemed like forever. It was laughter. A quick snort of it, to be sure, but still it was laughter. It brought a smile to his face. "Now, that's more like it." He shifted his head in an effort to look at her. "But I wasn't kidding."

She laughed some more and he walked slowly on up the trail, carefully choosing where to place his big feet, smiling and recalling something his long-dead grand-mother used to say, "Boy, get your little bit of happy where you can, when you can, 'cause it's sure enough a world of misery."

Delia shifted on Charlie's back and nudged the side of his head with an elbow.

"Ow, hey, don't you forget I am suffering a horrible head wound."

"Oh, stop your complaining. You know, for a big fella, you are one mighty childish sort sometimes. You forget, I took a knock to the head as well."

"No, ma'am, I did not forget. And for a little bit of a thing, you have a mighty big mouth. Anybody ever tell you that?"

"Yes, Hester does. All the time." She was silent a moment, then said, "Well, she did."

"Now, don't go on like that. I said we was going to find her, and by gum, we will. I ain't likely to go back on a promise, now, am I? Don't you make a liar out of Big Charlie."

They trudged on in silence for a few moments more, slowing as the trail rose before them. Charlie continued to choose his footholds with care. He'd already slipped once, driving down hard onto one knee and striking a rock, despite the thick snow. He'd done his best to keep her from getting too jarred, but he could tell by the gasp she let out that it had hurt. He vowed to be more careful, even if it meant moving a little slower on the trail at times. He also vowed to make a travois so he'd be able to drag her. That should be more comfortable for both of them.

They wouldn't have to worry about that much longer today, as the shadows had been drawing out with every minute, and the air had taken on that peculiar late-afternoon chill. It would be dark in another hour or so, he reckoned.

As they topped the rise, Delia saw the abandoned wagon first. She rapped Charlie on the head and pointed.

"If you don't quit that . . ." But the rest of his comment faded on his tongue. There sat one of the wagons. He paused. She started to speak and he raised a warning finger.

"Hush a minute," he whispered.

They both looked left and right, saw no sign of anyone, no sounds but a far-off raven, its saw-blade squawk dying on an unfelt breeze. Charlie moved closer, approaching with a caution that he hoped wasn't necessary. They'd abandoned the wagon, it seemed, once again before the latest snowfall. But this time he saw the soft indents of footsteps that had pocked the previous snowfall. Last night's snowfall would carry those marks through, revealing them beneath, even as the snow piled up.

"Look, Charlie, they left the oxen behind."

He recognized the excitement in her voice on seeing the oxen as a way to get on up the trail faster and easier. But he knew those animals wouldn't be in any shape to do so.

Ahead of the wagon, they saw what looked to be pulling animals. But their hunched forms told Charlie they were likely dead. Unless they were so exhausted they couldn't stand, they wouldn't be lying down. And the biggest sign of all, on this bitter cold day, he didn't see any breath pluming skyward.

"Let me down now, Charlie."

He lowered Delia to the ground, stomping a place in the snow first for her to stand. "Let me go on up there, check it over," he said. "Maybe there will be something of use for us."

He was already giving thought to cooking beef over a fire.

Despite the obvious pain the boor beasts had endured at the hands of Rollie Meecher — who else could it have been? — Charlie was relieved when Delia suggested they not let the creatures go to waste.

"I'm pleased to hear that, but out here

they wouldn't go to waste — lots of critters would be mighty glad to tuck into such a toothsome treat."

Delia shuddered, drew her blankets tighter around herself.

"You cold? I'll have this fire blazing in a minute."

"It's not that. It's the thought of all those animals out here, living out here, and we can't even see them."

Charlie nodded, decided not to dip the thing in honey — the girl had to know the dangers of being in the wilderness. "I won't lie to you, Miss Delia. We are in their world." He blew on the tiny flames, then looked up at her. "The animals, I mean."

"Are there really that many of them out there?" She looked around, and if the concern on her face hadn't been writ so large, Charlie might be tempted to laugh.

He leaned back, put his palms out toward the licking young flames. "Well, let's see. There are wolves, coyotes, mountain lions, grizzlies — they're all the biggest of them. Oh, lots of smaller critters out here with us too. Course, some of them are denned up for the cold months. Grizz'll be snoring away somewhere, I expect."

He looked at her, but she didn't say anything.

"Speaking of hungry critters, I'm going to carve off some choice chunks for supper. I'll cook up some for walking food tomorrow too. I don't have no wine, nor flowers, but I reckon it'll be a tasty feed, just the same." He smiled and handed her a long stick. "Do me a favor and prod that fire once in a while, keep the flames working. I'll be back."

As he worked at the nearly frozen hide of the healthiest-looking ox, Charlie pondered about choosing a campsite anywhere near the dead beasts. He'd chosen a spot pretty far away, but now he wondered if maybe they should have camped even farther from the carcasses. He looked up-trail toward the camp, but only saw faint clouds of smoke from the campfire. No, late as it was and as dark as it would soon be, he decided they'd gone far enough beyond the oxen. He knew Delia was all but done in for the day. And he could barely keep his knife hand from shaking, he was so tuckered out.

He didn't doubt the bodies would attract wolves tonight, and was surprised they hadn't before then. But it had snowed; maybe that had kept the scavengers away. Still, if anything tipped them off that there was fresh meat hereabouts, it would be the scent of the cut-open hides, and the meat roasting. He thought of the shotgun and figured with that, his knife, and a few well-placed campfires, they should make it through the night without bother.

He made it back to the camp carrying hunks of meat nearly frozen through. They'd need thawing before they could cook properly, so he set them around the edges of the fire on a couple of rocks he'd managed to kick up.

"Charlie, I'm sorry you're stuck tending to me."

"Hey, now, don't you go saying things like that. I'm —"

"No, I mean it. If you didn't have to carry me for half the day, you might have reached them by now. I propose that you leave me here and go on. Then you can come back for me." She wouldn't look at him, but prodded the coals with a stick. "Besides, there's plenty for me to eat now."

"That's exactly why I ain't leaving you here, nor anywhere else."

"What do you mean?"

"Them?" Charlie jerked his head back toward the dead oxen. "How long you think all that fresh meat's gonna last out here before it starts drawing critters?"

"Oh, it's all but frozen. Honestly, I can't smell it at all. It's not like it's summertime."

"That's true, but your sniffer's a whole lot different than the nose on a wolf's face, Delia."

"But, Charlie —"

He stood, trying not to moan from the throbbing in his head and his shoulder. "No more arguing. I ain't leaving you anywhere, and that's that." His voice came out harsher than he intended. He dragged more wood over by the fire and said, "Besides, who else is going to rap me on the bean and keep me awake?"

Charlie had arranged a half dozen smaller fires in a wider arc around their campfire, and he'd done his best to drag a couple of decent-sized lengths from deadfall trees close by. They weren't much but would make a little something to hide behind. He didn't want to light the smaller peripheral fires unless he had to.

They'd eaten well, too much, as they each said, but it felt good to have food in the belly. Charlie missed a big, hot meal like that. The only thing that would have made it even better would be a cup of steaming hot coffee to top it off. But the thought didn't trouble him for long. The taste of the meat was still fresh in his mind and on his lips. He'd even managed to sizzle up a couple more hunks. They'd keep in this weather for a few days on the trail.

The cans of food he'd found were nearly depleted, though they'd eaten sparingly. Charlie was always ravenous, an ache he'd grown used to throughout his life. It was not a feeling he particularly liked, but it was not unfamiliar to him. Given his size, it had always been a chore to keep himself satisfied where food was concerned.

He thought that if he wanted to keep himself topped up with vittles at his place in the mountain valley, he'd have to keep a few pigs, maybe rabbits and chickens.

And a garden. He could taste the fresh pole beans and corn. He'd never been much of a hand at such things, but with his own place, he felt sure he could turn his hand to gardening. And of course, his valley would have a number of game trails close by so he might never run out of fresh meat.

With all these pleasant, promising thoughts and a belly filled to brimming with roasted ox meat, Charlie's head began to bob, and soon his chin touched lightly to his coat's buttoned collar.

In his sleep, which normally offered few dreams, Charlie found himself breathing harder as something awful drew closer, closer, panting in his ear. Then he heard a low sound like gravel being scraped between metal. No, that wasn't quite it . . . and then he knew what it was — growling. The guttural throat-churning of a wild beast!

He uttered a small cry as he woke, tensed and gripping tight to the shotgun cradled in his arms. Delia was asleep beside him, the laudanum keeping her pain quelled for the time being. They were still in the dark. The fire at his feet had dwindled but was still flaming.

Charlie sat still, his chest working hard and his breath puffing out into the night sky. There it was again — only not in his head this time, not a dream at all. It was the rumble and snarl of animals fighting. Many animals. Wolves at the carcasses! He had hoped they might get away with one more night without them, but that was not to be.

There was plenty of meat there to keep them occupied — but in his experience, wolves were tricky creatures prone to unexpected behavior. Just like men. But though he had a healthy fear and respect of wolves, Charlie knew better than to trust that he knew what they'd get up to. Though even knowing that, he'd sooner turn his back on a wolf than on someone like Rollie Meecher.

He looked over at Delia again. He'd only

wake her if he had to. Otherwise he'd keep this big fire going and hope they didn't get curious. With all that raw meat to occupy them, it seemed they'd stick with that and not let their sniffers drag them elsewhere. But in case, he was prepared with a torch, the shotgun, loaded and cradled, and the shells at the ready in his coat pocket.

The snarling and yipping grew in intensity. Sounded as though more of the beasts were coming down out of the hills, and the more they all yipped, the more of them came. Seemed to Charlie like a foolish thing for the early birds to be up to — why on earth would they up and yell to anyone within earshot that they'd found a good feed? Maybe that was the human way of doing things, mused Charlie. Grab all you can, to heck with everybody else, and then brag on it.

That sure was the way Rollie had it figured. No, sir, ol' Charlie didn't picture himself sharing any similarities with Rollie Meecher. He pushed the end of a long branch farther into the fire. Without an ax, he had to resort to dragging anything that might burn over to the fire.

He was thankful that Delia was still asleep. He didn't know much about their upbringing, but if he had to guess he'd say they grew up working folks in a tough Irish family, maybe in a city back East. He wasn't much of a hand at placing accents. He could tell an Englishman from a Chinaman, and that was about it.

For all the time he'd spent in mine camps all over the West, where you were liable to hear a dozen different tongues all gabbling away at once on any given day, deciphering where folks were from and maybe picking up a few handy words was something he'd never developed a knack for. Charlie sighed and leaned back, an ear cocked to the oddly musical yelps and growls of the far-off wolves savaging the oxen.

If the noises were any indication, he doubted there'd be much meat left come morning, nor hide nor hair either. When a wolf tucks into something, you can be sure it will finish the job, or bloat up trying. Same with a grizz, though these carcasses would be much too fresh for a bear. An old-timer mountain man once told him that grizz like their meat rotted and swimming with maggots. The thought of it pulled Charlie's mouth into a wide grimace.

Then he sat up. Some of the quarrelsome yips sure sounded as though they were drawing closer. Down-trail, the night was as black as the belly of a bull. Every few seconds he heard soft sounds like panting, maybe footfalls in the snow. They started from the direction of the oxen and wagon, then seemed to quiet, only to start again off to the left, then right, almost as if whatever was making the sounds had wings and danced along the air in the frozen, dark night.

He ought to wake the girl, in case he needed help with the fires. Though how much help she'd be, he wasn't sure. At least she'd know what they were facing. Keeping low, Charlie slowly pivoted on a knee, scanning the dark. But it did no good. He'd only be able to see them when they were nearly on top of him. He kept the shotgun poised, butt rammed into his armpit, a sore finger featherlight on the twin triggers. With his free hand he reached down to tap Delia's shoulder.

And that's when he saw the first one.

CHAPTER 30

"Are you ready, brother?" Son of Cloud looked at his brother and couldn't help smiling. Despite the younger man's grim intentions, Son of Cloud relished the feeling of being out, on the trail with his brother. He would have preferred it if they were heading out hunting elk, but he would make the best of this task and continue to try to keep Blue Dog Moon under some sort of control. How much longer he could do this, he was unsure. But he would continue to play this game. He had no love for the whites, but he did not like to see them die and more so, he did not like that it was Blue Dog who killed them, and in vicious ways.

"They have but three wagons left. Perhaps if we leave them alone, that crazy man leading them will kill off not only all the animals pulling their wagons, but his own people too. Counting him there are four men and one woman. Though they have her tied up like a dog. That is because she is braver than the men."

Son of Cloud had seen them too and knew what his brother was saying. "That younger man telling the others what to do is a bad sort. Such a man would not last long as a Shoshoni. He does not know how to work with others. Do you know why that is?" said Son of Cloud.

"No, but I think you are about to tell me."

His brother nodded. "It is because of the whiskey. He drinks and drinks and so stays sickly and crazy all the time. Never once is his body without it."

Blue Dog knew why Son of Cloud brought this up. Whiskey had been a sore point between them many times. Whenever he found a bottle of it in the bags of one of the people he had killed, Blue Dog always drank it, and tried in vain every time to get his older brother to drink more than one swallow. But Son of Cloud would not indulge in much of it. He did not want to feel the warm feeling inside. That was a shame for him.

They slowly headed in the direction of the whites' camp, and slipped from their horses when they were still a long distance from it. Sound from the snow would work against them if they were not careful. Also, it would not do to have their horses try to talk with those of the whites. Son of Cloud whispered low and close to his brother's ear, "You run off the horses, enough to stop another of their wagons. I will bring back someone. If we scare him enough, we will learn something from him."

In the dark, he saw Blue Dog's teeth flash in a grin. "Or we could kill him, as I will do eventually anyway. This way, we will have to work less, you see? And maybe we can get more than one at a time."

"No! That is not what we agreed to do."

"I do not understand. I can kill a lot more than one man tonight. Then we would be done with it!"

"Again, I say no. I am the older brother here, not you. Until that changes, I will tell you what we will do and not do. It is important that we try to find out information from this man."

"Information? He knows nothing we care to know, has nothing we want — nothing useful except his whiskey. No, I do not care about him. I care about Father and Mother and the others of our people. Who will mourn for them? You will and I will, that is all. It is up to us to avenge their deaths and drive the whites from this land. They have no right to be here!"

Son of Cloud could only sigh and watch as his impatient young brother crept off into the night toward the camp of sleeping whites. Then he too moved low, from rock to tree, aware that on such a dark, clouded night, the snow would not share much of the moon's light. But that was no reason for him to not use caution.

In his opinion, whites were tricky creatures prone to deceit at the best of times, and were frequently much worse because most of them were drunk on whiskey. How they ever bested great Indian warriors in battle he could not figure out.

Long minutes later, something passed before the low flames of the campfire. Son of Cloud froze, crouching, holding a Colt revolver in his hand. He liked how it felt, as though it were made for his hand. Yet another thing the whites did that he could not figure out. A few of them must be very good at making the most of what little time they had when not drinking whiskey. If Blue Dog was not careful, the white half of him would win the game in his head and Son of Cloud would lose his brother to whiskey.

It was a still night, only a soft breeze whispering in the trees. He sniffed at the air — mostly wood smoke, sweat from the unwashed whites, and the warm smells of horses. It pained him to know his brother would kill horses and mules, not merely run them off. But in the end, it would be one more thing to help frighten the whites, to make them scream when they awoke.

These whites still had a day or so before they would get to the town in the hills. He wanted them to be so frightened by the time they arrived that they locked themselves up in those smelly log houses with the rest of the whites. It would not take much to make that happen.

Somewhere in the dark across from him, he knew that Blue Dog would by now be trailing down past the camp. Son of Cloud shifted his eyes back to the campfire. One of the white men had awakened and now leaned against a tree, fumbling with his leggings.

Staying downwind and crouching, Son of Cloud used the man's own animal sounds of grunting and coughing to mask the slight noise his soft-soled moccasins made punching through the snow. This would leave a trail, but there would be no way for the whites to follow once daylight came. He knew, from watching them for many days now, that they would be too frightened to follow.

He came nearer now and recognized the man as the tall, thin one wearing buckskins that carried the smell of sweat and smoke and the bloody gut-stink of many animals. The man also had been a bent, lame creature since he swam in the river days before. He would be easy prey.

Son of Cloud slipped the pistol back into the holster and thumbed his tomahawk up and out of his belt. He waited until the man jigged up and down, nearing the end of making his water; then Son of Cloud ran full out, one, two, three strides, his feet making no more sound in the soft deep snow than they would in tall, summer grass. He did not wait for the man to jerk his head around in wonder at the new night noises close and coming closer.

The blunted end of the tomahawk rose in Son of Cloud's grip, sure and true. It dropped down toward the side of the smelly crippled man's head. His homely fur hat fell to the snow as the ax smacked hard into the freighter's head above his right ear. The softest spot and a place where success in knocking out someone was nearly guaranteed. Son of Cloud slipped closer and encircled his long hand over the white's gasping mouth, already close to blurting out an oath that would rouse the other whites.

Beyond the far side of the sloppy camp, where the others lay in their sleep, Son of Cloud knew, his brother was even now busy slicing his knife deep into the throats of the animals. Soon they would become agitated on the picket line, the stink of blood clouding their faces. This would wake the rest of the whites, unless they were so drunk they snored through it. The woman, though, she would be another concern. She was smart and seemed to hate the other whites as much as the brothers did.

The buckskin man collapsed into Son of Cloud's arms, against his chest. He spun, grabbing the thin man about the neck, and dragged him back the way he had come. He would lash the smelly man to the back of his horse, wait a few minutes, and then when he sensed his brother's approach, Son of Cloud would mount up and ride back down the trail. A day behind, the big white man and the sickly white woman would find this smelly man waiting for them, hopefully alive, if Son of Cloud could keep Blue Dog from killing him.

If Blue Dog had his way, the smelly white would be killed, and it would not be quick or kind. Son of Cloud was halfway back to their own horses when he heard the animals of the whites begin to nicker and fidget. It would not be long before the whites, if there were any not laid low by the whiskey, might try to come after them.

He guessed instead that they would stand around their camp like dumb cattle and carry on and cry and wonder if the Indians were still around — and what they would do next to them. This was the part that Son of Cloud liked — making the whites shiver and sweat in fear.

"Brother!" Blue Dog whispered in the dark.

"Did you have luck?"

"Yes, I only slit the throats of two — the ugliest beasts. They were mules. I have never liked the look of them. But the others were once fine horses. I could not do it."

"That is a relief to hear. Seeing two and hearing the fear in the others — as I can now — that will be enough. Plus . . ." Son of Cloud waved a hand at his horse, on which he'd draped the man in buckskins.

"Good. I knew as soon as I saw that one get up that you would have him. Is he dead?"

"No. We may make use of him yet. But let's go before they decide to trail us. But, Blue Dog . . ." Son of Cloud looked at his brother.

"What?"

"We do not need to kill this one. If we kill again, there may be a war with the whites — and that would be a war we cannot win." Son of Cloud turned from Blue Dog and lifted the unconscious white man's head to peer at his homely face.

Blue Dog Moon felt the muscles in his neck tighten, stiffen as if made of wood. Once again Son of Cloud made him feel as he felt when a white looked at him before he slid his knife into his soft belly. And Blue Dog felt the red rage drip down inside his own head, coloring his eyes and making his head tremble.

He stared at his older brother's back and it was as if he looked upon a weak old woman, fussing and simpering over her cooking. And it felt so very good and right to him to slip his tomahawk from his wide leather belt, raise it high, and drive it once downward, hard and fast, into Son of Cloud's head.

His brother stood upright, stiffened, and turned to face him. Son of Cloud's eyes opened wide and gleaming in the mooned night's reflection off the snow. "Brother . . . ," he gasped. "Why . . . ?" Then he collapsed to the snowy ground. His horse fidgeted and sidestepped away.

Blue Dog Moon grabbed his dead brother

under his arms and dragged him to sit against a tree. "Because," he said, bending Son of Cloud forward and yanking the tomahawk from his head. "You are too white and I am not. I am nothing and I am everything."

He led Son of Cloud's horse, burdened with the white man, over to his own horse. He mounted up and walked his horse back toward Son of Cloud. "Good-bye, brother. This war was not your fight."

While the booze-addled men were slowly roused by the thrashing and whinnying of the wounded and freed animals, Hester O'Fallon lay still, hardly daring to breathe during the previous few minutes.

She had heard Norbert get up — it was difficult not to, what with all the groaning and grunting each of the men did every time they moved in their sleep or awake. Norbert had more reason than most, though, having been dunked in the river days before, and then whipped raw by Rollie that day. She had heard him make water close by and had hoped she wasn't lying downhill of him.

The thought disgusted her — until she heard another noise, also close by. As if something were hurrying toward her. She held still, not daring to open her eyes, and heard a soft, thudding sound, quiet grunts, then dragging, and finally heavier soft footsteps in the snow. They receded and she finally dared to open her eyes. And saw the shadowed shape of one man lugging another. One of the freighters? She shifted her eyes, saw no one where she had guessed Norbert had been.

It was then that the low sounds of pain came to her. The horses were in trouble. But she didn't dare move. What if it was Rollie, gone mad and killing everyone? He seemed the sort of man who might lose reason and become more of a monster than he already was.

Then a new thought stabbed her and she knew with certainty it had to be the answer — the Indians had found them. Maybe they had been following them for some time, and had only now begun to move in on them.

Her hands and feet were bound tight. Long ago they stopped aching and now throbbed, but she was unable to free herself, was unable even to stand. She counted herself lucky that Rollie cared too much for his liquor to remember his threats to molest her. She also knew that could only last for so long before the foul man eventually approached her.

But if it was the Indians, and since she

had slept away from the men, as Rollie had ordered her, trussed and tossed aside, should she make a sound? She did not care a thing for any of them. Not after they had left her sister and Charlie behind, both long dead now, the blaze consuming them.

She bit the inside of her cheek hard enough to draw blood. Anything less and she knew she would cry out at the horrid memory of it. As much as she would have liked to hear Rollie and Bo and Shiner and Norbert scream in agony as the Indians tortured and killed them, she also didn't want to alert them to her own location.

If she couldn't see far into the night, she didn't think the Indians could do any better. She had heard tales about them, people saying that they could see in the dark, change shape and fly like owls or buzzards, wiggle around like snakes, and travel in packs like wolves. She didn't much care about or believe any of it. She wanted to not be seen and to hear those bastards die. Hearing the four freighters give up the ghost would barely begin to make the hurt go away.

With no parents left, Hester had had no one else in the world but Delia. Then Delia married that bum, Vincenzo — without telling Hester. And then he left her and Delia became ill and begged Hester to help her find him again. All of that was bad enough, and yet it was all Hester had. And then Rollie stole it all from her.

Lying on her side behind a log in the snow, frozen and shivering, Hester vowed that if the Indians didn't finish the man's life, she would. She felt bad for whatever had happened to the animals, and hoped Mabel-Mae wasn't among those hurt. But she also felt a strange satisfaction when she heard the half-drunk freighters come awake at the sounds of the animals stamping loose around the camp, then stumbling their way out into the night.

"What's happening? Someone tell me what's going on here."

It was Rollie, and Hester wanted to shout to him that he was going to die. Sooner or later, she would see it done, or see to it herself.

CHAPTER 31

"Delia!" Charlie hissed, nudged her hard in the shoulder. "Delia! Wake up! Get up now, girl — we got company!"

And that was all Charlie had time for. The first wolf loped into view close enough for the firelight to bounce off its eyes, sniffing and surveying the curious fire and the big man staring at him, waving a torch and shouting.

"Charlie? What's happening?"

Delia sounded confused, and he reckoned that within seconds she'd be more frightened than confused. "Wolves, Delia. Stay calm. I didn't want you to wake up confused. Now, take that long stick there and burn the end up good, get a flame going on it. Good. And take this." He tossed his knife beside her. "Keep it in one hand and that burning stick in the other. And angle yourself so your back's mostly to the fire, so you can see out."

"What am I looking for, Charlie?"

He stole a glance at her. For a sickly girl, he was shocked to see there was almost a smile on her face. "Wolves, I told you. You'll see their eyes glowing, reflecting the light from the fire. Now, keep a sharp lookout. I have to light those other fires I set up. Then if you're up to it, you can help me tend them. We should have enough wood to keep them at bay."

"What about the meat? Wasn't there enough oxen for them? Charlie — you're not saying that there are so many wolves that all that meat isn't enough for them?"

Now she sounded scared, and for that he was glad. Wouldn't do to have her think this was a game. "No, I reckon not, Delia. But we'll get a few curious ones here. Maybe nothing more."

But as he turned to light the first small fire, a sharp bark, close by, made him crouch low. He saw a glint of wetness and the shine of an eye as it leaped, open-mouthed, at him. Charlie had enough time to drop his torch and touch off a trigger. *Kaboom!* The sound pulsed outward like the sound big rocks make cracking together underwater. For a handful of moments, all else was silent. Charlie heard no other close-by wolf sounds. He snatched up the torch. "Delia? You okay?"

"Yes. Did you get it?"

"I believe I did. Hang on, I'll take a look. . . ." He kept the shotgun at the ready, but jammed the torch outward quickly. There at the edge of the firelight lay a sprawled heap, out of reach, surrounded by spatters of darkness on the snow around it. He hoped they would not see more blood before morning. But Charlie knew better than to trust in hope. Every time he had in his life, it seemed to let him down. No, sir, it was better to rely on your strength and a good shotgun.

It felt odd to heft one again, and it felt very odd to have once again shot something with one. But — and he hated to admit it, hated the thought of revealing that old, buried side of himself — it felt good too to have a shotgun in his hands. And besides, he reasoned, using it to defend a young lady seemed fitting somehow.

"Why did it want to attack us?" Delia appeared by his side, holding her own weakly flickering torch.

"Might be it got caught up in the frenzy up there and thought there was more grub to tuck into down here." He gestured with his chin. "Keep low, now, and stay behind me. No telling what's next."

"You don't think that was the only confused wolf out here, do you?"

"No, and I hope you're not thinking this is a game, Delia. Confused or not, those wolves have teeth and they mean business."

"The wolves or the teeth, Charlie?" They'd been crouched side by side, talking in low whispers, scanning the black night around them, which seemed to press in, sending wavering shadows from the weak light from their torches and the scattered fires around them.

"What?" said Charlie.

"Nothing, I'm fooling with you." Delia grimaced, held a hand to her belly.

"Hey, I told you about kidding around — Delia, what's wrong?" Charlie hesitated, but leaned the shotgun against a log to help the girl ease back down to her blankets. "You overdid it, huh?"

She nodded.

"You want some of your medicine?"

She shook her head. "Can't."

"Why?"

"It's gone," she said through gritted teeth.

"But I thought you still had some left."

"Wasn't that much. I'll be fine, Charlie." She looked up at him, her eyes glazed and a forced smile on her mouth. As she looked past him, her smile turned into a scream.

"Charlie! Look out!"

Charlie spun, his right arm arcing out, the glowing torch whooshing. The first thing he saw was a large lobo, too big by half, stiffened in a crouch, poised between two smaller campfires as if they meant nothing at all to it. The beast's eyes danced dark, then bright with the reflected flickering light.

Charlie fancied he could smell the beast from across the few feet that separated them. It reeked of blood and hair and raw flesh and something more, a stink overriding all the others — something he couldn't name, as if the word *animal* had its own smell. And it was a sharp-toothed thing.

They stared at each other's eyes, but Charlie also noticed its long, pointed ears were angled back. Its wide head appeared to flatten in rage as if it were willing itself into a living wedge, ready for attack. Its lips were raised impossibly high, the long, curved teeth beneath flecked with spittle and small snags of gristle. One of its long teeth, he saw, had snapped off down near the point, and it made the creature appear even more menacing.

But it was the perfect, rattling sound rising from deep within the creature's chest that froze Charlie's blood. That, and the fact that the shotgun sat propped against the log, the butt of it not four inches from the wolf's right front paw. Charlie took all this in within seconds of turning, of catching the wolf in the act, as if he were a shopkeep nabbing a schoolkid with his hand in the gumdrop jar.

Charlie knew he had to get to that gun, but all he had was a torch in his hand. He'd wasted vital seconds staring down the wolf, and then it occurred to him that it might have been a game on the wolf's part to let others creep in silently behind the girl.

Charlie also knew that the second he moved, he'd have the better part of a hundred pounds of savage fury launch right at him. Nothing for it, he figured, and thrust the torch at the beast while he shouted, "Heeyaaah!"

The wolf leaped straight at him, gnashing its teeth and emitting a snarling sound more menacing than anything Charlie had ever heard from a town dog. He missed jamming the torch down the beast's gullet by mere inches. Instead it glanced off the leaping wolf's shoulder, singeing hair and causing little other damage.

Charlie dropped the sputtering stick and kept his bulk firmly positioned before the beast, and despite his size, the impact of the thrashing wolf — all muscle and hair and rage — rocked him back on his heels. He dropped to one knee and worked to keep his face away from the lunging, snapping head. Its foul breath clouded his face, but he kept his left forearm between his face and the wolf's, under the snapping jaw.

Behind him he heard Delia screaming and hoped she wasn't being attacked too, but he had his hands full. He let go his precious hugging hold around the wolf's ribs and jamming his right arm higher, pushed back against it with his left arm, pinning the thrashing wolf's neck between his arms. He felt something snapping, heard the ravening growls become gagging sounds, and still he didn't let up.

The wolf's legs all the while thrashed and clawed. Charlie felt some of his previous wounds open, felt the wash of hot blood, some from new gashes in his gut, chest, and legs, and still he squeezed. More snapping, he felt the wolf's windpipe collapse, and soon much of the fight ebbed from it.

Still Charlie squeezed, and standing again, he gave one mighty bellow and jammed his arms together. The wolf's head popped backward at an unnatural angle, and Charlie heard a sound like a carrot snapping; then the wolf went limp in his arms. He grabbed its thick coat in his fist and peeled it away from his chest, holding the fresh kill aloft.

The big man stared at it a moment, his chest heaving, his groaning voice a ragged sound. Then he swung the dead creature back and tossed it with a shout as far as he was able into the black night.

He seemed to regain his senses then and he spun to look at Delia, expecting the worst since he no longer heard her screams. His heart clawed its way up his constricting throat — she was gone!

"Delia!" he shouted, not seeing the log before him. As he sprawled forward over it and into the snow, a gunshot boomed in the night, the flash blooming but a few yards ahead.

"Charlie . . . are you hurt?" Delia rushed back to him, dragging the shotgun by the smoking barrels.

Charlie struggled to his knees. "What happened?"

"You were fighting off that wolf and I saw another one coming up behind, so I did a stupid thing and threw my stick at it. Then I saw the shotgun, so I crawled over and got it. The other wolf came closer as I grabbed the gun, and as it was about to leap at me, you snapped the neck of that one you were fighting with! I didn't take my eyes off the other wolf, though. But it must not have liked what it heard, because it backed up. Then you shouted and it turned away. I don't know what came over me, Charlie, but I . . . I took off after it!"

"But you're okay? You're not hurt?"

"No, I'm fine, fine. . . ." Her voice grew weaker and she dropped before him in the snow.

"Oh no, no, no, girl, I promised I'd take care of you and ol' Charlie ain't doing a very good job of it, is he?" He scooped her up, grabbed the shotgun, and retreated to the fire.

Once again, Charlie found himself nurse-maid to the sickly girl. Her color was the worst he'd seen it. In all his days, he'd never seen a person look so gray. Even in the weak firelight her coloring looked like a stormy sky. He shucked his big coat and wrapped her in it, something she'd staunchly refused to allow him to do before. He snatched a handful of shells from the pocket, cracked the barrels, and stuffed two more into the shotgun.

Charlie didn't dare look down at his own chest, legs, and arms. He knew what he'd see, shredded clothes and blood and welts from the wolf's thrashing claws. He jammed more wood into the hungry sparking and snapping fire, and stuck another long branch in to make a new torch. Then he dragged more wood to the smaller fires, several of which had petered out to mere glowing coals, all the while casting an eye toward the dark around them. He was bothered and confused by the sudden attacks of the wolves, but he was even more bothered by the fact that now he didn't hear a thing.

"Charlie?" Delia's voice was little more than a whisper.

He kneeled by her side. "Hey there, Miss Delia. How you feeling?"

"Like I could drink some water."

"Okay, then. Here we go." He retrieved one of the tins he'd had close by the fire melting snow into water. "Nice and warm for you."

She sat up and took the can from him, sipped from it. "Thank you, Charlie. I hate being thought of as someone who's useless."

"Oh, Miss Delia, you could never be —"

"Charlie, please." She held her steady gaze right on him, her mouth set in a hard line, and she looked like her sister, Hester, when she did that. He nodded.

She closed her eyes a moment, then opened them again. "Charlie, I have a cancer. Somewhere in my belly." She patted her midsection. "Two different doctors said so. And it sure hurts sometimes. I didn't want to say anything, but now with the laudanum gone, I am afraid I will be of even less use to you, and you deserve to know why. I had half a thought to using the other barrel on myself when I'd finished off that wolf, but you didn't reload that first barrel after you fired it, Charlie."

He tried to smile, but couldn't do it. "I reckon . . . I'm out of practice, Delia."

"Can you . . . let me lean against you, Charlie? Maybe sort of hold me awhile? Hester used to. It helps a little."

"Why, sure, sure." He scooched over, his back partially to the fire. He arranged her so that the crux of two logs shielded her from another attack, and he vowed to himself to stay as close as he could to her for the rest of the night. He wished morning was a whole lot closer.

She leaned against him and he wrapped his right arm around her, gently patting her shoulder and arm. Such a tough little thing, he thought. And so young to have such a bad thing happen.

The shotgun stood upright on his left thigh, both hammers peeled back, his finger outside the guard in case he dozed and touched off the triggers.

313

A few minutes passed. The dark, close up, was quiet. Far off, he heard the yowling and arguing sounds of the wolves having their fill of the oxen carcasses. *Must be like Christmas to them,* thought Charlie. He and Delia had managed to kill three of them, but he reckoned that wasn't but a smidgen of the whole pack. He figured Delia had gone to sleep, but then she spoke.

"It's all my fault, you know." Her voice was quiet, as if she were talking to herself.

"You okay, Delia?"

She nodded. "I'm the one who wanted to come all the way out here. If I hadn't been so desperate to see Vin, Hester and I would still be back East. None of this would ever have happened."

Charlie felt her shiver, heard a sniffle. Had to mean she was crying. He patted her shoulder again. "I tell you what. I for one am glad you all came along. Oh, I'm not happy you have had such a rough time of it, but if I learned anything this last week, it's that bad things happen, for sure. But good things tend to follow up right on behind 'em. You know what I mean?"

"No, I don't think you're right, Charlie."

"What? How's that? I met you and your sister, didn't I? And I ain't no ogre."

Delia pushed away from him, looked at

314

him. "Oh, Charlie I didn't mean that. Of course you're the best thing about this terrible journey, but . . ."

Charlie smiled at her. "I'm joshing you, girl."

She laid her head back against him.

"Now, don't you mind. I know what you're driving at and I can't say you're right either. So let's call it a conversation we can have tomorrow when you're a-whomping on my head."

"Okay, Charlie. . . ." And by the sound of her voice, Charlie could tell she'd finally fallen asleep.

CHAPTER 32

Norbert came to and the first thing he saw was a stream about twice as wide as a man was tall, a cutbank sagging directly across from him, clumps of snow stiff and unmoving curling over the iced flow. Most of the stream had frozen over, damping the sound of the flow. It all had a familiar look to it — and then he realized that the snow made everything look the same.

None of this made sense. He felt as if he'd been beaten with big sticks and trampled by buffalo, a whole lot of them. Norbert closed his eyes again, ran his thick tongue around his mouth. Same old teeth, but he tasted blood — what from?

Someone sighed nearby. Norbert forced his eyes open and saw legs, clad in tall moccasins, buckskin pants. He let his eyes travel up, squinting at the brightness of the sky. They ended up staring at an Indian who stared right back at him.

This could not be, could it? Norbert tried to speak. The words fetched up something awful. His mouth was so dry. He cleared his throat and tried again. "You savvy American lingo, Injun? Hey? I . . . I might could get you some money or whiskey. Maybe you like gold? I know of a place where there's heaps of it. We was headed there." Norbert looked at the man, more convinced with every second that this was one of the rascals who did all those horrible things to that body they found on the trail.

He felt his legs shake even more, knew they were about to give out on him. He had to do something, had to get away from him somehow. Had to let him know he wasn't a threat. "I don't want anything from you. Heck, I didn't even want to be here, you savvy? Me . . . uh, I want to go away. I got kin back in Tennessee. That's about all I got, I reckon. You set me free and I won't bother you or anyone here, for the rest of my days. That's a promise."

Still the savage stared at him. He was even smiling, but not the sort of smile Norbert would guess meant anything friendly.

Norbert's eyes skittered up and down him. Saw the mix of Injun and white clothes on him. Beaded buckskins. Couldn't hate a man for wearing such practical attire. He'd sported them himself for years. Wore like iron, they did. Maybe he could appeal to him that way.

"Them folks I was with, I got no ties to them. Don't owe them a thing. In fact, they owe me." Norbert's eyes widened. Here might be the way in. Might be he could convince him that he had promise, could make him money somehow. If only he knew what the Injun wanted.

The man circled around the tree so that he stood out of kicking reach, and every few seconds, he'd feint to either side, as if he were about to dart behind the tree and . . . what? Norbert had no idea what the man might do — lop off his hands? Bite him? Knife him in the back? *Oh no, what if that Injun starts cutting skin off me like he did to that man on the trail?*

Norbert, you have been in a pile of messes in your day, stuck behind Union lines in the war, hiding in that pile of corpses, then found and stuffed in that Yankee prison.

He watched this Injun, who was obviously more than Injun, and felt there was something odd looking about him, almost as if he had a touch of white man. It had something to do with the fact that he was decked out in white gear, had long reddish brown hair and odd-looking skin, and wore a Colt revolver and all.

But Norbert didn't have time or inclination to think on that too much, because the Injun scared him right to his core, looked as though he knew everything going on in his mind. Looking at him, Norbert got the feeling that even if they could understand each other, there wouldn't be a thing he could say or do to prevent what he might do to him.

Might? *Fool, Norbert,* he told himself. *This boy is, sure as the sun comes up each day, going to gut you like he did that man back on the trail.*

All of a sudden having a face full of beard and a topknot that he'd always been proud of, a full head of it like his pap and his mam's pap too, didn't feel like such a good thing.

He struggled against the rawhide thongs, but they were lashed too tight. The more he squirmed, the worse grew the cuts on his back from Rollie's whipping. Soon he felt them open up again and seep. Blood began to drip into the snow. The sight of it, coupled with the shooting pains in his legs he still had from his dunk in the freezing river and the pictures in his mind of the body they'd found on the trail, all came together so hard that he couldn't hold himself up any longer.

Norbert felt his legs go, first the left, then the right. He went with it and sagged, slumping down against the tree, the weight of his slight body jerking his arms high behind him, scraping against the rough bark. He didn't care, could not even cry out. He was done for and he knew it.

The Injun spoke. He'd said a few words before Norbert realized he was hearing his own tongue. He'd been weeping silently, his chin on his chest. He looked up.

The man had moved closer, stood over him, looked down on him. The man repeated himself. "You weep, white man. Like a woman."

"You . . . you speak American?"

"No," he said.

Norbert looked over at him, his brow pulled tight in confusion.

"I speak English. Better than you, from what my ears tell me."

"How is that? You one of them reformed savages?"

The Injun laughed. Norbert stiffened back against the tree and tried to stand.

The Indian spoke again. "If your ignorance were not so sad, it would be funny."

"I don't understand a thing about this at all," said the wayward freighter, his voice wavering and whimpering. "Is there any-thing I can help you get? You want them wagons full of stuff? I could maybe help you pull off stealing them. Hey, hey, they got a white woman there. You want her? I bet Rollie'd part with her. Ain't nobody wants any trouble with you all."

"I do not want anything from a man who would trade a woman for himself."

Before Norbert could respond, the Indian slipped behind him. Norbert struggled, clawing with his fingers at the too-tight leather wrappings. He felt the cool flat metal of a blade rest against his hand and stopped. But he couldn't stop his breathing from sounding as if he'd run up a mountain without stopping. What was he going to do with him?

Then the Indian bent low, spoke in his ear: "You are the one who likes to swim, is that correct?"

CHAPTER 33

"I knew it! I dang well knew it!"

Those were the first words Hester heard, the words that forced her eyes open. And everything that had happened a few hours earlier in the dark of the early, early morning came back to her. And within seconds, she knew exactly why Rollie's hoarse voice was once again rasping out rage.

"Now that I can see, it's plain what happened here!" Rollie stood at the dead, cold fire, hands outstretched toward it anyway, as if the black coals would, by his will alone, spring to life and offer the warmth he wanted.

"What's that, Rollie?" Bo said, walking back toward the cold camp, buttoning his fly after relieving himself a few feet away behind a tree.

"You idiot. It's Norbert."

"What? Naw, it ain't neither," said Bo.

"Do you see him anywhere around here?"

322

Rollie stared wide-eyed at Bo, then at Shiner. "Do you?"

Both men looked at the trees, as if their friend might wander out. "Nope," said Shiner.

"That's because he killed them mules and took off! He was riled because I grazed him with the whip. I reckon he didn't like that."

Hester couldn't help herself — she snorted back a chuckle.

"You think this is funny?"

"No, Rollie. In fact, I think it's plain sad."

"What's that supposed to mean?" He walked over to her.

"Why would Norbert leave? Where would he go? Did he take his gear with him?"

Bo went over to the wagon, lifted the corner of a tarp. "His war bag's still here, boss!"

"Shut up, Bo. And get away from there." Rollie turned to face them all. "Course he left — and he took one of the horses, rode on out of here."

"You really believe that?" Hester knew she was pushing her luck with him, but she couldn't help it.

Rollie folded his arms and stood hipshot over her. "Well, now, Miss Smarty, what do you think happened?"

"Indians," she said without hesitating.

"Oh no, no!" At mention of the word *Indian,* Bo pulled his pistol and hustled off toward the dead mules. "We got to get going, Rollie. This is bad."

"Shut up, Bo. Go find the other animals."

Shiner slowly turned in a circle, eyeing the thin, Snow-filled scape around him.

"Don't just stand there, you idiot," yelled Rollie. "Go help Bo to round up them others. We only caught four so far and that ain't enough to drag both those wagons, you hear me?"

He nodded heartily and stomped through the snow to the sagging picket line and the blood-spattered mess beneath it.

Rollie turned his attention back to Hester. He crouched down beside her, pulled his pistol, and ran the cold steel barrel tip up and down her face, tracing her strong chin. He smirked at her and gently dragged the snout of the barrel up the side of her face until it rested in the middle of her forehead. "Seems to me you know a whole lot about what happened here last night."

"You would too, if you hadn't been drunk."

Instead of hitting her or shouting, as she expected, Rollie surprised Hester by nodding in agreement. "I reckon that is so, yes, indeed. But you got to understand something." He leaned even closer, so that his mouth was inches from hers.

She smelled his breath, a gagging reek of tobacco, stale whiskey, food smells, and what seemed like vomit topping it all off. His teeth were clouding gray from neglect and several had pitted and were blackened in the middle. She tried not to look, tried not to breathe in as he spoke.

"You say the word *Injun* one more time in front of them two, or displease me in any other way, and I will kill you." He pushed her forehead with the pistol again and held it there. Hester tried to remain calm, tried to not show the fear she felt knotting her insides. But she had never had a gun pointed at her forehead before meeting him, never had one jammed hard into her.

"Oh, I will have me some fun first, but make no mistake, you will end up poorly. Now, nod if you understand me."

Hester felt her eyelids tremble and she could not help it. She nodded and hated doing so.

"Good." He stood and turned away.

"Please untie my legs," she said. "I need to . . ."

"Oh yeah." He smiled and nodded. "Just remember," he said as he slipped free his sheath knife and sliced through the binding wraps at her ankles. "Don't try to run, 'cause a bullet travels faster than any person I ever seen."

She told herself she'd keep that bit of information in mind, then test it on him as soon as she was able.

Twenty minutes later, Bo and Shiner had managed to round up seven animals, one of them Mabel-Mae. None had strayed far.

"Well, this'll be cozy, won't it? All of us riding in two wagons." Shiner rubbed his stubbled head and looked at the haggard-looking animals.

"Can't put three on a wagon. Ain't enough to pull. And that mule belonging to Big Boy is bound to be useless in the traces. Have to go on with one wagon."

They all looked at Rollie. He was red faced and shaking his head. "You and Bo empty that rear wagon, and the woman'll ride up front with me." Then as quickly as his rage emerged, it dwindled again. Rollie winked at Hester and patted her behind.

Impulse grabbed her, and Hester spun and kicked Rollie. She caught him on the side of the leg, below the knee. He buckled into the side of the wagon, clutching his leg, and howling in pain and anger. It didn't take him but a moment to launch himself back at her.

She had already spun and headed off the trail into the trees, but the snow was deep and with her hands bound behind her, Hester's balance was off. Rollie closed the gap, limping and cursing her. She looked over her shoulder as he lunged at her, his arms out to grab her by the shoulders. Hester sidestepped, lost her balance. He fell one way, she the other. They both struggled to stand in the cold snow.

Rollie was faster and she felt his fist slam clumsily into her shoulder blade, sending her back down into the snow, face-first. She thrashed, waiting for the second blow, guessing that she'd really stepped over the crazy man's line this time, that he would do terrible things to her and then kill her. Without Delia, what would it matter. Still, she tensed and waited for the blow.

What she heard was a scream. But not from Rollie, from one of the men. It was a horrible sound. It reminded Hester of a child's cry of terror at seeing something frightening, something it had never before experienced. But there was also pain mixed with the scream.

She opened her eyes and raised her head up out of the snow. Rollie stood above her, crouched with his arm raised to pummel her again. But he'd stayed his blow and looked toward the scream.

For a few seconds she saw nothing but the dark stalks of the trees rising from the stark white snow, a steel gray sky above seeming to push down on everything below it. The only things that moved in those few seconds were plumes of breath from the horses and mules, and then she saw Bo's arms wagging up and down from behind a tree as if he were trying to fly.

"Bo? What in heck are you doing?" Rollie asked, but quietly, as if he were unsure if it were safe to shout.

Hester didn't move, stayed crouched low. Then she saw Shiner rise from where he must have been crouched down in the snow by the animals. He strode hard through the snow, big strides bringing him to the wagons. He reached the nearest and ran around it until he was on the far side.

"What are you doing?" yelled Rollie, over his initial fear. "And what is going on with Bo?" He loped back down the slope, his Colt drawn. Hester heard him thumb back the hammer.

"Oh no, no, no, Rollie, don't!" Shiner shouted, gesturing wide-eyed toward where Bo still stood behind a thick tree, his arms not flopping as rapidly as they had been.

Hester didn't like the looks of any of this.

She rose to her knees and crept upslope several feet until she reached a large tree with a snow-humped rock at its base. She angled low beside it and huddled there, unsure why she was doing so, but sensing that something was very, very wrong.

Rollie looked from Shiner to Bo, then shook his head and walked toward where Bo hid behind the tree. He was still a dozen feet from it when Hester saw him stop, as if jerked tight by an invisible rope attached to his back.

He stood that way for a few moments; then with arms spread wide, he stepped backward, once, twice, then turned and ran for the wagons.

Hester looked back to where one of Bo's arms was still visible from behind the tree. And that's when she saw blood drip, drip, dripping from his twitching, trembling fingertips.

Then, as she watched, he slipped into view, facing her. He held himself up, canted at an angle as if peeking out from behind the tree. The look on his face was something she was sure she would never forget. His eyes were wider than she'd ever seen anyone's, his eyebrows arched high, and his black, rotten-toothed hole of a mouth had stretched tall in a silent scream. Beneath it, brilliant red blood gushed out as though a miniature waterfall over his bottom lip and down his stubbled chin, cascading down the front of the tangled mat of his buffalo coat and black wool shirt beneath.

Those frightened eyes seemed to stare right at her. Hester heard her breath drag into her throat and lock there as if pulled by an invisible hand from her gut.

Bo stepped once, twice from behind the tree, his full body visible. He made a sound like a failed shout that pushed a gout of blood spuming up from his mouth. It arched high into the air, spraying scarlet feathers across the white snow before him. Then he pitched forward, facedown in the snow. And from between his shoulder blades thrust upward a long, slender arrow, the feathered tip quivering rigid and final.

Hester stared at the scene for long moments, then forced herself to look beyond Bo's body toward the direction from which the arrow would have come. But she could see nothing. No Indians, no movement in the snow, nothing but the humps of snow-covered rocks and slope and stunted pines and the winter-stiffened silvery arms of aspens.

But instead of being gripped in dread, Hester instead felt a creeping weariness.

What a strange few weeks this had been. Here she was, on a trip she hadn't wanted to make, and now she was the one making it while the one who had wanted to make it, her deathly ill younger sister, had been left to die . . . by the man who now held her prisoner!

If Rollie Meecher was to be believed, the one kind person she'd met in the past many months, Big Charlie, was apparently some sort of outlaw. He certainly didn't seem like one. And she'd always been a pretty good judge of people, so she felt pretty sure Charlie had been a good man. But he too had been left for dead by these foul freighters — they were the bad ones. And now here she was, staring at a man freshly dead, with an arrow sticking out of his back. Indians were hunting them, picking them off one by one and killing their animals.

Hester decided she had to either get away from these men, somehow cut the leather wraps tying her hands tight behind her, and take Big Charlie's mule, Mabel-Mae, and ride down out of these mountains, somewhere far and away, but not back to Monkton. That town could rot and all its inhabitants with it. Starting with that thief, Jasper Rafferty, and his business partner, Marshal Watt.

"Hey, woman!" Rollie's low growl broke the silent spell.

Hester didn't want to look at him. She was too tired, cold, wet, thirsty, hungry, and sore. But she knew she was kidding herself — he held all the cards and she didn't even have a penny to sit in on the game. Heck, her hands were still tied behind her back.

She shifted her gaze from the dead Bo to the wagon. Rollie nodded, gestured to her to come to the wagon. "Come on, we got to make a run for it! We'll get all the best stuff into this here wagon." He clunked the wooden side of the wagon and turned to Shiner. "You hitch the animals. I'll cover you."

Rollie looked back at Hester. "Woman! Get on over here. You got to help move the goods into this wagon, you hear me? Else I will be sorely tempted to leave you here to deal with the savages."

"I already am," she said, not breaking eye contact with the reprehensible man. He squinted at her, clearly not understanding what she meant. She sighed and pushed herself up to her knees. Before she rose into the open and headed down the slope to the wagon, she said, "I'm not comin' down there unless you untie me and do not tie me again."

"We'll see," he said.

"No, that's not a deal. I have no problem with staying here alone. And you can re-arrange your precious loads of junk your-selves."

"Fine, fine," he said. "But no tricky busi-ness."

Who does he think he is? she thought. *He killed my sister, killed Charlie, whipped others, drove his own uncle to death. Of course I'm going to resort to tricky business. In my own good time. After all, I have nothing to lose.* Hester suppressed a smile and, crouching low, made her way back to the wagon, half sliding in the deep snow.

It took the three of them most of an hour of hard work to get what goods Rollie selected transferred to the wagon. Not surprisingly to Hester, he made sure plenty of liquor made the grade, along with most of the flour, sides of bacon, coffee, beans, and tobacco. The wagon wasn't exactly light, and the snowfall so far had been significant, so she was curious to see how far the poor remaining pulling animals would be able to go. Hester guessed that another storm would make the going nigh on impossible.

That very thought must have niggled at Rollie too. "Shiner, and you, woman!" he yelled when they all but had the load covered. "Both of you, out front, busting trail."

"What? I didn't hire on —"

"What about Bo?" said Hester, despite the fact that she hadn't liked the dead man.

"What about him?" said Rollie, climbing up into the wagon seat.

"You can't leave him there."

"Watch me."

Hester didn't move. Rollie sighed and drew his Colt. "Now, look, that old boy's dead. And that's an affliction he ain't never going to recover from. Unless you want to come down with the same creeping sickness, you'll shut your mouth and get on up that trail and start a-stomping."

Any sense of rebellion she'd felt seconds before fluttered then died in her breast. There would be no escape today, she thought. But she would continue to keep her eyes scanning the trees, her ears perked for sounds that might mean danger, and her mouth shut — any other way and it would only land her in hot water.

He'd had her tie Mabel-Mae to the back of the wagon once again. "If it really was Injuns on our trail and not ol' Norbert all pissed off, then that soap sack of a mule will be the first thing to get it."

"Why you keeping that mule anyway, Rollie?" asked Shiner.

"Because, fool, it's in decent shape and we might have need of another one for the traces." Hester suspected that Rollie's real motive where Mabel-Mae was concerned was that if the Indian attackers continued nibbling away at his wagon train, his animals, and his men, he would eventually need a reliable animal to make his escape on. Hester vowed to make sure that didn't happen. She'd kill the mule herself if she had to before she'd let Rollie escape the fate she craved to dole out to him.

"One more thing, woman." Rollie chucked a couple of straggly lengths of hemp rope to Shiner. "Tie her hands again."

"No! I will not have my hands tied again. I cannot walk properly in the snow with my hands tied! Besides, you gave your word."

Rollie slapped his knee as he swigged his liquor bottle. "You honestly think I'd give such a thing? Or that if I did, it would be worth something? Lady, have I once given you cause to trust me?" He didn't wait for her to respond. "Shiner, tie her hands, will you?"

"Boss, it ain't necessary. There ain't nowhere for her —"

Rollie peeled back the Colt's hammer,

waved the sidearm in Shiner's general direction, and sighed. The bald underling retrieved the rope from the snow where Rollie had tossed it.

"I am feeling generous," said Rollie. "So you can keep your hands in front, but tied. That way if you fall you'll be able to catch yourself before you break your nose." His chortles echoed through the stark landscape. Rollie seemed to have forgotten the Indians completely, but Hester kept her eyes looking between the trees.

"If it's true that God does protect fools and drunks," said Hester to herself, "then that idiot is doubly safe."

They headed on out, the two sullen figures in front, stamping halfheartedly in the snow, making slight trails for the pulling animals. Rollie hunched below the humped bulk of the covered load, the snapping whip all but frothing the chill air above the beasts' backs. He stroked it snakelike, made it sing a vicious cracking note, over and over. The wagon lurched in fits and starts, never quite reaching a steady, rolling pace.

What would Rollie do when he could no longer move forward? Surely this was not working out as he had hoped. Hester guessed she would find out soon enough what his plans were, probably within hours.

She doubted they would be able to go on much farther. And especially if the snow began again. The weather felt as though it was growing grim once more, the sky darkening all around, pressing down at them. Even the air felt close, tighter somehow.

She reached up with her bound hands and tried to pull the old saddle blanket she'd managed to keep around her shoulders. But her feet were so cold, it felt as though she were walking on wooden stumps. She felt sure she would lose toes, maybe worse. Maybe death at the hands of the Indians wouldn't be so bad. Maybe it would be quick, painless. She hoped Delia hadn't suffered in the fire. Hoped the laudanum had kept her all but unconscious during it. . . .

Unbidden, tears built up in her eyes. She closed her eyes tight and squashed them away. It wouldn't do to give over to emotion now. Now that it no longer mattered, now that nothing really mattered except somehow getting revenge on these remaining two killers. Then the Indians could have at her; she didn't care. So long as she was able to do for Rollie what he had done to so many others, but mostly to dear Delia.

CHAPTER 34

Norbert swallowed and considered what the man had asked him. Liked to swim? What did that mean? And then a cold feeling seeped through him.

"Yes, I believe this is true, brother." The Indian — he looked strong — bent low and studied Norbert's face up close. The freighter tried not to look away. He had to show him he wasn't afraid. But what was that remark about swimming?

"Now, fella," said Norbert. "I don't rightly know what you think you know, and I'm all for kiddin', believe me. But I've had a rough time of it lately. You might have noticed I was whupped by my boss. Wasn't nothing I did wrong, on account of him being ornery, especially if he has been drinking. And then if he ain't, oh boy, look out. I reckon I look stronger than I am. I been in the water recently and it took a mighty toll on me. I —"

But the Indian wasn't even listening to him. He was busy at some task, gabbling on as if he were having a conversation with someone else right in front of him, but Norbert never heard more than the one voice. *Must be an Injun thing,* thought Norbert, *to talk to yourself. Maybe to Injuns it ain't a sign of crazy.*

Suddenly the Indian jerked Norbert to his feet with no warning and dragged him down to the stream. A sudden bad feeling — a very bad feeling — gripped Norbert inside by the throat and he started scrambling his legs, pawing them backward, doing anything he could think of to keep the Indian from doing what Norbert hoped wasn't going to happen.

"You ain't gonna put me in that water. No, sir, I been in freezing water and I ain't over it yet!"

"You will be warm, trust me." The Indian stepped in close, at the riverbank and, with his face an inch from Norbert's, he whispered, "Blood is warm, very warm."

Norbert couldn't seem to look away from those eyes. Even when he felt a strange feeling of stinging, almost like whiskey poured in a cut. It flowered up slowly from his belly on up to his chest. He jerked away from the Indian and took a half step backward.

Norbert looked down at his gut and couldn't believe what he saw.

The greasy smock front of his buckskin overshirt had been sliced open from side to side, it looked like a big gaping fish mouth. But it was what wagged out of it, like a big bloody red tongue, that stopped Norbert from screaming, thinking, or crying out at all. But only for a moment. He was staring down at his own guts, slowly becoming a gut pile as they tumbled out of him and slipped down his leg fronts to land on his feet. Steaming in the cold air.

Norbert recovered his ability to scream, but only for a few seconds, because a gush of something warm, so warm, pulsed up and out of his mouth.

The Indian leaned close and said, "You will not die right away. This is so you can feel the good warmth I told you of. It is cold out here. We are doing you a fine favor." Then the Indian smiled and dragged the stunned, wobbling Norbert, whose mouth had filled with his own blood, down the riverbank.

At the water's edge, the Indian stomped through the ice. Then he lowered Norbert's bottom half, up to his gut, into the swift-flowing stream.

Norbert felt the constant, hurrying tug-

and-push of the freezing water. But the Indian was right, he only felt warm, not cold.

Then he jerked Norbert's arms forward, retied the leather strapping, and staked him facedown, his arms apart on the bank.

The man appeared beside him again. Norbert felt very fuzzy headed, as if he'd got hold of a bad bottle. The Indian had a long pole in his hands. No, no . . . it was a bow, an Injun bow. No, maybe a lance, he wasn't sure. Then it went up in the air, came down, and Norbert felt another hot flash of pain, then a long stinging feeling.

He managed to look over his shoulder, saw something protruding from his side. Then the warm feeling started to go away. He couldn't understand it. The Indian had said he'd be warm. But he had lied — the warmth was going away, being chewed up, like a rat on a soda cracker. It left Norbert with a creeping cold, the like of which he'd not felt since falling in the river.

And then the cold became freezing cold. Hot blue stabs of pain lanced up his body, jerked him stiff, pulled any fuzziness that had been clouding his mind clear away. He knew exactly what was happening. Oh no, he was being tortured to death by an Indian, staked out on a freezing-cold riverbank and there was nothing he could do. He could maybe scream. . . . Norbert tried, but only managed to cough as blood backed up inside his mouth, flooded out his nose.

He finally pulled in long, gagging draughts of air and wished for death. He watched the Indian walk away from him and he couldn't even curse him, beg him for mercy, nothing. Could only watch as he walked away, not even once looking back at him.

And the entire time, Norbert stayed awake and the stabbing cold grew worse and worse with each passing second. And still he was awake, staked half in, half out of the rushing, icy mountain flow.

CHAPTER 35

"We all of us are, eh, how you say . . . waiting for something, no?"

Rogers, a burly man half a head taller than most of the other men in Gamble, scratched his ample mustaches and cocked his head to the side. "What are you talking about now, Vinny?"

Before the surly young Italian could respond, Clayton Eldridge said, "That's the problem, ain't it? We're all waiting. Setting up here in the hills with blizzard weather coming square at us, waiting for supplies that will help us wait some more, and make the time we spend waiting more tolerable."

"So?"

"So . . . it isn't right, is it?" Eldridge shook his head as if what he had been explaining had been so very simple.

"You make it sound as if there isn't a payoff at the end of it all," said Rogers. "You seem to be forgetting that come spring we're

all going to be rich as . . . well, darn rich!"
Judging from the looks he received from the
rest of the folks in the room, they remained
unconvinced. *Ah well,* thought Rogers. *Their
loss.* He swallowed another mouthful of
tepid water. The tea floating in the bottom
of the cup had been used so many times it
looked like a clot of something a cat had
hacked up.

"Rich isn't worth spit if you're dead," said
Eldridge.

Rogers didn't want to rise to the bait. He
pushed away from the table. "I'm going
hunting. Anyone care to join me?"

Eldridge cleared his throat. "Be sure to
use your shells judiciously. There are only
so many of them in camp and we can't afford —"

"By Golly," said Rogers, shaking his head
and pulling a wide, grimacing smile. "If I
needed another mother, I reckon I'd knock
on your door, Clayton Eldridge. Thankfully
I had one and that one was enough. She
was also polite enough to never tell me what
to do with my life. Or my bullets."

He bent close and pointed a thick, bent
finger in the air before the man's face. "You
may have elected yourself mayor, but there
ain't nobody in Gamble or on the rest of
God's snow-covered earth who is going to

344

tell me when and where to shoot my gun." He strode to the door, paused to take down his hat and coat from a wooden peg.

"I only meant —" said Eldridge, beginning to redden. He thrust his jaw out.

"Let it go," said Sheila Trudeaux. She poured more hot water all around. The door closed and she said, "He's right, you know. We're going to make it through, we have to hunt. And there isn't a better shot in Gamble than Rogers."

"But we need all our ammunition for fighting off the Indians."

"Who we haven't seen in quite some time, as I recall. What's more important? Starving or fighting?"

"It seems as if we are doing both."

Everybody looked at the Italian, surprised to hear from him. No one quite knew what to say. Finally he pushed away from the table. "Maybe I will go hunting with Rogers. It would not do to have our best shot lose himself in the coming storm, no?" He winked at them as he left, a mirthless smile on his face.

CHAPTER 36

"Pawnee's at my office, Jasper. Like I said, I gave him a bottle. He's no fool, though," said Marshal Watt, stopping in the street. "So don't you talk down to him as if he were a simple child."

"Whatever do you mean, Marshal?" Rafferty's eyebrows met in the middle.

It seemed to Watt that Jasper truly didn't know what he was getting at. The marshal sighed. "Look, Jasper, you have a tendency to act like your visits to the outhouse are holy affairs. You understand me? By and large, people aren't dumb, but you do your darnedest each day to make 'em feel as if they are. Not sure if you know this, but you only end up with a whole lot of people who aren't fond of you."

"I have no idea what you're talking about, Watt. The entire town passes through my doors in a week's time, and I manage to elicit smiles from most of them, talk with each of them as if we were old friends."

The marshal began walking toward his office. "The townsfolk all come through your store because it's the only one in town, Jasper. Believe me, if they didn't have to, they might not." He stopped and turned to the puzzled merchant again. "You ever wonder why no one asks you over to supper? Or out for a glass of beer?"

"You do."

"Yeah, but I have to. I'm married to his sister. That makes us kin, of a sort. You see?"

"You . . . you don't like me?"

Marshal Watt sighed again and closed his eyes. "That isn't what I'm talking about, Jasper. You're fine, you're my brother-in-law. Of course I like you. Look, don't get all fancy and highfalutin with Pawnee Joe, okay?"

They reached the edge of the street and climbed up onto the sagging sidewalk. The marshal made a point of banging the snow off his boots outside the door to his office, then rattling the latch a couple of extra shakes longer than was necessary.

He leaned into the room. "You in here, Pawnee? Ah, there you are. Keeping warm, I see."

Jasper followed him in. The marshal could tell by the tight look on Rafferty's face that he hated the very idea of pandering to the raggedy mountain man.

"Yeah, I'm here, Marshal. I heard you clunking outside the door, figuring to wake me up, let me know you're here, is that it?"

"Something like that, Joe. Something like that. I see the bottle helped keep you company while I tracked down my associate, Jasper Rafferty." Marshal Watt turned to the merchant, his eyes forced wide. "Jasper, I daresay you know Mr., uh, Pawnee Joe, isn't that right?"

Before he could respond, Pawnee splashed another glug into a tin cup. "I know that one all right. Gouging bastard, got a stranglehold on the town being the only store with any amount of stock in these parts. And his prices show it." Pawnee smiled, leaned back in his chair by the stove, the wood creaking under his middling weight.

"Now, Mr. Pawnee. I guess we all have a right to a fair profit on our goods," said Jasper through a tight-set smile.

"Fair, sure thing, fella. But every time I reprovision there, I leave bleeding and dizzy! It's almost as if I been scalped, but —"

"Okay, then, gents. I think we all understand each other here." Marshal Watt sat down heavily behind his desk. "Thing I want to know, and I'm sure you do too, is how we're going to deal with this . . . situation that has come up."

The bearded man chuckled and poured himself another splash of whiskey, then touched a finger to the side of his nose. "Now we're getting to it."

Jasper sighed, rolled his eyes at the marshal, who did his best to ignore him.

"Way I figure it, you two men have a valuable thing going on up in the hills. But it's at a precious spot now." He bucked the chair forward and it landed with a thud on the worn planks. "Might say it's a bit of a gamble, huh?" But he wasn't smiling.

"And?" said Rafferty, his arms crossed.

"And, Mr. High-and-Mighty, I could do one of three things." He eyed both of them.

The marshal didn't move a muscle in his chair, but returned the mountain man's stare. "Go on."

"I could call your bluff, I could raise the stakes, or I could sit tight with what I got. Hold for a spell."

"Now, see here," said Rafferty, springing to his feet, his long face under his bald dome bright red and popping dewy beads of sweat. "I will not tolerate a man such as yourself threatening me or my legitimate business venture. You have no authority, no say in the matter, do you understand? You've only been granted an audience here at Marshal Watt's behest and against my better judgment!"

Throughout Rafferty's little speech, Watt had tried to shout him down, but the merchant was too heated to have any of it. Finally the lawman sagged back in his chair and rubbed his forehead.

Pawnee Joe had leaned back in the chair once again, his buckskin-clad torso wrapped in his long arms until it looked as though he were hugging himself. It appeared to the marshal that he was doing all he could to not break into a grin and laugh.

"You about done, haughty man?"

Rafferty was set to pull in a second wind and start in again when the marshal bellowed, "Enough, Jasper!" The two business partners glared at each other.

Pawnee Joe sprang to his feet, still smiling, and headed to the door.

"Where are you going?" Marshal Watt stood, his fingers steepled on the desktop.

"Thinkin' maybe I'll go over to the Royale. Why?"

"Pawnee, I'd prefer it if you stay here now, at least until we hammer out this, uh, agreement we all need to come to."

The mountain man leaned against the

door. "Oh, Marshal. You really wanna dump lamp oil on this fire?" He regarded the lawman with a grim smile and a headshake. "Seems to me you and your uppity friend here ought to have more regard for me than that. I'll be thinkin' things through, but on my own, in my own way. Don't need no mother-hennin' from you." He left the office and the marshal watched the door close behind him.

"Why did you let him walk out of here, Watt?"

"What would you have me do, Jasper?"

"Why, you are the law in this town, are you not? You could have . . ."

"Could have what?" The marshal filled a cup with hot coffee from atop the stove.

"You should have detained him. Yes, that's it — you should have locked him up so he wouldn't wander around town drunk and blather all he knows about Gamble."

"Lock him up, eh? On what charges?"

"Who cares? You're the lawman, you think of something for a change." Rafferty stood and faced the wall, rubbing his thumb and forefinger into his eyes.

As the marshal returned to his desk, he heard the muttered word "incompetent" from Rafferty. That was all it took. He grabbed a handful of wool overcoat at the man's shoulder and spun him around. He didn't wait for Rafferty to settle and square off, but drove a solid right-hand jab into his jaw.

Rafferty's head whipped to the side, cutting off a strangled, confused shout. The tall shopkeep staggered, caromed off the door, and folded to the floor, one arm thrown up to protect his face.

But the marshal had finished with him. He walked to his desk and once again, sat down with a tired sigh. To think, this day had begun so promising. . . .

CHAPTER 37

After a few hours of hard struggle, it seemed they hadn't gotten all that far. And with the promise of snow greater with each minute that passed — the sky had turned a deep gray that reminded Hester of gun steel — they were all ready for a rest, especially the horses.

"Find us a spot where we can fetch us some water for these no-account horses." Rollie shouted the command forward, and Hester could see Shiner's shoulders slump. He'd heard too and knew it meant Rollie had selected them to fetch the water. It also meant that Rollie would remain seated in the wagon, drinking whiskey.

Without acknowledging Rollie's request, Shiner walked on another dozen yards, glancing toward the barely audible babble of the brook down a slight slope to their left. They'd been traveling alongside the thin but frigid-looking flow most of the day since leaving behind the horrible campsite where Bo and the mules had been killed.

Shiner headed down to the water, Hester made certain she was well out of range of Rollie's whip, should he take it into his head to lay the lash on her as he had been doing to the horses and as he had done to Norbert. She wondered where he'd been taken by the Indians.

It was Shiner's strangled scream that answered her question. Hester ran toward the stream, but Shiner ran back toward her. "No, no, no, you can't go down there. It's terrible!" He was nearly hysterical, breathing in short gasps and shaking all over. He'd only been gone from sight for a few seconds. What could he have seen that was so bad?

Hester shrugged away and pushed past him to see for herself. She didn't have to go far before she saw a figure crawling up out of the frozen stream. But no, that didn't make any sense. . . . The stream was mostly frozen, and the figure, partially covered in snow, wasn't moving, now that she looked harder at it. She walked closer. Even from that distance and under a dusting of the newly fallen snow, Hester saw that it was Norbert, facedown, arrows sticking from him.

"Aw, now, don't that beat all?" It was Rollie. He'd come up behind her and looked over Hester's shoulder at his former friend and employee.

"We should cut him free." Hester turned to Rollie and Shiner, a sudden thought occurring to her. "He might still be alive. We have to check. Cut my hands free so I can try."

"It's no use," said Shiner. "I already did — he's gone. I lifted him up to see if he was breathing, but . . . he'd been gutted."

"But —" said Hester, taking a hesitant step toward the body.

"No! Dang it, girl, you leave him be! I said he's dead!" Shiner shouted the words and they all froze. The man had to this point been a quiet sort, rarely raising his voice, except to curse and laugh. Hester guessed he was telling the truth.

"Well, there you have it," said Rollie, shaking his head and walking back to the wagon. "Let's get going before we're forced to stay right here at this gruesome spot."

"But aren't we going to —" Again, Hester was interrupted, this time by Rollie.

"Going to what? Bury him? Too frozen. Besides, we ain't got Big Boy here to dig for us!" He chuckled and climbed up into the wagon. "Now let's go!"

Shiner didn't move. He shook visibly and

kept stealing glances down toward the brook.

"Shiner! Woman! Get your asses moving. Now!" Rollie cranked back on his Colt's hammer and fired a shot. It whistled, a tight shot, between Shiner and Hester. They both yelped and headed back up the trail, the snow thickening slightly as they resumed their places before the horses, breaking a feeble trail for them to follow.

Hester hoped the trip would not get any worse. She didn't think it was possible to live through any more horrors and still remain in control of her mind. And then she knew that such a hope was foolish. Of course there were more horrible things to come, if only for the fact that there were still people alive for them to happen to . . . including herself.

CHAPTER 38

"Charlie?"

"Yeah, Delia?" Charlie paused, worried about the new snow that had begun to fall, and looked back toward the travois. He'd rigged it up — two long poles that crossed at the top and a third about four feet wide at the base, all lashed together and dragged by him with straps he'd retrieved from the last wagon they'd come across.

Truth be told, he was relieved for the rest. The task of punching boot heels in the snow had been anything but easy. Now with the definite promise of another fresh storm on the wind, the snow already falling, Charlie wanted to gain as much ground as he could before it hit fully. Something in the air — an extra-sharp snap when he breathed in, a tang, told him that this new snowfall was the early edge of a coming storm, and that it might well be a corker. He had been tromping in the high mountains for far too long to not recognize such hard-to-define symptoms.

"Charlie, what do you think was wrong with those wolves?"

She was still thinking about the attack. He had been mighty impressed with her and how she kept cool in the situation, but now he wondered if maybe her sickness wasn't playing with her mind a little. She kept asking him about it. It was a good question, but one for which he had no answer that would satisfy anyone who knew much about wolves.

"I believe they were caught up in all the excitement with the carcasses of those oxen." At the mention of them, he thought back to the amazing sight that had greeted them when they inspected the carcasses the next morning.

He had expected to see much more than he did see. But what they found were picked-clean bone racks surrounded by blood-pinked snow. True, there was still plenty of hide and gristle, some meat, but only in the hard-to-reach places. Charlie reckoned that by the following day there wouldn't be much left but picked-and-licked bones, gleaming yellow-white against the cold snow.

"You think they might follow us, don't

you?" said Delia.

"I never said that, Delia. But you did — a handful of times already. I didn't know better, I'd swear you are trying to get me to walk faster." He smiled down at her, laid out on the travois. He'd managed to truss her in with soft wraps of cloth over the blankets, and all on top of a cushion of pine boughs for comfort. At least he hoped she was comfortable. He guessed that Delia wouldn't complain if she had a mouthful of glass.

What a trouper she was. And her sister too. He'd been heartened to begin seeing tracks that he could read, and he was sure of a couple of things — they were still following the freighters, and Hester and Mabel-Mae were still alive.

But as good as it was to see tracks he could recognize, he hardly needed them since there was only the one trail for them to travel to get to Gamble. Charlie had never been much of a hand at tracking and trailing and reading sign. He reckoned he'd learned enough over the years to get himself into trouble.

He decided to change the subject, get Delia off haranguing the topic of the wolves and worrying herself in circles. "You know how a while back I told you I believe I saw

359

Hester's boot prints?"

"Yeah," said Delia, as more of a hopeful question. She squinted up at Charlie, the sky's clouded light keeping her eyes half lidded.

"Well, I was right. And it looks like they still have Mabel-Mae too." He smiled, hoping the good news would perk her up. It seemed to, but he knew she was in pain. And he had nothing to give her for it. "We best get cracking on if we're going to gain more ground before snow or nightfall, whichever catches up with us first."

"Or wolves."

"Now, enough of that talk," said Charlie, not a little irritated. He repositioned the travois straps over his shoulders and wrapped them around his meaty fists. And trudged slowly onward, each step sure and deep.

"I'm sorry, Charlie. Tell me about Mabel-Mae. How'd you get her?"

"Oh well, that's a good story. But I tell you right now, you don't 'get' a mule like Mabel-Mae. You find her, sort of like you find a good friend and you know you're going to be friends for a long time."

"Sort of like us, right, Charlie?"

"Yes, ma'am. Exactly like us. Fast friends for life." Then as soon as he said it he felt bad — her life wouldn't be all that long. But if she caught onto his slip, she didn't say a thing.

"I'm glad to hear that, Charlie. Now, about Mabel-Mae . . ."

"Well, I was in a small mine camp in northern California, place called Bluebell, though there wasn't a thing pretty about it, not like such a name would indicate anyway. More rock and mud than anything else — except for dumb rock hounds like me. I was doing myself some digging, not having much luck, and not doing myself any favors howling at the moon at night and waking up thickheaded and poorer with each sunrise." He grinned and shook his head at the memory.

"Well, along about my fifth month there, with my meager claim all but dug away, I was thinking about selling up, heading out, when an old man showed up at my claim. He was riding old Mabel-Mae. No, that's not quite the truth. More like he was falling off her, hanging on to her neck with a couple of skinny old arms. I'll never forget the sight. I'd had a few dry days — no money for whiskey, and not much around the place to do but shoot rabbits and work the rocker and a pan, hoping for gold with each swirl. So I was stone sober — otherwise

I might have thought I was having what the Indians call 'visions' — and I looked up and seen this old man a-hanging off this mule."

Charlie glanced back at Delia to make sure she was listening.

"Go on," she said, her face eager for more.

Good, he thought. *It might help keep her mind off her pain.* "The old man raised his head. He had a shaggy knot of long gray hair that sort of mixed in with his beard, and he looked at me. I could tell he was sick and not long for the world." Charlie clamped his teeth tight together. This wasn't the sort of thing a dying girl should be hearing. Would he never learn?

"It's okay, Charlie. I want to hear the story as it happened. Don't whitewash anything."

"Okay, then," he said, keeping an eye on the trail, pressing his lips together to melt the ice on his beard and mustache whiskers. They were running close by a stream and he thought he might stop in a few minutes. They could drink their fill and he could catch his wind again. Ever since Rollie and his boys took a few rounds out of him, he'd been healing but mighty slow. At this rate, it would take a long while.

"The old man fixed me with a look and then groaned and fell right off that mule. I dropped my pan and stomped on over to hm. He'd fallen half in that old silty stream, so I yanked him out of there and laid him on my bed. He was a skinny drink of water, not much more on him than raggy clothes and hair."

"Then what happened, Charlie?"

"Well, I was convinced he was going to . . . well, that he might up and die on me. I looked him over, didn't see any signs of a fight, nor wounds of any kind. So I guessed he had a sickness of some sort — that scared me, I can tell you. But I couldn't turn him away, so I tended to him as best I could. No one would come around once word got out that I was harboring a sick man. Some folks claimed he had cholera, others scarlet fever, still others said pneumonia. One crazy old woman who prospected by herself shouted to me that she was sure he had something called leprosy. Said parts of him was going to fall off, can you imagine?"

"Did he fall apart or die on you?" Delia asked.

"No, sir, the old rig lived. After a while, why, he up and lived! Got better and better. I reckon he was old, tired, and hungry, though maybe not in that order. Insisted on paying me once he got well. Course, I didn't want nothing, only happy to see he was alive. He didn't have much to his name anyway. Turns out he was an old prospector name of Mac Winkler. He had taken to prospecting when his wife died years before. Named every mule he ever had after her — Mabel-Mae."

"So what happened to him?"

"I swear, Delia, you sound disappointed that he didn't turn out to be a wanted man or that his head or legs didn't fall off." Charlie chuckled. "Well, ol' Mac told me he was too old and tired to keep on moving. Said he wanted to settle down. I, on the other hand, felt the opposite. I was too young to be stuck on my claim, trapped there with nothing to do, no way to leave. So you can guess what was coming, right?"

"You didn't swap your claim for Mabel-Mae?"

"Naw. I give him the claim, fair and square. I was getting close to up and walking off it anyway. So I came up with the idea that he would have to put me up whenever I was in town."

"So how did you get Mabel-Mae?"

"Well, like I said." Charlie blinked hard to melt the snow from his eyelashes. "Ol' Mac insisted on paying me for helping him get well. Then when I up and gave him the claim with my little shack on it, why, he insisted. I didn't want the mule, truth be told, figured she'd be another mouth to feed and I have trouble enough keeping myself in vittles. But in the end, he grew downright ornery. I never saw such a cross old man. Acted like I was insulting him. Can you imagine that? So I took the mule off his hands to keep him quiet, figured I'd sell her down the road somewhere."

He trudged on, slowing more with each step, ready for a break. "Funny thing happened, though."

"Hmm?"

"Mabel-Mae ended up helping me out more ways than I can say. She provided me with transportation now and again, though in case you hadn't noticed, I'm on the big side, so I don't like to burden her with too much of that sort of thing. But she also carried freight. I began hauling light loads of goods up into the hills for lone miners too poor, too busy, or too plain dumb to come down and get their own supplies. They paid me gratefully in dust and I got by. She's also a pretty good listener. A lot like you."

"I will pretend you didn't compare me with a mule, Mr. Chilton. Now, whatever happened to Mac Winkler?" said Delia.

"You won't believe it, but a while back somebody told me that old man struck a sweet spot on that worthless claim of mine and made himself a tidy little sum. Enough to get him to Frisco. Now, I don't rightly know what happened to him there. Could still be there to this day. Could be he owns the whole waterfront. Myself, I never did cotton to big towns, so I reckon I'll never find out what happened to ol' Mac Winkler. But I do know what happened to his mule."

Charlie smiled, looked back at Delia, but her attention had been pulled away by something else. She was squinting down-slope to Charlie's left, toward the half-frozen brook they'd been traveling alongside for most of the day. She had a sock-covered hand visoring her eyes as they focused on something down there.

Charlie followed her sight line to the mostly frozen brook, one of the feeder streams that flowed to the Salmon River down below. Hard to tell through the thickening snow, but it looked to Charlie as if it could be a man half in, half out of the brook. But that didn't make any sense.

"Must be a stump," he said. "Reckon I'll check on it, to be safe. We need water anyway. I'll bring you back a drink."

Delia struggled feebly to uncinch herself from the travois. "I can help, Charlie. I'll go down there with you."

"No, you won't neither." He laid a big paw on her head. "You keep still. I will be right back." He unslung the cloth-wrapped shotgun from across his chest and turned to go. He tried to keep his big body between her and the thing at the brook, in case it turned out to be something hard to take. With each step closer, the thing looked less and less like a stump or a rock, and more and more like a man.

"I mean it," he shouted, looking back once at the frustrated woman on the trail.

He chose his steps with care, as the new snow had begun to obscure everything before him. But not enough to hide the fact that when he got to the brook side, he was looking at a dead man, facedown in the snow. Shafts of two arrows were driven down into the man's sides.

Charlie kneeled down, brushed snow off the man's head, and his suspicions were confirmed. "Norbert, what has happened to you, mister? By gum, you can't keep yourself out of the water, can you?"

Charlie shifted his knee off something hard, a rock or root, and happened to look down and got a fright. He'd been kneeling on the dead man's arm. He brushed more snow off it and saw that it had been tied about the wrist and staked with leather stretching off to the base of a nearby sapling. He looked to the other side and found the same thing.

"What did you find, Charlie?" Delia shouted from back on the trail.

He swallowed, nibbled his mustache, and hesitated before shouting back, "Hang on a minute. Give me a minute here."

Charlie bent low and, keeping the shotgun gripped in one hand, he stepped closer to the brook, angled himself so that he kneeled with one leg beside the man. It looked to him as though Norbert had been cut in half. But why tie off his arms? Norbert hadn't been scalped. His head where Charlie had brushed the snow away to get a look at his face had looked to be bruised up a bit, but not cut up and peeled. So was it the Indians or Rollie? From what he'd seen of the handiwork of both of them, he'd not put anything so foul past either.

Charlie brushed more snow from the man's back, saw the grimy buckskin tunic had been slit in ragged cuts crosswise, as though by a knife. He guessed it didn't matter who had done it at this point, but that someone had done something bad to the man.

Charlie inched lower and gingerly tested the ice with his boot, then his knee. It was solid all right, as he guessed it would be close to the bank. It was barely crusted over in the middle, a few feet away. He heard the gurgling, saw the cold flow bubbling here and there through holes up and down the length of it in the slowly forming ice.

As with most mountain runs, he guessed that what it lacked in width it made up for in depth, gained in the spring when the freshets ran, gouging and carving their way downslope with the melt water.

He cleared away more snow and saw a vague, dark outline, murky under the ice, of what he assumed was the lower half of Norbert's body. "Oh, Norbert, whatever you did wasn't hardly deserving of this end. You have my hearty sorrow, fella."

"Charlie?"

It was Delia. He reckoned he owed her some explanation about now. "I'll be up directly. Sit tight."

Charlie eyed the situation, decided not to slice free Norbert's stiff, frozen arms, the fingers clawing as if in the middle of trying to drag himself out of the freezing water. But the arrows at his side had him pinned in place. He must have been sufficiently weakened at that point to not be able to snap the arrows, drag himself out and to safety.

The ground hadn't frozen so hard that the shafts, loosed at such close range as they'd required, wouldn't sink deep enough to prevent an injured man from yanking them free. The pain must have been hard to take. Up to then, Charlie hadn't looked closely at Norbert's face, but when he did, he saw the buck skinner's long face drawn even longer in a rictus of agony, his eyes, yellowed and wide, staring with glassy intensity at something Charlie hoped he'd never see himself. From the man's look, it must have been the worst terror imaginable.

If only those eyes could show him the last people Norbert had seen. Charlie looked back upslope toward the trail, but the snow had covered over anything that might be a useful track to him.

Charlie laid the shotgun alongside Norbert's prone top half and slipped his knife from its sheath. He used it to chip at the ice, a couple of inches thick, around Norbert's waist, where it disappeared into the stream. Within minutes he had a ring cleared around the man's midsection and pawed chunks of ice away, freeing the crusted-in buckskin. Soon the body was loosened enough for Charlie to drag him free. But first he had to remove the arrows pinning Norbert's sides.

Charlie gripped one low and gently worked it back and forth, but it soon snapped off. He cursed, then did the same with the other, snapping that one also. He sliced through the leather thongs tethering Norbert's outstretched arms, then turned his attention back to the arrows. They had broken off low enough that he could raise Norbert up slightly off the jagged nubs. He gently lifted the body up by his arms, close under his shoulders. It was then that he saw the blackened snow and earth under Norbert's body, saw the man's guts frozen tight to the riverbank.

Charlie froze for a moment, unsure what to do. He wanted to drop the man's body and bolt back up the trail, drag that girl to someplace safe, anywhere — he had no idea where . . . anywhere.

But after the moment of shock at seeing the frozen intestines and closing his eyes and pulling in a deep breath, he looked back to his task and set the man down gently. He would have to free the frozen parts of the man before he could finish dragging him out of the frozen, barely burbling brook.

He also realized that the few minutes he'd spent dealing with the man were precious minutes they could have used on the trail, to once again find someplace to hole up for the night, make a shelter.

But he couldn't leave the dead man like this. Charlie thought for a moment, then lowered Norbert's body back down to the ground. He fished in his mackinaw's large outer pocket and pulled out a tin can, one they had been using to drink from. Charlie had a devil of a time doing it, but he kept ferrying water from the slurry of slush he'd made around Norbert's body at the surface of the river. All the while he lifted with his other arm, trying to keep freeing the frozen man's guts from the riverbank.

Charlie splashed the water under the man, pushed up, splashed, pushed, loosening the frozen parts more with each dose of freezing water. He had to work quick or it would all freeze up again. Three, then four more inches and he'd have it. And finally Norbert lifted free of the frozen mud as Charlie had stretched as far as he could.

He leaned back, out of breath and trying not to look at the frozen clot of gut and the blue-gray face with those shocked eyes staring wide open.

"What are you going to do with him?"

Charlie spun, breathing heavy and clawing for the shotgun. "Delia!"

The girl had freed herself from the travois and had made her way down the trail. Her face was white and her hands trembled from the effort, but she stared at Norbert with a squint-eyed look, more curiosity than fear or disgust.

Charlie sighed, rose to his feet. "I don't know. But I'm about tired of finding death along this trail. I'd give a whole lot to be someplace else right about now."

"Me too," Delia said, covering her mouth with a hand. "Hester would say, 'If wishes were horses, beggars would ride.' "

"I reckon she'd be right too. And no, I don't know what to do with him. But I couldn't leave him like that." Charlie looked at Delia. "I'm not sure how much you saw, but it was a grim sight."

"Hasn't gotten much better, has it?" Delia finally turned away, hugging herself and pulling her blanket tight around her shoulders. She'd draped it over her head too, forming a sort of hooded cape, but now the entire affair was quickly being covered in the thick, falling snow.

"Ol' Norbert'll have to make do with leaning against a tree and knowing he'll fortify some animal or other in these hard, cold days of winter. Nothing else we can do, except maybe try to remember the good things about him. And we best get to it because the weather's not waiting for us.

You feel that breeze picking up?"

Delia looked up toward the treetops, but ducked her head back down quick. The only thing Charlie knew she'd see was snow, snow, and more snow, coming down faster with each passing minute.

CHAPTER 39

It wasn't far up the trail that Charlie and Delia found yet another wagon. The thick snowfall had covered much of any sign that might have let him know how many people and animals were still trekking toward Gamble. But a bit of ciphering told him that they would be down to their last wagon, down to how many horses and mules he wasn't sure, since some could have run off or died along the way and they'd not seen them under the snow.

"One thing is for certain, Delia. Ol' Rollie Meecher can't be too happy right about now. From the looks of it, they left this camp with their last wagon, and from the lumps in the snow, he left behind a lot of the goods he'd planned to gouge the Gamble folks with."

Delia didn't respond. She was hurting, and this time she couldn't even pretend the episode would pass soon. Charlie was thankful the abandoned wagon had more usable freight goods than ever. He laid Delia up under the wagon and set to work on building a windbreak on the north side of the exposed wagon. He tore off a few boards from the south side of the wagon and managed to deflect the wind and snow enough to keep the worst of the gale off the girl.

The space under the wagon was far from cozy, but if he could get a fire going and maybe find some food to supplement the last of their meager ox meat left, they should make out okay. This blow was shaping up to be a corker. He finally managed to kindle a small blaze and fed it with hunks of boards he'd snapped braced against the wagon tongue.

Then he checked Delia once again, found her wide awake, but in considerable pain. Her eyes were nearly shut and she held her mouth in a tight, hard line. She nodded in annoyance when he asked her a couple of questions.

"I'm going to find you something to eat, don't you worry," he said.

What he really wanted was to find something to help her with the pain. He didn't know a thing about natural remedies, much less how to find the ingredients and concoct a tincture in the middle of a blizzard.

He climbed up into the wagon and pushed snow off the odd shapes within. A couple of crates of tinned food, not bad. And there seemed to be plenty of it. He loaded his pockets. He could make do with tinned fruit, milk, and a couple of cans of corn. And then he saw something promising . . . but it couldn't be.

Still, he reached for it, brushed off the cold, clotted snow, and there it was — a bottle of whiskey, brand-new and standing in the corner of the wagon, behind the seat. Might have belonged to one of Rollie's men, maybe Rollie himself, and they'd left it behind. But it might help with Delia's pain. He dang sure doubted it could hurt.

Charlie took another look around, scattering other items that would be useless to them — a set of three glass oil lamps, a few candles. He stuffed a couple into his pocket with the tinned food. You never knew when something might come in handy.

The rest he'd do his best to burn for warmth. Some of these meager pickings would have been the very food and gear that Rollie had been so set on using against the residents of Gamble. Holding it hostage so they would be desperate enough to venture out in hopes of getting it from him. Until he killed them for trying.

So if he was leaving all of these potentially valuable goods abandoned on the trail, what was he up to now? No doubt he was running scared, what with all the abandoned wagons, dead animals, and even a lost man — unless it was Rollie who did such terrible things to Norbert.

Charlie left off with such thinking and dragged a pile of crates over to the edge of the wagon, then hopped down. Some he broke up for firewood, others he jammed in the snow to help keep the wind from gusting out the young fire.

"Delia, I found some tasty food for us, girl. And something else, something that will help with the pain."

"What is it?" she said, her voice muffled from under the blankets and scrap of tarp he'd tucked around her.

"Whiskey. Now, I'm no doctor, but I do know that this will help dull the worst of it, that much is for certain."

Delia spoke, but Charlie had to lean close to hear her. "I don't know, Charlie. Hester wouldn't think very much of me drinking."

"Well, girl, Hester ain't here. And ol' Charlie is. So I reckon we'll have to risk disappointing her, because I know a thing or two about snake juice and it's the best thing we have for helping you right now, Delia."

She didn't say yes, but then again, she didn't say no either. Then he saw her pale hand grab at her belly, heard her pull a sharp breath in through her mouth.

"That tears it, girl. Not only is it the best thing we have for your pain, it's the only thing we have." He uncorked it and glugged a few liberal splashes into the drinking tin, then held it before her face. She nodded and he helped her hold the cup. Soon he saw her hand relax, her shoulders loosen a bit.

"That better, Delia?"

She nodded and like a little bird, moved her head forward. He helped her with another sip. "If you think that's enough for now, I'll heat us up some food. Scare up more wood before the storm gets worse."

"Thanks, Charlie. I feel better already."

"Well, good. But be careful. That stuff will sneak up on you. Best to ration it so you'll have some for tomorrow too."

She nodded and he heaved his bulk back out from under the wagon. Once he felt the wind slicing at him, driving stinging flecks of snow and ice into his cheeks and eyes, he realized what a decent little shelter he'd made, and he was relieved for it. The girl

379

would need a night's rest, and so would he. For what, he had no idea. Whatever lay ahead, he hoped Lady Luck would keep them in favor.

He'd tromped into the trees and kicked at the snow, hoping to turn up windfall branches, anything that might burn. He stumbled over a snow-mounded rock, landed on it with his knees, and realized it didn't feel like a rock or a log.

After clearing away snow, he felt the softness of hide stretched tight over a frozen body. There beside it lay another. He cleared more, got to the head, saw the stained snow under the fresh snow that he'd pushed away, and also saw the telltale oversized ears of the mule. His heart did a double dance in his cavernous chest and he mumbled a low "Oh no, not Mabel-Mae. . . ."

The nearest one wasn't. He stumbled over that carcass to the next, his mouth set in a grim line at the prospect of finding her dead. But it wasn't. And while he hated to see these two had been laid low by something or someone, he didn't mind admitting his relief that neither was Mabel-Mae.

As near as Charlie could tell from low-scanning the terrain close by, there were few other beast-sized lumps in the snow, save for one smaller rise a ways behind the wagon. Looked to be a sizable bit of wood, something like a branch sticking up from it. He blinked away the snow crystals collecting on his lashes and struggled one step at a time through the knee-height snow. He tried to clear away the snow with a boot, but soon had to drop to his already-wet knees and use his hands. And he wished he hadn't.

Once the upright stick of a branch was closer to his face, he recognized it for what it was — an arrow. Just like the ones that had been sticking out of Norbert's body, pinning him in place at the brook. Who was this, then? Despair and fear drenched down over him all at once. *Please don't let it be Hester. . . .*

For long moments, Charlie Chilton didn't dare clear away any more snow from whoever might be before him. If it was Hester, what would he tell Delia? It couldn't be Hester. He didn't want to live with himself knowing he'd been the one to let her down. She'd trusted him, counted on him to . . . no, he knew that wasn't exactly the truth. She was a strong woman capable of taking care of herself. Wasn't she?

He forced himself to look down again, and then as if seeing his actions slowed down no faster than the sweep hand on a clock, Charlie watched as his mitten-covered paws dug and brushed the snow from the person.

And as with the mule a few minutes before, Charlie felt guilt-tarnished relief at seeing it was a man's body, Bo if he wasn't mistaken.

As with Norbert, he would not shed tears over this man's death, but he did feel bad. No man begins life as a rogue and an ill-intentioned fool. He ends up that way as a matter of his own choosing. But Charlie figured Bo deserved more than to be left out here. He might well deserve better, as did Norbert, and all the rest of the bodies, human and animal alike, they'd left along the trail, but they wouldn't receive anything special from him. Charlie had to care for the living.

And unless he found Hester's body somewhere hereabouts, he'd have to assume she was still alive and still with Rollie and Shiner, the only ones left. He had to find them before the vicious, killing Indians did. But everything seemed to fight against him — the weather, his traveling companion's illness, hunger, and mostly the fact that both Rollie and the Indians were ahead of him.

Then a thought occurred to him. An image of the drunken Bo came to mind, and Charlie recalled that the man had worn a holstered sidearm. "Sorry, Bo," said Charlie as he dug out more snow around the body, but he found no gun belt. While he was at the grim task, he flipped the stiff body on its side and made a quick search of Bo's coat pockets. He'd been hoping for matches, but found nothing that might be useful to them.

He flopped the body back to its facedown pose and covered it over with snow, in case Delia should look in this direction. But with this snow, he doubted she'd see much farther than the campfire. And at the thought of the warming element, he rose, stiff and slow to his feet, and returned to the wagon to strip away more wood in preparation for a long, cold night.

Chapter 40

From behind Hester, Rollie's already-slurring voice rose above the whistling snow, the blowing of the struggling mules and horses, and the random squawk of a wheel begging for grease. "Get walkin', woman! Or I swear I will lay this lash right down on you, you hear?"

Hester picked up her pace and raised her head to make sure she was still on what looked like the trail. The snow had begun to come down harder over the past few hours until seeing more than five feet ahead had become difficult. She wasn't even sure what time it might be, not that it mattered.

An image of Norbert popped into her mind and she felt a tug of sadness. Yes, he'd been one of the hated freighters, but there had been something about him that was almost decent. As if he had struggled with the very idea of being Rollie's so-called friend. And now he was dead. Or was he?

Had that even happened? Had they really seen him dead on the bank of the brook, as if he had been trying to climb out of the frozen water? Of course it had happened, she told herself. But the dizzying effect of the snow, the cold, her throbbing hands, her tired legs, her weakness from lack of decent food — it all seemed to work together to make her confused somehow. Then a gust of raw wind sliced straight at her like a slap to the face and roused her once again. She blinked hard and walked on.

If they kept on like this, they might well totter off the edge of one of those spots she'd seen earlier, off to her left as the trail narrowed and wound along a steep drop-off. It wouldn't take much for the wagon and Rollie to pitch to the side and crash down a rocky slope. The phantom vision brought a smile to her face, only to disappear at the thought of Mabel-Mae, who the last Hester knew was still tied behind the wagon, still trudging along silently, without complaining, mile after mile.

And thought of the kindly old mule brought Charlie and, so, Delia to mind. It was all Hester could do to not spin and run straight back at Rollie, with but one thing in mind. But that would only get her killed, of that she was sure. He had shown no worry or concern over harming others.

Maybe she could wander off into the snow and hide from Rollie, then sneak up on him later and . . . *Foolish woman,* Hester chided herself. There was no way that was going to happen. Not with Shiner up ahead, looking back on her every now and again, and with Rollie snapping his whip and shouting his drunken anger at her back at odd times, as though he did it to keep her frightened and confused.

Hester trudged on for more lengthy minutes. Some time later she looked up, the wind doing its best to peel the blanket from her shoulder and head. Loose strands of her hair whipped away from her face, and icy snow peppered her face. Where was Shiner? As much as she despised the filthy man, today she had grown to rely on seeing his back a dozen paces ahead. But he was gone.

Hester took one more long step, sinking up to her knees in the thick, dense snow. She half turned and looked behind her. She swore she heard a voice other than Rollie's, maybe a high-pitched shout, like a scream. Probably that squawking wagon wheel.

The wagon was farther behind than ever. Through the snow she saw Rollie still in the seat, heard his whip cracking and Rollie's drunken shouts urging the beasts onward. Maybe Shiner had gone back to the wagon for a drink from Rollie's bottle. Maybe he had wandered far ahead. Or . . . did she dare hope? Maybe the man wandered off one of the steep-sided stretches of trail they'd passed along earlier. With this snow and with Rollie's drinking, no one might know.

Hester's heart beat faster. In the span of a few slight seconds, she had all but decided that this was her time to escape, to keep low and scramble off the trail, down the slope, somehow cut through the rawhide straps around her wrists — maybe on the edge of a sharp rock — and make her way . . . where? What was out here? Did she care? No, as she'd told herself time and again, there was but one thing left for her to do, and that was to kill Rollie Meecher.

And then she thought of the Indians stalking them. What if they got her? No, she couldn't let that happen, not before she took care of Rollie.

Then she caught a whiff of something, smoke maybe. And as quickly, it was gone.

"Hey! Where's Shiner at?" Rollie spat into the snow as the exhausted team dragged closer. "Woman! Where's he got to? Takin' a leak, is he?" This struck Rollie as funny and

Hester watched as he leaned back in the wagon seat and shook with silent laughter.

The blowing snow made it increasingly difficult for Hester to see the wagon. She heard the beasts' harsh breathing, their chuffing and blowing, groans and low neighs as one or another slipped, driving an already bleeding knee back to the unforgiving snow and ice pack beneath. And yet, because of the guttural shouts and painful whistle-and-cut of the whip, they continued to lumber forward in the thick white piling snow before them.

It was now above her knees and halfway up the wagon's wheels. And still Rollie, after his laughing fit, had resumed the lash. Hester refused to go on and instead stood in the middle of the trail, as defiant as she could look in such conditions. The wagon ground to a squeaking halt, the horses and mules hanging their heads as if bowing in deference to her.

Hester reckoned the hour barely past midday, but the exhaustion of the animals was evident. Their pink tongues thrust outward, stiff and trembling, their rubbery mouths steaming and flecked with foam. Great clouds of smoky breath rose from them as though they were trains huffing after an uphill stretch. Hester raised her bound hands and gently rubbed them on the head of the horse before her.

"I tell you what, they are near useless. Time was you could get animals with some sand, some bottom to 'em. Nowadays you got this!" He popped the whip over their heads. Hester felt the air whistle and crack. The animals lunged, but in their stalled and exhausted state the best they could muster was a halfhearted few inches of momentum. The wagon slowly rolled back to its earlier ruts.

He laughed again. "I swear I am hungry for some meat! Something in the air reminding me of a thick cut. You hungry, woman?" More laughter.

Hester was about to curse him, no longer caring of the outcome, whether he whipped her to death or shot at her in his drunkenness. But she never got the chance to give voice to her rage because, from the hillside above them, to the right of the wagon, far too high to see in the whistling, wind-driven snow, something large and dark dove out of the white gloom and straight down on Rollie.

Hester saw it all, watched the shape emerge from the snow, into view, and fall heavily. Rollie saw none of it, as he was busily sucking on a bottle that seemed to have reached its end. But when the large, dark shape slapped with a loud crash partly on him and partly on the bench beside him, causing a loud cracking sound, the wooden-plank seat snapping like a gunshot, that's when Rollie reacted.

The freighting boss screamed high pitched and long and loud, as if he were a young child seeing something in the shadows that wasn't there. But there was something there, and Hester saw it at the same time Rollie did. They both screamed.

It was a blackened, smoking man. And in the following seconds that it took Hester to figure out that it was a burned man, she knew with certainty that it was Shiner. Burned and thrown down at them from on high. She looked up, into the dizzying, driving snow, but saw nothing.

As soon as Rollie figured out what had dropped down on him, his screams took on an even harsher edge, a higher-pitched squeal as he tried to slide from beneath the flopped, charred, smoking remains. The pulling beasts lunged, each trying to run in an opposing direction, resulting in none moving too far from any other. They ended up standing in their same spots, blowing and champing, not at all comfortable with the raw stink of burned man.

Rollie made it to the ground, fell into the snow, and flailed his arms trying to stand. He finally accomplished the task and slid his Colt, fast and easy, from its holster. Despite the fact that he'd been drinking for hours, in smooth motions he cocked and fired, cocked and fired far above, up into the driving gloom, until his gun was empty. He stood staring into the snow, his Colt's barrel smoking, his mouth agape. His dead friend lay sprawled, broken and awkward, across the splintered seat of the wagon.

A half hour later, unable to force the beasts to move in any direction, Rollie and Hester made camp on that spot in the trail. Rollie had not tried to move Shiner, nor had he asked Hester to do so, even though she had fully expected it.

They left the animals in the traces and Hester had had a few moments when Rollie was still babbling, drunk and confused and scared, to check on Mabel-Mae. The mule was still there, standing with her head down, hip-shot and quiet, behind the wagon. Hester rubbed the long nose, spoke soft meaningless words of apology to her. If any of it mattered, the mule made no sign, save for the flick of an ear. Hester chose to believe that meant she was forgiven for whatever her part in this nightmare trek had been.

Hester untied the mule and moved her to the downslope side of the wagon, where she retied her.

"What are you up to, woman?" Rollie belched and gestured at the mule as he sloppily reloaded his pistol.

"I'm getting her out of the wind." In truth, Hester wondered if whoever had killed Shiner was still up there, most likely the Indians, then they might attack from up above, and moving Mabel-Mae was the only thing she could think of doing for the animal. She felt responsible for her somehow. As if she owed it to Big Charlie Chilton to do what she could to keep the sweet beast safe, little though the gesture would amount to.

"Leave off that foolishness and cook me some food, curse your hide!" Rollie spat the words and gurgled back more whiskey.

Hester considered untying Mabel-Mae and riding off, but dark was fast descending and she didn't think they would make it far at all. They'd be lucky to not topple off one of the steep cuts, let alone stay on the trail.

She was exhausted, and imagined Mabel-Mae was too. And besides, if he wanted her help with all those chores, he would have to cut her hands free. And who knew what that might bring? Still, she convinced him she needed use of her hands, and he complied, though he railed about how he'd be watching her for any sign of treachery against him.

Hester did her best to ignore him and went about the business of setting up the camp. She didn't know what tomorrow would bring, or the rest of the day, for that matter. But she was relieved that they had stopped. The animals were in desperate need of rest and she felt as though she could hardly go on.

True to his word — and his character thus far on the trip — Rollie did very little but drink and wag his Colt revolver in her direction whenever she caught his eye. It seemed he was always watching her.

Which is why he didn't see the man watching them from the trees on the slope above the camp.

The snow still fell thickly, but not so much that Hester couldn't tell it was an Indian, mostly from the way he stood, unafraid, arms folded across his chest, staring straight at her, as if daring her to scream or drop to the ground in a faint.

She did neither. Instead she regarded him fully, a frying pan in one of her hands, a hunk of side bacon in another.

"What you staring at, woman?" Rollie was facing her, with his back to the Indian.

Hester looked at Rollie, shook her head, then looked back to the Indian, but he was gone. She looked hard at the trees, but she only saw snow and trees and little else. Had she really seen him? Yes, she decided she had. Just as she had definitely seen poor dead Norbert earlier in the day.

Hester bent to her task at the fire, smiling. She had a feeling something was going to happen that night. One way or another, good or bad — though she suspected it would no doubt be bad — something was going to happen to them that very night, and maybe even sooner.

Rollie had seemed much drunker earlier than he was, now that the light had faded and the small fire was snapping. She had stretched the canvas tarpaulin, tied to trees and the wagon, to help cut the wind. It helped. She cut open two tins of meat and they ate in silence, across the fire from each other.

Rollie's wobbling head occasionally looked up, focused on her across the guttering blaze, and he would try to smile. But she knew that he had been rattled to his boots, no mistake. She didn't think he'd try anything foul that night. He was far too bothered by what the Indians had done to Shiner.

For long minutes, Hester stared into the fire. There was a sickened, deranged part of her that envied Shiner the escape he'd made, burned to death in a blizzard. She was gripped with the sudden urge to laugh. If she didn't she might well cry and cry and never stop. And crying was not something Hester O'Fallon had ever had the luxury of doing. So she gave full and free rein to her laughter, long loud bellows of it.

She leaned back and into it until she cried from the throat-aching laughs that bubbled up and out of her. Rollie regarded her as if she were some sort of attraction at one of the mystery tents at the traveling circuses, the sort of show that only the daring ever ventured forth to see. And still she laughed, didn't give a whit what Rollie Meecher thought of her. Let him shoot, let him whip.

But Rollie Meecher did watch her. And he did not have shooting or whipping on his mind.

It didn't take long for Rollie to sidle on over to her. Hester didn't try to evade him. He was drunk, no doubt seeing double. But Hester's hands were still untied, and in her right hand, stuffed tight into the waist pocket of her dress, she gripped the handle of a short knife she'd managed to filch from the cooking crate. In fact, as he approached, she tried to quell a grim smile, knowing soon he would get something of what he'd earned for himself.

He sat down beside her and leaned close, the boozy reek of his breath clouding her. "I expect you know what's about to happen."

She stared at him a moment, her eyes half-lidded in a sultry look. "I don't care."

"You don't? Why not? Why you smiling, girly? Could be you know what sort of fun you are about to have?"

She shook her head. "No, that's not it. It's because we're being hunted, you idiot. And each person so far on this trip has died in a horrible manner. Some of them by your hand, some of them not. Unless you are going to kill yourself, that means you will likely be killed next."

That seemed to have the effect of cutting through Rollie's drunken fog. His eyes opened wide. "Why me?"

Hester smiled. "Because each one so far has been a man, and you are a man. Last one left, in fact. That means you are next." She couldn't help herself — she laughed right in his face. Laughed at the fear she saw hovering there, twitching his mouth corners, tugging at his cheeks, raising his eyelids high.

She didn't expect that he would react as he did to her brazen, half-formed deduction. She expected he would shrug it off and attack her. She had steeled herself for it, had clenched tight to the short knife in her hand, ready to end the pig's life.

But he disappointed her.

Rollie scrambled backward, one hand on his revolver, the other clutching his bottle. He retreated to his side of the fire. "You're crazy. Yeah." He nodded, as if agreeing with himself. "You're sure enough a crazy woman. You keep away from me, you hear?" He pulled the revolver and aimed it at her across the flames of the campfire.

CHAPTER 41

"Did you hear about Jasper Rafferty?" The young man at the end of the bar slid a fresh beer to the old man who'd walked in.

As Perton, the bartender at the Royale Gaming Hall, walked back up the bar after delivering the two beers, he couldn't help smirking. If he'd heard that question once, he'd heard it a hundred times in the past few hours. And it had only been a couple, three hours since the shooting.

The entire town of Monkton was buzzing like a hive full of bear-bothered bees. He thought back on the events that had led up to this not-so-pretty pass. Who would have thought that Jasper Rafferty had it in him to do anything more than overcharge and annoy people with his holier-than-thou attitude? But apparently there was more sand in the man than anyone had given him credit for.

"Yeah, it's true." The excited young man

down at the end of the bar smacked a hand down on the bar top.

The newcomer, ol' Shakes the wheelwright, stared wide-eyed at the young man, still not believing him. "Say that again," said Shakes.

"I tell you," said the young man. "Jasper Rafferty and Marshal Watt — you know they're brothers-in-law, right?" The man didn't wait for Shakes to answer, but kept right on talking. "They had themselves a dustup, rumor has it on account of the news that Pawnee Joe told folks about Gamble being a big strike after all."

"But what about Rafferty, dang you! Stick to your story!" Shakes scratched at his smoke-stained beard and poked a wobbly old work-hardened finger into the bowl of his briar pipe.

"Right, right," said the young man. "So Rafferty, he goes off in a huff, all bruised up — the marshal's a solid fighter — and he goes to his store, gets himself a revolver, a box of bullets, and marches back to the jail!"

"No!" said Shakes, struggling with a box of lucifers.

"Yes, so help me, it's the truth! Then he all but kicks in the door. Marshal Watt, he's settin' at his desk, working on something, and without a by-your-leave, Rafferty shoots the marshal in the chest four out of six shots fired. The other two hit the wall behind the desk."

"I don't believe it!" Shakes looked down toward Perton, caught the barkeep's eye, and winked, then turned a furrowed brow back to the excited young conversationalist.

Perton had to admit, not having any love for Rafferty, nor for Marshal Watt, that the news didn't bother him terribly much. What it did do, he thought as he plunged a couple of beer mugs into the murky wash water, then toweled them off, was get him excited about all the money he was going to begin making as soon as his shift was over.

He'd already figured out a way to get himself up to Gamble before the rest of these saps in this town. Only thing he had to do was finish packing his gear into his sled, pull on his snowshoes, and hit the trail. He had a rifle, a sidearm, a couple of knives, and plenty of woods know-how.

This was the sort of break he'd been waiting for since he came down from Winnipeg two years before. He'd ended up in Monkton, nearly broke, and taken the barkeep job as a way to keep grub in his belly and as a way to reprovision himself for extended prospecting forays into the promising reaches of the Rockies. He'd scramble to places where a single man with no pack beasts could get to better than anyone else, except maybe a mountain sheep.

But reprovisioning had come hard, mostly because of the prices Jasper Rafferty charged. But all that had changed in the past half day. Beginning with the news that Pawnee Joe had told them last night at the bar. It was the single-most exciting bit of information Perton had heard since arriving in the dismal little river town.

To think that Watt and Rafferty had been holding out on them all, keeping the promise of the little mine camp of Gamble all to themselves. As if providing the start-up money for the folks up there, then keeping them hidden away once strikes had been made entitled them to think that sort of information was theirs and theirs alone. It was enough to make Perton spit.

"Where did Rafferty get to after he shot the marshal?" Shakes had a decent blue cloud boiling up from his pipe and he'd begun working on his beer. Perton guessed the old man would nurse that one for a while.

"He headed here, to the Royale," said the young man, looking around the place as if he'd been there.

Perton had been and the young man had been nowhere in sight. But he was right, nonetheless. Rafferty had stormed in, shouting a blue streak for Pawnee Joe's blood, claimed he was going to shut him up before he did any more damage to his well-deserved coming fortunes.

No one knew what he meant at the time, of course, but a pile of men jumped Rafferty and disarmed him. They hauled him off to jail, only to find that Rafferty had already been there and shot the marshal. That's when Pawnee Joe must have figured he had nothing left to lose, so he up and told everyone with ears all about the golden city that Gamble was about to become.

Perton looked at the mantel clock on the shelf high above the mirror-backed bar. Twenty minutes to go until his shift was over, and then he would head to his rented room, store with his landlady, Mrs. McGillicuddy, what few possessions he didn't want to bring with him, and head north, to Gamble. Perton figured he could make the trek in three, four days, depending on the weather.

Then he could get a feel for Gamble, take in the land, and lay claim to the most promising spots before all the talkers in town finally showed up. He guessed, from the hubbub of the last few hours, and the run on Rafferty's place, that a whole lot of folks were fixing to head to Gamble. But he'd get there before them all. *Pity,* he thought, *that I couldn't have the place to myself.*

Just then a boy still in short pants stormed in, slamming the door back on its hinges.

"Ho there, boy!" said Perton. "You ain't allowed in here, you know that."

"But I got news!" said the lad, his face red and his chest heaving. "Marshal Watt died. Doc did what he could, but the marshal's dead!" The kid bolted back out the door, banging it behind him.

Every man in the place fell silent. Then Shakes said, loud enough for all to hear, "Well, boys, that means Rafferty's earned himself a hemp necktie, wouldn't you say?"

The cheer that roared through the Royale Gaming Hall felt to Perton as if it were rattling the place's window glass. Within two minutes, the bar emptied. Perton smiled. He could leave even sooner now that the customers were gone.

Time to hit the trail to Gamble, Perton, he told himself as he untied his apron for what he knew would be the last time.

CHAPTER 42

The last thing Hester had expected she would do in daylight, sitting across a weak campfire from a man who wanted to do her harm, was fall asleep. And yet she did. Sleep got the better of her. She was awakened by an errant blast of gusting snow that hit her full in the face as if that was its sole intention from the moment it first gained speed. Jerked fully awake as if by ropes from behind, she felt her heart thumping hard.

"No!" she shouted into the breeze, snow clouding her face, flitting into her open mouth like mosquitoes in summer. She had no idea how long she'd been asleep — though it couldn't have been more than a few minutes. She cautiously crept over to Rollie's side of the fire. It wouldn't do to have him catch her slinking around on his side of the fire if he were only relieving himself off behind a rock or tree. But when she bent to investigate what looked like too many tracks leading away from the drunk's spot beside the fire, she saw smooth tracks as though made by . . . bare feet? No, not bare feet but feet wearing moccasins. And that didn't set well with her.

She shouted the single word "No!" again, harder and angrier, when she saw that Rollie was missing and had been taken by that cursed Indian. The very one she had seen, earlier, no doubt, spying on them and waiting for . . . what? Why hadn't he killed Rollie and her too? Why rob her of her prize? She had been so close to killing Rollie and being done with it. Why hadn't she knifed him when she had the chance?

She finally followed the tracks and saw they stretched well beyond the horses, who still stood hitched, leaning into the wind. At least the Indian hadn't killed them . . . yet. For a long moment she stared into the teeth of the wind-driven snow, her anger growing to a seething rage second by second. How dare that man steal her revenge!

With a growl of hate and disgust, she spun, firm decision guiding her actions. She stopped in her tracks. Passing the horses once again, she worked quickly to unbuckle them. Some of the leather gave her trouble, so she pulled out her stolen short knife and hacked through the leather. Soon the horses were freed, though they were so exhausted they didn't move.

She had no time to do more than smack them on the rumps to try to instigate movement in them, let them know they were finally free to at least seek their own shelter. She was sure they would die, but she had at least done what little she could for them. Especially given the fact that she was about to undertake a task that she doubted she would survive.

Skirting the wagon, Hester rigged up a hackamore on Mabel-Mae. Without taking the time to saddle her, instead she climbed into the wagon, then onto the tall mule's back. A single, somewhat-rested animal high-stepping in the snow would get her farther up-trail than her own weary legs.

The snow had already begun to fill in the tracks of the two men, one deep set and bold, the other, a dragging, half-stumbling set that looped wide, then left furrows and troughs in the snow. This looked to Hester as if the moccasin-clad man had clunked and dragged Rollie. The fact that his tracks showed he was somewhat able to walk meant to Hester that the Indian hadn't killed him.

Rollie's inebriation would certainly have aided the Indian in some respects, since

Rollie was, despite his drinking, a muscular, tense man who reacted with sudden, violent movements. But judging from their previous encounters with the Indian, he would be more than a match for Rollie. Especially a drunk Rollie.

Hester was also sure of two things: The man would eventually kill Rollie, and it would not be a pleasant death.

She had gone quite a distance before she realized she hadn't taken the time to rummage in the wagon for a weapon. She didn't think there was much of an arsenal secreted in there, but then again Rollie had been full of surprises. She cursed herself and patted her waist pocket — the short knife was still there. Good. At least she had that.

Hester looked down once again and saw no tracks. They had changed course several yards back. She paused Mabel-Mae, reined her around, and saw that the tracks angled to the right, into a cleft in the steep hillside. Visoring her eyes, she barely saw that they trailed all the way up the hill and disappeared high up, as far as she could see. How could that one man get another half-drunk man that high up without assistance?

For the first time, the flame of anger in Hester's belly guttered. Such a man would be powerful, too powerful to defeat. Mabel-

Mae angled her head out of the wind, and Hester snapped out of her daydream. No, she could not let unfounded thoughts of her new foe shake her from avenging the deaths of so many innocents. Come what may, she would succeed in killing Rollie.

With that renewed thought in her mind, Hester dismounted, patted Mabel-Mae once on the neck, and headed on foot up the steep cleft in the rocks, following the trail in the snow, a trail that almost looked as if it were left for her.

It took but a few minutes before Hester's breath dwindled to short gasps and sharp pains lanced up her legs and knotted hotly in her sides. Still she pressed on, following the ragged mess of footprints in the snowy hillside.

At least off the trail, up into the trees and between old piles of boulders, she found occasional relief from the gale and stinging snow. Her fingers had been numb for days, and the socks she'd worn for mittens had begun to shred against the jags of rock she used to drag herself upward. It felt as though she had ripped the very ends of her fingers off, but still she kept going.

Up ahead the thin trail looked as though it leveled off — maybe she'd soon reach the top. Then what? *Put it out of your mind, Hester,* she told herself. *And keep moving.*

She reached the top a few minutes later and despite the fact that she knew a murderous Indian lurked somewhere ahead, she was too exhausted to do much more than flop on her side in the snow and let her breathing calm down.

As she lay there, her breath pluming into the snow-filled sky, Hester noticed that the storm seemed to have slowed; certainly the wind had died down to stray gusts. She guessed they still had a couple of hours of daylight left, maybe less.

Then she heard a noise that seized her breath in her throat — a scream. A man's scream. She'd heard that voice before. Rollie. He was being tortured and he wasn't far away. While she lay there without breathing, she heard another sudden sound — two gunshots, followed by more screams.

The anger toward the strange Indian she'd felt earlier came back twofold, and she pushed herself onto her knees, wavered there a moment, then got her feet under her. Rollie was hers. She alone had earned the right to put him deep into his own misery before she ended it for him.

Hester pulled in a deep breath and, stepping high, she trudged forward, on somewhat level ground, toward the sound of a man's sobbing screams.

The land continued on, level and rocky, dappled with trees. Hester followed the fresh trail and within minutes of reaching the top found herself at the edge of a clearing that measured but a few dozen yards across before dropping off again at the edge across from her. She found herself peeking between trees at a scene that even her hardened heart could never have imagined.

A broad-shouldered man of average height stood with his back to her. His long hair, a curious reddish brown color, flowed loose down the back of his buckskin tunic. Spiking and wagging from the top of his head were a number of feathers and woven thongs that wagged and wavered in the breeze. Clutched in one hand, a long-bladed knife, smeared in bright red blood, dripped on the snow. In the other hand he held Rollie's Colt revolver. This was the Indian. The killer. The torturer.

Twenty feet beyond him, three men were loosely tied to trees. Those on the ends were obviously dead, perhaps had been so for some time. Trussed in sagged poses, they had been sliced and peeled and skinned and now sported wads of fresh snow spired atop their shoulders and heads. In the center, facing Hester, and also loosely tied to a tree, Rollie Meecher half stood, half sagged.

Arrows wagged from his upper legs, two in one, three in the other. The meat of his upper arms had been shot, as the blackened puckered wounds showed. Strings of bloody spittle drizzled from his battered mouth, from matching slices in his cheeks, from above his forehead. But where his hair had been, a bloody smear now glistened, almost as if he wore a knitted red wool cap. Hester realized Rollie had been scalped.

She stood, mesmerized, as the Indian pulled back an arm and let loose a short yip. Time seemed to slow for Hester as she watched the knife fly as if guided by an unseen string, straight at Rollie's gut. Rollie's head whipped upright, his bloodied mouth wide in surprise, his eyes wide, as well, two white-rimmed flashes in a reddened face. They seemed to see Hester, lock with her eyes for a finger-snap moment, then rolled upward before his head whipped side to side in agony's relentless grip.

Hester yelped, "No!" but was already on the move by the time the Indian began to turn. She hit him low, buckling his legs and sending him whipping backward to sprawl in the snow.

He growled in anger at the unexpected

intrusion. Hester rolled clumsily from atop him and felt his strong hand grab her ankle above her boot top, squeezing in a grip that she knew could never be loosened. But she kicked at his hand anyway and was rewarded with a bark of pain. She wasted no time in scrambling from his reach and watched as he tried to rise. He managed to push himself up on one knee, but wobbled and fell back, clutching the other leg, his mouth spread in a grimace of pain. She must have hit him harder than she thought, and for that she felt relief.

As Hester pushed backward away from him, she saw his face fully for the first time, and noticed he wasn't an Indian. At least not a full-blooded Indian. Couldn't be — he had blue-gray eyes, a honeyed tone to his skin, and the reddish brown of his hair was unlike the straight black hair she'd seen on Indians.

But if she thought she had rendered him incapable of movement, she was mistaken. For as soon as she took her eyes from him, shifted them back to Rollie as she stood in the deep snow, she sensed movement behind her and before she had time to turn, she felt two powerful arms lock tight about her.

The Indian stood behind her, squeezing the breath from her, lifting her off the ground until her boots wagged limply in the snow. She felt his face nuzzle her neck, close, smelled the sour, wild-animal stink of him, the breath of a wild meat-eater.

"Why have you done this? Why have you betrayed me? I let you live, white woman, so that you might hunt for a long time to come. Because you have endured cruelties that only whites might put upon other whites. You lived where others died."

Even as he squeezed the life from her, his voice confused Hester — he spoke better English than most men she had met lately, but there was something stilted about how he conveyed his confused — and confusing — thoughts, something edged in sharp rust, jagged and cruel. How had she betrayed him?

"And yet you have turned on me, betrayed me, left me to cleanse the mess from this lost place. . . . For that, you must now die."

And she realized he was correct — if she did nothing for a few seconds more, she would be all but dead. And was that so bad? No, she mustn't let him win! She had to avenge Delia, Charlie, who knew how many others? With the last of a strength she had not felt in long days of fatigue and drudgery and freezing pain, Hester convulsed in the Indian's arms, thrashing her arms, whipping her head backward into his. She felt the back of her head connect with his, heard him shout in pain. Still she writhed and slammed against him, kicking with all her fading strength, and landed a heel perfectly against something that caused the man to drop her immediately and fall away from her.

Hester fell forward into the snow, gasping and retching, sucking in icy breaths. Behind her the Indian moaned and forced air and spittle between his clenched teeth, suppressing mighty bellows of pain.

Hester worked to stand and breathe, and to ignore the sharp pains in her sides. Surely he had damaged her ribs. Never had she felt so tired or alone or helpless or sad or angry, all at once. And then she saw that in their struggles they had worked their way closer to the edge of the clearing farthest from where she'd entered between the trees. She guessed they were now a dozen feet from the drop-off. Was it a cliff? A slump of but a few feet before leveling off again?

While the man struggled to regain a standing position, in her mind Hester weighed caution and reason and found them both lacking. And even though she longed to do nothing more than lie in the snow and breathe her last, once more she rushed at the Indian. And once more, she caught him unawares, driving right into his damaged leg. It was bent badly at the knee in a way that nature never intended.

He howled in pain and rage, pummeled her with mighty fists, tried to push her away. But Hester had found a determination, the last of it in her body, in her mind, in her very being, and she dug in the snow with her legs, pushing against his unbalanced body. And inch by inch they went to the edge. And then they went over.

CHAPTER 43

It was still a couple of hours before dark when Charlie heard what sounded like far-off shouts. The wind blew a norther, driving gale-driven snow down at them from the upper cleft ahead in the trail, so he thought for a moment that the sounds might have been a trick of his hearing, something in nature made louder, stranger by the storm. But it also sounded an awful lot like screams, followed by a couple of echoing shots, as if someone had cranked a few rounds out of a revolver.

They'd stopped to rest and he'd positioned the travois behind a mass of tumble-down boulders that provided a decent windbreak. It felt good to get out of the wind and snow. Delia had sipped a little whiskey down to dull the pain in her belly, and she'd fallen asleep. Now that he'd heard the sounds, he felt more confident with each passing second that they had been gunshots.

But he hated to wake her, even though he was itching to investigate, and if it turned out to be nothing more than branches, ice, or a trick of the wind, they could at least put in another mile or so before they had to make camp. The going was slow enough, but the girl's bouts of pain seemed to him to be getting worse.

He shifted from one foot to another, the shotgun cradled in his arms. He let out a long, slow sigh as he looked uphill toward the source of the sounds.

"I told you I'd hold you back, Charlie."

He turned at the sound of her quiet voice. "Delia." He bent low over her, felt her forehead. "You okay?"

She closed her eyes and smiled. "Charlie, I am a long distance from okay." She looked at him. "I heard them too. Those sounded like gunshots, didn't they?"

He raised his eyebrows, nodded, then glanced back uphill. "Yes, they surely did. Might be them. . . ."

"You should go ahead, see if it is."

"You ain't in no fit state to do any more traveling now, Delia."

"I haven't been since we started our trip, Charlie. But here I am. Look." She struggled to prop herself up on her elbows. "You should leave me here. I'm out of the wind. I have a little whiskey left — all the comforts of home." She smiled again, then lay back down, drained from the effort she'd expended.

"I can't leave you, Delia. I won't do it."

She sighed, kept her eyes closed. "Charlie Chilton. Leave me alone for once. I don't need you nursemaiding me every minute of the day. I am a married woman, after all. What would people think?"

"I . . . I didn't think of it that way. I thought —"

"Well, maybe you've been doing too much thinking. Go on and see what's happening up there. We may well be close to Gamble. Did you think of that?"

He rubbed his wide, bearded jaw. Might not hurt to cross that little rise, at that. "You sure you'll be okay here, Delia?"

She sighed and smiled. "Yes, Mother Hen. I will be fine here. Certainly warmer and safer than on that trail." She opened her eyes and her smile faded. "Don't forget me. I . . . I don't want the wolves to come, Charlie."

He rested a big paw on her hand. "Delia, I ain't about to let that happen. Besides, who'd keep me awake on the trail, asking me crazy questions?"

He fussed over her blankets, made sure

her bottle was close at hand, then said, "I won't be long. You stay put." He tried to sound menacing, but she only smiled and nodded. He paused a few paces away from the hiding spot and was pleased to see that it was well concealed, in part because of the snow.

He was worried about the rogue Indians, but he wouldn't be gone long. He was probably kidding himself, but this weather didn't seem as threatening somehow as if it were clear out.

It didn't take him long to top the rise ahead, only to see another one. But the tracks they'd been following on the trail were still there, cut into the older snow, but covered over with fresh layers of the fast-piling white stuff. He trudged on, mindful of the distance he was putting between himself and Delia. He would only go a bit farther, then turn around. She'd need a fire soon, especially if this storm kept up.

As he angled off the trail and up a steep jumble of rocks, hoping to get a better view of what lay ahead, he wondered about life in the mountains. What had ever made him think that living in such rugged country was a good idea? All it brought lately had been misery and headaches.

Charlie shifted the shotgun to the crook

of his other arm and grabbed a stunted pine for support. He was about to jam a boot sideways into the hillside snowpack when he heard shouts from a gruff voice mingle with a woman's scream. The scream seemed to last a long time, before it stopped suddenly.

Charlie froze — had that been from back behind him? Delia? He almost bolted downslope, but something stayed his action. He felt sure it hadn't been Delia, had been from far ahead and the sounds had carried downwind to him. Something inside told him to finish climbing to the top of the rise, that he needed to see whatever lay ahead. . . .

CHAPTER 44

A blur of grunting, kicking, buckskin-clad half Indian, thick white snow, and jagged gray boulders ranging from a person's head to the girth of a horse in size, all rushed up to meet Hester before falling away again as quickly as it began. Over and over they fell, hitting what felt to Hester like every hard object she'd ever seen in her life. Her head, her arms, legs, chest, back, face, all slammed into things that did not move.

And then it stopped.

Long moments passed where nothing moved. Even the wind had stopped. Dark slate clouds blocking out the late afternoon light parted, allowing gold light to slice downward and reflect in every direction.

If I am not dead, thought Hester, *then I am surely on my way. I don't dare move, but I don't dare lay here for long. If I can live through such a fall, surely the Indian did as well.* She opened her eyes and risked moving her head, pleasantly surprised to find she could do so.

Her arms and legs all appeared unbroken, though she knew they would surely ache forever because of this. She didn't care. All she needed was one more shot at Rollie Meecher· before the bum expired from wounds she had not been able to deliver.

Hester saw that she had landed at the base of a massive boulder — gray-black and jutting enough for snow to form on one long side-slope edge. She also noticed that blood had smeared against some of the snow. The sight of it made her touch her own temple. Her fingers, through the frayed end of the sock, came away red. *Lucky is what I am,* she thought. Then she heard a noise.

Piled alongside the uphill edge of the rock lay the Indian. He looked to be in bad shape. One arm looked broken and his head looked to be bleeding far worse than hers. He moaned again. Hester grabbed at the big rock with shaky hands and pulled herself up, groaning and moaning in the process.

The Indian's eyes fluttered, opened, and he looked up at her. "Why?" he said in a small, raw whisper.

Hester continued hauling herself up against the blood-and-snow-smeared rock.

"You took the only thing that matters to me now."

"You . . . love that man?"

When Hester realized what he said, she laughed and shook her head. "It is revenge, nothing more."

"You know . . . nothing of revenge." He coughed, closed his eyes, and sagged, unmoving, against the rock.

After all those tortured men and slain animals, this is how the great frightening Indian meets his end? Hester looked at him and envied him. She had nothing left to live for, and now not only was she still alive, but she was battered and alone in the wilderness. Alive . . . alive? And that's when a thought occurred to her that kindled the flame of revenge deep within her once more.

She barely paused to take a breath and began clawing her way back up the rocky slope, back to the clearing at the top. Back to where she knew a Colt revolver lay lost in the snow and a man who might not yet be dead soon would be.

CHAPTER 45

"Hester! No! Don't do it!"

She recognized the big, booming voice in
an instant, but knew it had to be nothing
more than a voice in her head, echoing from
the past. It could be trying to change her
mind, some last remnant of her conscience.
Well, it wouldn't win, not when she was so
close to taking from this man the only thing
he had left, the only thing he apparently
ever valued anyway — his own life.

The haggard woman, her hair caked and
sopping with muddied snow, her dress a
limp, torn thing, her hands begrimed and
thrust through shredded socks that hung
from welted wrists circled with raw, bleeding wounds from the rasping ropes that
bound her much of the past days — this
woman who had endured more hardship
than most people do in half a lifetime,
trembled, but only from fatigue. In her
resolve she was solid as oak as she peeled

back the hammer.

"Hester! Delia needs you! Listen to me, girl — Delia's okay!"

That could not be — her mind was playing bad, bad tricks on her right now. But what if it wasn't? What if . . . ?

"Hester."

The voice was closer, nearly beside her. She didn't dare take her eyes from the simpering, bloodied and snotted mess that was the crying Rollie Meecher. Oh, she wanted to end him right now, in the worst way. But she could not take her eyes from Meecher. He was that slippery. . . . But what if the voice was real? *Whisper something, she told herself. Whisper his name and prove that it's nothing more than your mind playing bad games.* Hester licked her lips. She could only hear her own breathing, rasping in and out, hard, like a train that might not make the grade. "Charlie?"

The voice drew closer. "It's me, Hester. It really is. Look at me." A shape appeared beside her on the right, moved slowly beyond her, drawing even with the Colt's jittery barrel. Blood from the gash on her forehead had soaked the eyelashes on her right eye. She didn't dare blink but slowly turned her head to see a person, a big person, a man . . . Hester jerked her eyes back to Rollie. He was still crying, nearly soundless, down on one knee, his bloodied head trembling.

"Charlie? Is it you?" She whispered it, didn't dare speak it louder.

His big, dirty, bearded face bent down into view. "It's me, Hester. It really is."

"Delia? Is she . . . ?"

"She's with me — Delia is with me. But she needs you right now, Hester."

She saw a big hand reach slowly for the Colt. "No!" She jerked it away, kept it pointed at the simpering wreck that was Rollie Meecher.

"Hester, don't do this thing. Don't ruin your goodness on this man. Every second you waste on him is a second you ain't helping Delia. . . ."

"Is she really alive, Charlie?"

"Yes, yes, she most certainly is. And she's full of vinegar, I tell you. But she needs you now, Hester. What do you say? Let's stop this. Look at him. Ol' Rollie ain't nothing to nobody right now. He's reached the end. We got other things need tending, Hester. Like Delia."

He reached again for the revolver. Slower this time, and without grabbing it, he pushed it down with his palm, feeling her resistance the entire way, until it pointed at the snow-covered ground. Then he closed his hand around it and took it from her.

Finally Hester looked up at him and it seemed to him that for the first time in a long while, she let herself truly lose control of her emotions. Her chin quivered and her eyes filled with tears. She reached up, touched her hands to Charlie's wide face, then collapsed into his arms. He hugged her, patting her back for a few moments. Then she pushed away from him. "Delia? Is she really . . . ?"

Charlie nodded and said, "We'll go get her. One thing to do here first."

As they turned to face Rollie, they heard him moan, saw him try to raise his head. Charlie walked closer to him, bent down to his face, then looked at Hester. "He's trying to talk."

Hester stepped closer, her teeth set tight, as if she had smelled something bad and wanted to get away from it right away.

Charlie bent close to Rollie's face. "What's that, Rollie?"

"All them . . ."

"Say it again, Rollie."

"All them . . . golden eggs." His eyes grew wide again and he smiled a wide, bloody smile. Then his eyes glazed and his head dropped forward and the blood slowly stopped drizzling from his mouth.

They were both quiet for several minutes on their way back down the trail Charlie had made a short time before.

Then Hester said, "What did he mean by that 'golden eggs' comment, Charlie?"

"Oh, I reckon it means he died greedy."

By the time they reached the trailside cleft in the rocks where Charlie had secured Delia, Hester was almost running. She'd stumbled in the snow several times and would not listen to Charlie's urges that she maintain a steady pace.

Delia was there, bundled as Charlie had left her. But she did not look good to him, paler and thinner, as if she'd lost weight in the short time he'd been gone. Still, she recognized her sister and smiled. Charlie hated to do so, but he cut short their tearful reunion. "I believe we had best make camp. It's going to be dark and cold soon."

"We have, or that is to say, there's a camp up the trail a short ways where we had stopped. It should do for the night."

It didn't take the straggling trio long before they found the camp that Rollie and Hester had set up. With a roaring fire, food, and whiskey for Delia — though she barely sipped any — they settled in for an evening of slow renewal of hope and happiness tinged with the shadow of gloom that Delia's illness brought with it.

Hester made her sister as comfortable as she could, mothering over her for far longer than she needed to. Finally she sat back, her raw hands and feet to the fire, and accepted from Charlie a plate of food and even a small glass of whiskey. They ate in silence, and then slowly their separate ordeals unfolded and they filled each other in on all that had transpired.

Hours later, they fell asleep leaning against each other, facing the fire, Delia bundled and sleeping a pain-free sleep.

A dragging sound woke Charlie. His eyes snapped open to see low flames and a broad bed of pulsing coals in the fire before him. The dragging sound continued not far off in the dark, to his right. He reached for the shotgun he'd propped beside him earlier and felt its reassuring, solid heft in his big hand.

Still, the scuffing, dragging sound approached. Charlie pushed Hester gently away from him. She roused, mumbled something that wasn't a word, but didn't awaken. He got to his feet as quickly and as quietly as he could. The sound Hester made had surely given away their position should it be someone or something unwanted that approached.

He walked as quietly as he could, angling slightly away from the noise, hoping that he could come upon whatever it was from the side. In the dim glow of the firelight, a large, dark shape approached and before Charlie could raise the shotgun and thumb back the twin hammers, it pushed into him. And Charlie knew it for what it was — Mabel-Mae, nosing his torso, probing his jacket as she always had for an apple, soda crackers, anything he might have hidden in there.

"Sweet girl." He rubbed her head, lowering the shotgun. "Hester said you were up-trail somewheres — I figured I'd find you in the morning. I'm sure glad you came back this way, though."

He'd no sooner gotten the words out than another dark shape launched down on him from atop the friendly mule. But this dark shape swung a tomahawk. Charlie saw the outline of the man and weapon, as if sketched there against the clear night sky, stars winking on high, before the man, with no sound other than a grunt, dropped on Charlie.

He batted away the fast-swinging arm, heard the man grunt, but the weapon was still there, arcing and swiping at Charlie's head. He tried to push the struggling man away with one arm and raise the shotgun with the other, but that was his weakened side.

He used the only thing he could, until he could get that shotgun raised up to touch it off — he drove forward with his entire formidable body, forcing the struggling man backward, away from the campfire and the women, and into the dark.

Mabel-Mae sidestepped back into the shadows, as if knowing she must get out of the way.

By that time, he heard Hester calling his name in desperation, heard another sound, must have been Delia, also shouting. But he couldn't afford to think about them now. He had to defeat this fresh attacker. The near silence of the man was downright scary. Who fought like a demon and barely grunted?

"His legs, Charlie! Go for his legs!"

Must be Hester, shouting something about legs. . . . Of course, she must guess it was the Indian, the very one she'd busted the leg of. He drove forward, snaking a boot out as he could to kick at his attacker, but it didn't seem to help. Was it the same Indian? Was it even an Indian? Was it even a man? He didn't believe in spooks or spirits, but this one was too odd by half.

Hester had stoked the fire and now light from the blaze spilled onto the struggling pair.

Without warning, the man broke off, seemed to melt away, farther into the ink black night. Not a sound rose from him. Charlie heard his own heartbeat in his head, pounding like a steel driver's hammer. He raised the shotgun, tucked the stock under his armpit, and crouched as he swept left to right toward where he guessed the devil would be.

"Charlie?" Hester called.

In the next second, he heard a light whooshing sound, as if silent wings in the night, to the left, close by his head. Charlie dropped to his knees and swung the brute of a weapon upward toward the sound. The roaring fire lit the left side of the silent dropping form of an angry, bloody-faced Indian like none Charlie had ever seen, with eyes of ice and hair of flame. The man's tomahawk whooshed as it swung down at him.

Charlie squeezed both triggers at the same time. The Indian's body seemed to fold over the end of the barrels as gouts of flame bloomed straight into the dropping man. Charlie tucked low and rolled onto his shoulder, kept rolling out of the way of the man. He lay still, the shotgun clutched in his left fist.

"Charlie? Charlie Chilton?"

"I'm okay." He sighed and slowly got to his feet and walked to the spot where the man had fallen. He was there all right, and Charlie could see his mangled body. The firelight showed him enough to tell him that was one fella who wouldn't be swinging any tomahawk again.

He walked back to the fire. "I gave him a double. I reckon even that magical Injun can't live through two barrels of this ol' family heirloom." He patted the big gun's thick stock.

"Are you hurt, Charlie?" said Hester, feeling his arms, patting his chest as though she were drying a ham.

"Naw, ma'am. I'm just tired. So tired. You know, I can't remember ever feeling this plumb tuckered." They stood in silence for a minute, staring into the flames.

Finally Charlie spoke. "I hope that's the last angry person set on attacking us tonight. I sure could use some sleep." He yawned, a long, deep sound that tapered to a sigh. "I reckon things can only get better from now on. In fact, I have a feeling we'll get to Gamble tomorrow."

"You never cease to amaze me, Charlie

Chilton," said Hester.

"How's that?"

"You are the most optimistic person I've ever met."

"If by that highfalutin word you mean that I am chatty, I will admit to being prone to talk when I'm tired or worked up."

A small voice from deep within a bundle of blankets beside them said, "Uh-oh, don't get him started about his mule."

"Hey, now, Delia, you rascal!" said Charlie. "Just for that, I reckon I about have enough steam left in my lungs for a nice, long version of how I come to meet ol' Mabel-Mae."

"Oh no," said Delia.

Hester laughed. "How about we hear it tomorrow, Charlie?"

"I reckon . . . ," he said, and within seconds he was snoring.

CHAPTER 46

The paltry structures of Gamble looked more impressive to the haggard travelers than the grand hotels, banks, and gambling halls of an enormous coastal city. Hester and Charlie forced their legs up and out of the snow, one step forward at a time. Charlie held tight to Mabel-Mae's reins, Hester stepping low beside Delia, who lay bundled in blankets on the travois, jouncing and jostling behind Mabel-Mae.

A handful of people appeared, one at a time, opening doors to dark log huts half buried in the drifted snow. None of them spoke as the odd little procession struggled into the middle of the small cluster of buildings.

The late-day sun angled low over the trees, shading half the street, leaving the rest in bright light made blinding as it bounced off the glittering white storm-smooth surface. Charlie finally stopped a few yards from a low building with what looked to be fancy uprights holding up a sagging porch roof.

The heads and shoulders of three people were visible over the snowdrift before the building. An older woman with a whole lot of hair piled on her head, and two men, one dark-skinned and fat, the other smaller, bald, and with a large oiled mustache, stared at him from the porch. Someone had already shoveled a narrow path leading to the entrance.

"Howdy," said Charlie, nodding, matching the suspicious stares with his own.

Hester pushed past him. "We're looking for Vin. Vincenzo Tantillo. We were told he was here."

No one said anything for a moment. Hester continued. "This is Gamble, I take it?"

Finally the small, bald man with the mustache cleared his throat. "Yes, ma'am. You have reached Gamble. May I ask your business with one of our residents?"

"No, you may not. But I take it that means he's here."

"Oh, for heaven's sake, Clayton," said the large woman with all the hair. She looked at Hester and smiled. "Yes, honey. He's here all right. Up yonder, last hovel on the left.

But he ain't alone."

Hester nodded her thanks. "I didn't expect he'd be. I'm obliged to you." She touched Charlie on the arm. "Come on. We don't have a lot of time left."

Charlie heard her voice shake. He tugged Mabel-Mae forward.

Hester led the way to the cabin and pulled the Colt from her belt as she bent low before the door. She lashed out with a worn boot and kicked once, twice; then the wooden thing spasmed inward.

Charlie untied the ropes holding Delia on the travois and lifted the girl. He held her face close to his, praying to feel breath on his cheek — he did, the faintest. But it was there.

"You there, girl," said Hester in a matter-of-fact tone. "Get up and out of this man's bed right now."

"Who died and made you all bossy?"

Hester pulled in a sharp breath and laid a quick backhand across the slattern's mouth. "Much as it pains me to say it, I am his sister-in-law," she said in a low growl, jerking her chin at the half-naked hairy man who'd retreated to the corner beside the bed. "The good Lord help me."

Hester leaned closer and hissed, "And my sister is here to see her husband."

The woman in the bed leaned back, stroking her red cheek. "Big deal. I'm here now. Tell her to come back later. Or better yet, never."

Hester leaned in so close her nose touched the other woman's, her voice shaking with barely contained rage. "She's dying. And you will be too if you do not get up this second." She cracked the woman another one, then whipped the covers off her naked body. Charlie turned toward the wall, holding Delia gently in his arms.

"But I ain't clothed!"

"That seems to be your professional preference," said Hester, pushing the woman out the door and into the snow. She slammed the door, then saw a pair of woman's worn boots on the floor, hole-riddled wool socks on top, and snatching them up in one hand, she opened the door and fired them out into the snow, then slammed the door again.

"What?" said Vin in a small voice, leaning forward, tears forming in his eyes. "Dying? Little Delia?"

"Yes, no thanks to you. And before she is gone, I would have a word with you." Hester had backed the swarthy little man farther into his corner, his handsome face inches from hers, his roguish eyes fluttering at the barrel of the cocked Colt jammed tight to him, the tip of the barrel dimpling his chin.

"Now," said Hester in a low voice. "You are trash, pure and simple. But for some reason my sweet sister Delia set her hat on you from the start." Her voice cracked, but she kept on. "It is true that she is not long for this earth, and the only thing that will make her happy is to see you again, so I want you to hold her in your arms, so that she dies thinking that she is still in love with the only man who ever swept her off her feet. Even if that love is one-sided, you will hold her in both your arms. Do you hear me?"

"But —"

Hester's gun hand lashed upward with snake-strike speed and she rapped Vin hard on the side of the head with the pistol's barrel. "No buts. You will do as I say. Now nod your pretty head so I can see you understand me."

He wobbled to the bed, holding a hand to the side of his head.

"Lay her in the bed, Charlie," said Hester, arranging the rumpled blankets. She looked at Vin. "Now, you, settle alongside her and hold her gently, or so help me . . ." She lowered her quavering voice. "And remember that this was her last wish, you scoundrel."

Vin nodded, his eyes, wide with fear, darting from the massive bulk of Charlie Chilton glaring down at him to Hester's hard-set face to the Colt revolver held tight in her fist.

Delia responded slowly to Hester's voice whispering gently to her, and Hester's fingers softly stroking her sunken cheek. "Delia, honey, we made it. We made it to Vin's. Open your eyes, honey. Vincenzo's holding you."

Delia's eyelids, purpled and thin as flower petals, flickered, then parted. Her eyes roved unfocused for a few moments, then settled on Vin's tearful face. He smiled, wiped his eyes, and said, "Hello, little Delia. How are you? I'm so glad you found me. I was going to come back to you in the spring. I made us a fortune, you see. . . ." He glanced at Hester, who nodded for him to continue.

Delia smiled. Her voice came out soft and quiet, but all three could hear her. "It's good to see you once more, Vin. I'm glad to know you'll do well." She tried to raise her head but couldn't. "Kiss me, Vin."

He did, and they stared at each other for a moment.

"Now please go," said Delia, breaking the

spell. "I want to talk with my family." She looked to Hester and Charlie.

Vin rose from the bed, confused. He pulled on a ratty old wool mackinaw and boots and left the cabin.

"Hester," said Delia. "I am so sorry for making you come all this way . . . so sorry for everything."

Crying herself, Hester wiped away Delia's tears. "Hush, now, I would do it all over again a hundred times if you asked me to."

"I know. . . ."

"Besides," said Hester, "it has been a most memorable adventure for us all."

Delia's face relaxed and she smiled. "And you never would have met Charlie."

"That's true." Hester glanced at Charlie, who had kneeled by the bedside.

He felt his face heat up and couldn't do a thing about it.

Delia raised her thin hands and they each took one. "You take good care of each other, you hear me?"

"Oh, Miss Delia, you have my promise," said Charlie, "and when you get better —"

"Charlie, no." Delia's voice grew a little louder. "This is good-bye. And it's all right. It's all right."

The big man nodded, tears dripping off his nose. He tried to speak, but his voice tightened in his throat and came hard. He held her little hand tight between his two big paws. "I've enjoyed every second of our time together, Delia. You are dear to me, girl, and I will never forget you." Charlie rose from his knees, leaned over, and kissed her forehead.

He stood and cleared his throat. "I'll leave you two gals alone now. I expect you have things to talk about." He squeezed Hester's shoulder lightly. "I'll be right outside."

Charlie saw Vincenzo standing in the snow away from the cabin, looking small and weak in his long-handles, his old coat, and his slumped shoulders. For all the man's faults, Charlie reckoned he must have cared for Delia at one time, maybe still did. Charlie walked up beside him and clapped him gently on the back of the neck a couple of times. They stood quietly, not able to speak, not needing to speak, both choked with the overwhelming emotion of the moment.

Hours later, a shiver worked its way up Charlie's spine and he looked around. Dark had begun to pull its cloak over the sparse settlement. The untouched white landscape took on a silvery tint and the pines blackened against it, disappearing into the bluing sky. Already stars began to wink. It seemed to Charlie that he'd never seen so many all at once.

Vin was gone, probably to that little cabin with the porch that looked as though it doubled as Gamble's meeting house and saloon. Light pinched through one small window and colored the snow beneath.

Charlie heard boots slowly descend steps behind him. Snow squeaked, and then Hester stood beside him. Neither spoke for long minutes. The little cabin sat dark and still behind them.

Finally, in a quiet voice, Hester said, "Delia is . . . her pain is all gone now."

Charlie nodded, said nothing. The clouds of their breaths rose and broke apart in the dark around them.

"I can't be too far from her, Charlie." Hester's voice was quiet, almost as though she hadn't spoken but had only thought it.

Charlie nodded. "I know. Me either." His hushed voice matched hers.

"Where is your valley?"

"Not too far, I can feel it."

"You haven't ever really seen it, have you?"

Charlie scuffed a boot in the snow, looked toward the black outline of the close-up peaks. "I'll know it when I see it."

"Then Gamble isn't it."

He looked at her. "Not hardly. Come

spring, this place will be crawling with all manner of gold hounds, turning this pretty little spot to dust." He grew quiet a moment, taking in the dark hills around them. "Might take some time, but I'm close, I can tell."

Hester O'Fallon slipped an arm through his, leaned her head on his shoulder. "Then we'll know it when we see it."

For a moment, Charlie's eyebrows rose. "Yes'm, I reckon we will."

"Hold me, Charlie Chilton. Hold me tight."

He felt his face heat up, but he wrapped both of his big arms snug around her. "Yes, ma'am. I ain't about to let go."

They watched the silhouette of the peaks sharpen against the blue night sky and the last of the far-off storm clouds parting, revealing a promising and clear pearly moon.

ABOUT THE AUTHOR

Ralph Compton stood six foot eight without his boots. He worked as a musician, a radio announcer, a songwriter, and a newspaper columnist. His first novel, *The Goodnight Trail,* was a finalist for the Western Writers of America Medicine Pipe Bearer Award for Best Debut Novel. He was also the author of the *Sundown Riders* series and the *Border Empire* series.

The employees of Thorndike Press hope you have enjoyed this Large Print book. All our Thorndike, Wheeler, and Kennebec Large Print titles are designed for easy reading, and all our books are made to last. Other Thorndike Press Large Print books are available at your library, through selected bookstores, or directly from us.

For information about titles, please call:
  (800) 223-1244

or visit our Web site at:
  http://gale.cengage.com/thorndike

To share your comments, please write:
Publisher
Thorndike Press
10 Water St., Suite 310
Waterville, ME 04901